The
Tinderbox

Books by Beverly Lewis

The Tinderbox

The First Love • The Road Home

The Proving • The Ebb Tide

The Wish • The Atonement

The Photograph • The Love Letters

The River

HOME TO HICKORY HOLLOW

The Fiddler • The Bridesmaid

The Guardian • The Secret Keeper

The Last Bride

THE ROSE TRILOGY

The Thorn • The Judgment

The Mercy

ABRAM'S DAUGHTERS

The Covenant • The Betrayal

The Sacrifice • The Prodigal

The Revelation

THE HERITAGE OF LANCASTER COUNTY

The Shunning • The Confession

The Reckoning

ANNIE'S PEOPLE

The Preacher's Daughter

The Englisher • The Brethren

THE COURTSHIP OF NELLIE FISHER

The Parting • The Forbidden

The Longing

SEASONS OF GRACE

The Secret • The Missing

The Telling

The Postcard • The Crossroad

The Redemption of Sarah Cain

Sanctuary (with David Lewis)

Child of Mine (with David Lewis)

The Sunroom • October Song

Beverly Lewis Amish Romance Collection

Amish Prayers

The Beverly Lewis Amish Heritage Cookbook

The Beverly Lewis Amish Coloring Book

www.beverlylewis.com

The
Tinderbox

BEVERLY
LEWIS

BETHANYHOUSE

a division of Baker Publishing Group
Minneapolis, Minnesota

Published by Bethany House Publishers
11400 Hampshire Avenue South
Bloomington, Minnesota 55438

Bethany House Publishers is a division of
Baker Publishing Group, Grand Rapids, Michigan

Printed in the United States of America

Scripture quotations are from the King James Version of the Bible.

This story is a work of fiction. Names, characters, incidents, and dialogues are products of the author's imagination and are not to be construed as real. Any resemblance to any person, living or dead, is purely coincidental.

Cover design by Dan Thornberg, Design Source Creative Services
Art direction by Paul Higdon

To
Claudia Ferrin Muniz,
sweet friend and partner
in prayer.

That Time could turn up
his swift sandy glass,
To untell the days, and to
redeem these hours.

—Thomas Heywood

Prologue

*M*y earliest recollection of *Dat* was of going with him to Root's Country Market when I was no taller than a buggy wheel and surprised to see so many fancy folk there. It was the first time I'd asked about his other life as an *Englischer*, before he came to Hickory Hollow. He was mum for a while, then hemmed and hawed a bit, seemingly reluctant to say much.

We wandered from one produce stand to another as I finally got up the courage to ask, "Do ya ever miss bein' fancy, Dat?"

"Miss living out in the world?" He glanced down at me, grinning. "Well, one thing's for sure, I can't imagine missing out on *you*, Sylvie."

I giggled as we proceeded through the crowded marketplace. *Ach*, I couldn't have been happier to be his little girl—the firstborn and the apple of Dat's eye. Most Amish families I knew had oodles of girls, but in our family, there was only me.

Now, at eighteen, I sometimes contemplated that long-ago conversation, wondering why my father still seemed reluctant

7

to discuss his past. I've marveled at his ability to accept the Old Ways so readily, considering his modern upbringing. Hadn't it been hard for him to leave it behind? Mamma says it's like he was *born* to be Amish. Maybe so, but all the same, I wished I knew something more about his family.

Just now, finishing my kitchen chores, I stepped barefoot out the back door, waving to my father coming across the newly planted field of sweet corn. Walking quickly, he waved back and headed toward his clockmaker's shop, the House of Time, a structure separate from the main house. There, he made timepieces large and small, not only for our Plain folk but for *Englischers*, too. Some customers traveled from as far as Philly and Pittsburgh after word spread through the years that Dat was a fine workman and his integrity second to none.

Moving toward the porch steps, I called, "Busy day?"

"*Jah*, but never too *fleissich* for my Sylvie-girl," he said, blending his English and *Deitsch* as he sometimes did. Grinning, he removed his corn silk–colored straw hat, revealing that his dark brown bowl cut was in need of Mamma's scissors.

Following him over to what had always been his work haven, as well as a small showroom, I found myself in the area where old and new clocks lined the walls and where clock parts filled shelves; an array of tools for the exacting work he was so well-known for were on his work desk and organized in cupboards nearby. In this cozy yet cluttered room, complete with its own small fireplace, Dat had worked from early morning to suppertime, and occasionally into the evening, for as long as I remembered. Sometimes, when the work was especially intricate, he hummed unfamiliar melodies while leaning close to the clock in hand, his black-rimmed magnifying loupe pressed to his right eye, his left eye squeezed shut. And all the while, the pendulums swung, and the clocks ticked their familiar pulse in this magical place.

Dat took his seat on the wooden swivel chair and gave me an appraising look. "Itching to tell me something, *Dochder?*"

Nodding, I said, "Susie Zook stopped by earlier while I was shaking out rugs." I hoped that what I was about to disclose wasn't news to him. "Preacher Zook's taken a turn for the worse."

My father lowered his head briefly and sighed. "I just returned from seeing Mahlon." Raising his head, Dat gave me a thoughtful, sad look. "The poor man is suffering."

The potential loss of Preacher Mahlon Zook seemed to trouble Dat more than I would have expected, given the minister's seventy-seven years on earth.

Even so, one of the many things I loved about my father was his attentiveness . . . and his patience. For instance, when I was very little, he would sweep me into his lap and listen while I made up a story for him, not yet able to read the picture book in his hand—the one he was waiting to read to me. *"Tell me more,"* he would say again and again, smiling encouragingly and raising his eyebrows at my tales. Oh, I could have sat there forever while Dat listened patiently.

But I wasn't the only one who clamored for his attention. Dat was also highly sought after amongst the People; there were many who came for his assistance. Generous beyond belief, he was always so eager to help anyone in need. Why, according to my beau, Titus Kauffman, even some of the ministers looked up to Dat. To think Dat had come as a seeker when he first set foot on fertile Amish soil more than twenty years ago, and now he was known as one of the most upstanding church members in all of Hickory Hollow! For several years now, he had even assisted Deacon Luke Peachey with the alms fund.

Leaning against the work desk, where I'd stood so often as a little girl watching his nimble fingers at work, I glanced at the shelves above. Once, when I was just seven, I had stood barefoot on this very surface, stretching high on tiptoes to reach the old brass tinderbox on the top shelf. Like a hen warming eggs, Dat's family heirloom always nested in the same spot. And it was always locked.

While I remember asking about the beautiful tinderbox that day when I was so young, I had often wondered *why* it was kept locked. If fire-starting material was needed, shouldn't it be at the ready?

My father had once warned me never to snoop, and Mamma had cautioned my childish curiosity. *"Ain't your business, Sylvie. Besides,"*—and here she'd looked me straight in the eye—*"how do ya know it's locked?"*

I kept mum about my efforts to pry it open; I'd even shaken the scuffed-brass treasure that had so tempted me. *Nee,* I just scrunched up my little face at Mamma like I couldn't remember, hoping she wouldn't ask more.

And in spite of my silence, Mamma leaned down and kissed my forehead. *"You've never been a Duppmeiser, Sylvia,"* she said. *"Now's not the time to start."*

Eleven years had come and gone since that embarrassing day. And I had been mindful to heed Dat's warning.

Presently, Dat reached for a mantel clock and studied the back of its case. "Is there something more on your mind, Sylvie?" he asked as he reached for a specific tool. "Dirk Jameson's dropping by soon, so I should prob'ly make sure his clock's keeping perfect time." Dat glanced at me.

I quickly told him that Titus Kauffman and I had been courting for nearly a year now. After all, Dat had likely put it together already, and he was often the first person I wanted to share with, even before Mamma at times.

"*Des gut . . .* Titus is a fine young man," Dat said approvingly.

I glowed inwardly, happy with his response.

"I'll be over for supper right on the dot," he said, still tinkering with the clock. "Be sure to tell your Mamma."

"Okay." Moving toward the open door, I slipped out to the side porch just in time to see Bishop John Beiler, the blacksmith, pull up in his enclosed carriage.

The man of God climbed out and immediately tied his mare to the hitching post. Waving at me, he smiled and hurried up the walkway lined with pink tulips toward Dat's shop. "*Wie geht's,* Sylvia?"

I replied in *Deitsch* that I was fine and glad to see him. *He'll likely tie the knot for Titus and me come November,* I thought, my face warming at the possibility.

"How's your hardworkin' Dat?" Bishop Beiler inquired.

"Keepin' real busy." I smiled and motioned toward the shop, guessing he was here to pay Dat a visit. "By the way, there's a fresh pitcher of root beer in the fridge. Care for some?"

"You're as thoughtful as your father." Bishop nodded, his blue-gray eyes twinkling. "And bring a tall glass for your Dat, too."

Agreeing, I went over to the back door of the utility room, then through the narrow hallway leading to the kitchen. There, Mamma was wiping her face with her white work apron, smiling-happy to see me.

"Bishop's come to see Dat," I said, also mentioning the offered root beer.

Mamma turned back to the counter, where she was grating cabbage for slaw. "I hope he's not bringin' worse news 'bout Preacher Zook."

"Well, he didn't look glum, if that's what ya mean." I poured the root beer and told Mamma I'd be right back to help. "Oh, and Dat says he'll be on time for supper."

Mamma laughed softly. "We'll see 'bout that."

As I carried the two tumblers of root beer out the door, I smiled fondly, thinking how caught up in his work my father often was—able to repair any clock to perfect running order. But now I wished I'd also revealed how much Titus reminded me of him—the most wonderful man I knew.

When the time's right, I'll tell him.

CHAPTER
One

*I*t was the first day of May in Hickory Hollow, and the sky was so bright Rhoda Miller wished she owned a pair of sunglasses. Thanks to the warmest spring in years, farmers had already planted both their sweet corn and their field corn.

Rhoda was not only delighted with the gorgeous weather, she was also excited about celebrating the twentieth anniversary of her engagement to dearest Earnest. *Just two weeks away, on Ascension Day,* she thought, trying to imagine what her husband might have in store to surprise her, not sure how he could top what he'd gotten last year—an antique Dutch cupboard made in 1742. And then there was the year before, when he had custom made a lovely cherrywood grandfather clock. It was almost as if their engagement anniversary was somehow more important than their actual wedding date in mid-November. But she knew better. Unlike folk who were born and raised Plain, Earnest just had his own unique way of doing certain things.

Smiling at the memory of the whirlwind Earnest Miller had

caused in her life more than two decades ago, Rhoda finished her preparations for supper while Sylvia took the ice-cold root beer to Earnest's shop. Rhoda let herself daydream about their very special relationship, feeling blessed beyond her fondest hopes by her wonderful man.

From their first meeting, brown-eyed Earnest had had such a winning way, quickly gaining her trust, as well as that of every church member, including the ministerial brethren. He had even gotten approval from Preacher Zook and Bishop John to join church after only a single year of Proving, during which he'd learned the *Ordnung*, as well as such necessary skills as how to hitch a road horse to a carriage and carpentry skills to help with barn raisings and whatnot.

Who would've thought an Englischer would make such a fine Amish husband? she thought.

With Ernie Jr. and Adam over helping the neighbor bring in the cows for the late-afternoon milking, and Calvin and Tommy out in their own barn, Tommy milking Flossie, the kitchen was too quiet. *Has it ever been this still?* Oddly, Rhoda could almost *hear* the silence, and she moved toward the screen door to stand there for a moment.

Just then, she heard Earnest talking with the bishop out on the porch. Doubtless both men were concerned about Preacher Zook's fragile state. She prayed silently, asking God to carry the faithful minister safely over Jordan when the time came. And to help his wife and family cope with the great loss. *Bring comfort and peace to the People,* she thought, not adding anything for herself. After all, she had much to be thankful for in a close-knit family, five healthy children, an attentive and loving spouse, and plenty of customers for his clock-making business. Rhoda's prayers were for others' needs—body, mind, and spirit. She believed the Lord God and heavenly Father expected nothing less of her.

While the pork chops topped with mounds of stuffing baked in the middle of the gas oven, she washed her hands at the sink and set the table, still counting her numerous blessings . . . this hand-crafted table, for one. As a teenager, she had secretly coveted the table made years before by her great-uncle. Then, lo and behold, when he passed away, the table was bestowed on Rhoda's *Mamm*, who later offered it to Rhoda after Mamm became a widow and pared down to move into the *Dawdi Haus* at Rhoda's eldest sister's.

It'll belong to Sylvia someday, Rhoda thought, wondering if the spring in her daughter's step meant there was a special fellow. If so, Earnest might have to surprise Rhoda with a different table. Either that or have a new one made for Sylvia's wedding present.

Who might be courting her? Rhoda mused as she poured cold water into a large pitcher, since most of the root beer had gone to her husband and the bishop just now. Goodness, she'd felt downright jumpy off and on all day, thinking of Preacher Zook so near death's door. She was glad Earnest had gone to see him, close as the two friends had been all these years. *Even longer than Earnest and I have been together. . . .*

"Mahlon wants you to come alongside his family when he passes," John Beiler told Earnest in the privacy of the clock showroom. After drinking their fill of root beer, they had moved inside from the porch for this private conversation.

Earnest pushed his hand through his dark beard, feeling awkward hearing this while his friend still drew breath.

Bishop John looked toward the only window in the room, then returned his gaze to Earnest, a solemn smile crossing his wrinkled face. "Mahlon trusts ya like a *Bruder*."

"I'd say the same about him," Earnest admitted. From their first encounter, his friendship with Mahlon had come about effortlessly. Mahlon had been the one to usher Earnest into the community of the People so long ago. The two men had never argued that Earnest recalled—never even spoken a cross word. Rare for any friendship, let alone for two men brought up in such vastly different cultures. And now Mahlon lay dying. *My closest friend,* Earnest thought with a great sigh.

Bishop John stayed around a few more minutes, then mentioned the batch of horseshoes he must finish making before day's end. Without saying more about Mahlon, he turned to leave.

He's already missing his other preacher, thought Earnest, returning his focus to Dirk Jameson's contrary clock. Dirk would be arriving in ten short minutes, and once the transaction was complete, Earnest would head over to supper with his wife and their children.

I'll be eating like a king when poor Mahlon hasn't been hungry in weeks, he thought guiltily.

Earnest's visit to see Mahlon that morning had had every mark of a deathbed visit. Recalling it, Earnest leaned back in his work chair, closing his eyes. His friend's words were still in his ears. *"I wonder who the Lord will choose to replace me as a preacher,"* Mahlon had said, motioning Earnest near his bed.

Earnest realized the man was thinking ahead to the casting of lots that would take place if Mahlon should pass away. He had leaned closer to hear what more his friend had to say, assuring him that he was praying for his recovery.

But Mahlon shook his head. *"My dear brother in the Lord, be ready to pick up the mantle, if it should be Gott's will."*

Earnest had struggled to keep a poker face as he inwardly shrugged the notion away. *"The People need you,"* he had insisted. *Not a man like me . . .*

Sitting to the left of her mother at the supper table, Sylvia couldn't help observing her father after the silent blessing. He had surprised Mamma by being on time for the meal, but there was something off in his demeanor, and Sylvia couldn't rightly discern what. While he seemed downright blue about Preacher Zook's failing health, something else behind his dark brown eyes hinted at a deeper misery.

Mamma passed around the baked pork chops, and Sylvia's youngest brother, Tommy, just turned eight, soon began scraping off the browned bread crumbs mixed with onions and seasoning, muttering that he didn't like his pork chop that way.

The other boys—eleven-year-old Calvin, thirteen-year-old Adam, and Ernie, fifteen—snickered. Dat let it go, maybe not even noticing. *His mind's elsewhere,* Sylvia thought.

Calvin spoke up to ask when Tommy was getting a haircut. "'Tis gettin' mighty long . . . an' curly, too," he said, his eyes dancing while he seemed to hold back a laugh.

Dat smiled a little then and scratched his wavy brown beard. "Say, I had curls like that once," he told them, looking at Mamma. "'Course, I didn't have a bowl cut when I was Tommy's age." He chuckled. "I missed out on that."

Sylvia smiled.

"Well, you need a haircut, too, dear," Mamma said, surprising them. By the looks of it, this took Dat off guard.

He flipped his hand through the back of his hair and laughed a little. "Been too busy, I guess."

Right then and there, Mamma scheduled Dat and Tommy for haircuts on the porch tomorrow evening. "Can't be puttin' it off any longer," she said.

Tommy pulled a face and reached up to tug one of the curls Calvin had complained about earlier, but Mamma had spoken, and that was that.

"Tell us more about what it was like growin' up English, Dat," Calvin said, taking his table knife and fork to his pork chop.

Instantly Sylvia was all ears, hoping to hear something about Dat's family—especially his younger sister.

Dat glanced at Mamma, then back at the boys. "Well, it wasn't nearly as much fun as you and your brothers are having, I can tell you that."

Adam's smile was nearly identical to Dat's. "Ya mean, you never had a mouse run up one pant leg and down the other when you were little?"

Dat shook his head. "Nope. And I didn't learn to bow hunt or help plant a big potato field, either. None of that." He made the saddest face just then, comically shaking his head in mock dismay.

Sylvia smiled. Truth be told, Dat had acknowledged numerous times the many things he'd missed out on—churning butter, playing corner ball, building a chicken coop, or going through eight grades of school at a one-room schoolhouse. His growing-up years had been so different from everything Sylvia knew, there were times when she wondered how Dat could *not* miss the fancy life.

I'm glad he doesn't!

"See? You kids have *all* the fun," Dat said, using one of his favorite expressions, and Mamma nodded as she sat there eating and enjoying the silliness.

"Seems to me we get all the hard work, too," Ernie said, rubbing his forehead.

"Hard work puts meat on your bones," Dat said, "and builds strong character."

"What do *curls* do?" With a grin, Calvin turned to look at Tommy's hair. "Make ya look like a little kid?"

"Now, son," Dat chided.

Sylvia didn't say what she was thinking, which was that, with such a mop of hair, their baby brother somewhat resembled a girl.

"In the blink of an eye, Tommy will be a young man," Dat told them.

Tommy beamed like he'd won a foot race.

"But looking young is a *gut* thing." Dat grinned at Mamma. "Just take a look at your pretty Mamma here . . . still as youthful as the day I met her."

"For goodness' sake," Mamma said, blushing as Dat lightly touched her cheek.

Sylvia had never heard any other person talk like Dat did. Scarcely anyone amongst the People would call another person pretty, not right out. But she couldn't deny appreciating the way her parents treated each other, like a young couple still in love, different from most other couples their age. It seemed an awful lot like Dat was still courting Mamma. Why, there were moments he looked at Mamma the way Sylvia sometimes caught Titus looking at *her*.

She had to wonder if this was because of her father's upbringing, raised outside of their cloistered world and only becoming

Amish in his twenties. Listening now to Dat's familiar teasing, she couldn't imagine having more fun around the table at any of their kinfolk's homes, or with any other family for that matter—Plain or fancy. And Mamma and Dat's enjoying every minute of their time together made Sylvia dismiss the notion that her father had been troubled earlier.

CHAPTER
Two

*A*fter the last of the dessert dishes and lemonade glasses had been washed and put away downstairs in the kitchen, Sylvia had turned in early, saying her familiar "Sweet dreams, Mamma and Dat" as she hurried to her room with a book tucked beneath her arm. Now that the boys were also in bed, Rhoda gave Earnest a back and shoulder massage, sometimes rubbing his neck beneath his dark brown hair.

The gaslight flickered on the walls of this large bedroom where Rhoda and her husband had loved so dearly, and where she still hoped to conceive at least one more baby. She had often wished for another baby girl, but seeing as their youngest was already eight, Rhoda wondered if five children might be all the Lord had planned for them. In that moment, she thought how wonderful it would be to sit and rock another little one in the old rocker passed down from her grandmother. Her heart ached for her youngest sister, Hannah Riehl Mast, who'd suffered a miscarriage last week. Her second in two years . . .

Rhoda kept kneading her husband's shoulders and neck like

bread dough, smoothing away the lumpy knots. "You've been awful tense lately," she whispered. "Ain't so?"

His answering murmur was more like a sigh.

"It's been years since you've taken even a little time off work." She hoped Preacher Zook's illness wasn't the reason Earnest was so stressed. Her husband was a giver who was always doing for others and dropping everything to help anyone in Hickory Hollow who needed looking after or just befriending. Through it all, Mahlon Zook had been the one person he turned to outside their family. And when the time came for Mahlon to take his last breath, Earnest's clock making would likely become his solace . . . that and his family, of course. She just hoped he wouldn't lose himself in his work like some folk seemed to do during hard times.

When she'd finished the massage, Earnest rolled onto his back and took her into his arms. She smiled in the dim light. "Who would I be without ya?" she asked softly.

"Shh, my love," he said, kissing her cheek, her forehead, her eyelids. "Rhoda . . . my sweetheart." His lips met hers.

The background of night sounds—someone's mule in the distance and a light wind in the trees near the eaves—began to fade as Earnest's kisses became more ardent.

"I love you so," he whispered, and if she wasn't mistaken, his cheeks were damp with tears.

For the life of her, she could not remember a time when their hours together had been so tender. It was as if her husband's heart was breaking.

Before breakfast the next morning, after he had hauled hay down from the barn loft for the livestock—one cow, two driving horses, and the field mules—Earnest plodded back to the house and sat down on the back porch steps, Mahlon's words repeating in his mind. *"Be ready to pick up the mantle, if it should be Gott's will."*

He leaned forward, his hands pressed against his temples, trying to dismiss what his friend had said. *Truth be told, Mahlon doesn't know everything about me. . . .*

Earnest raised his head and looked toward the field that separated his house from the Zooks' brick farmhouse with its abundant rose arbors—the latter one of Mahlon's pet projects—and something welled up. He had an impulse to rush over there again to look in on his dying friend, now in the painful last stages of stomach cancer. But it would be selfish to disturb the household at this early hour, and on a Saturday, too.

Mahlon's impending death—and the possibility that Earnest could be nominated for the drawing of lots—had stopped him in his tracks and made him think about things he had not previously considered. Or if he had, he'd pushed them far into the recesses of his mind.

Getting up from the steps, he walked out to his red two-story barn, climbed up the long ladder to the hayloft, and perched himself on the edge. Earnest looked at the rope swing far below and shuddered as the past crashed down upon him.

Rhoda watched her husband through the kitchen window after breakfast that Saturday as he hitched up to run an errand. Without even a wave, he leaped into the spring wagon and rattled down the drive to Hickory Lane. She found it peculiar, since he always made a point of running inside to kiss her good-bye when he was leaving the house.

She shook it off, refusing to dwell on it. *Not after last night . . .*

Just then, Sylvia came downstairs from redding up her room and asked what she could do to help in the kitchen. "I was thinking we could bake some cookies or sticky buns for *Aendi* Hannah . . . and Uncle Curtis, too."

"Nice idea," Rhoda said, glad her daughter had suggested it, as they were fairly caught up with indoor chores. "We'll make snickerdoodles, Hannah's favorite."

So, while Sylvia wiped the kitchen counter, Rhoda set out the mixing bowl and gathered the ingredients. She hoped the cookies would put a smile on Hannah's face. Since the sudden loss of her baby, her dear sister had kept her shades drawn and wasn't eating much. This worried Rhoda no end. *Hannah's in desperate straits.*

Rhoda began to make a generous batch of cookie dough. "Some cheer-up cookies will be just the thing to give me an excuse to look in on her," Rhoda said, noticing again how very perky her daughter looked these days—brown eyes sparkling and a nearly perpetual smile on her dear face.

"Sounds good. I'll be headin' to see a friend in a little while myself," Sylvia said as she measured the vanilla for the cookies.

"Will ya be back for dinner at noon?"

Sylvia shook her head. "Not today, *nee.*"

"Oh?"

"Gonna have a picnic."

Given the pink tint to her daughter's cheeks, Rhoda was curious to know more. "Ain't picnic weather yet, is it?"

"Well, the sun'll be shinin' right nice by noon. Besides, we'll be picnicking in a gazebo."

Furtively, Rhoda made a mental list of the neighbors who had gazebos. But as much as she wished her daughter would reveal what was up, Rhoda kept her peace and didn't probe further. When Sylvia was ready, she would tell her more. Meanwhile, she may have already mentioned something to Earnest. *The two of them have always been so close.*

Rhoda had thought of inviting Sylvia to go along with her to Hannah's, but Rhoda knew her sister wasn't herself at all, and Sylvia would sense something more was amiss. Heartbroken and fragile as she was, Hannah didn't want the miscarriage to be known even amongst her nieces. *Most folk just think Hannah's been under the weather. . . .*

Dear Hannah had been four months along this time, and Rhoda prayed for wisdom to help bring her sister out of the doldrums.

Sylvia was staring at her. "You look awful sad, Mamma."

"Just thinkin'." Rhoda tried to put on a more pleasant countenance, wanting to keep her sister's secret.

"Well, let me know if there's anything else I can do." Sylvia removed the cookie sheets from the cupboard and greased them with freshly churned butter from their neighbors over on Cattail Road.

After they scooped out balls of snickerdoodle dough, rolled them in cinnamon sugar, and placed them onto the prepared cookie sheets, Rhoda opened the hot oven. "You really don't have to wait around for these to bake, Sylvie."

"*Denki*, Mamma." And without another word, Sylvia flew toward the stairs to change clothes—or so Rhoda assumed.

How unusual to meet a beau for a noontime picnic, Rhoda

thought, then smiled to herself, remembering the thrill of falling in love.

~~∽~~

On the drive over to Amos Kauffman's in Dat's enclosed family carriage, Sylvia passed the old water wheel just up the way on Hickory Lane, there near the grassy streamside beneath the stately trees, and recalled her father pointing it out to her as a little girl.

As the carriage rumbled along, Sylvia reveled in the sight of dozens of flower beds bursting with golden-yellow snap-dragons, as well as the sweet perfume of lilac bushes lining the roadside. There were times when the wondrous sights and sounds of nature made her want to stop and fall to her knees to pray. She wondered if anyone else ever felt so moved; it was as if the Lord was trying to say something to her through His creation. Could it be a sign of His blessing over her and Titus's growing love? Might he propose marriage today? Or perhaps the invitation was simply meant for her to get better acquainted with his family.

Mamma will soon know I'm seeing Titus, if Dat hasn't told her already. . . .

Presently, she looked around her at the Kauffmans' front yard, a sure slice of heaven. The immense rolling lawn leveled off to a small pond encircled by a narrow walkway that Titus and his brothers had created years ago, and neighboring trees towered over ducks, Canada geese, and two swans. Taking in the loveliness, Sylvia thought, *If I weren't Plain, I'd want our wedding to take place right here.*

She caught herself and felt a bit shamefaced. Such flights of fancy would never do. Once she joined church this September, she would have to keep her musings in check.

Hearing footsteps on the gravel lane, she saw Titus coming to greet her. And by the enormous smile on his handsome face, she sensed that something really wonderful was about to happen. Oh, she could scarcely wait!

CHAPTER
Three

"W*illkumm!*" said Titus, looking handsome even in his work clothes as he offered a hand when she stepped out of the carriage. The sandy brown hair peeking from beneath his straw hat looked recently combed. "It's *wunnerbaar-gut* to see ya, Sylvie!"

She smiled, touched by his enthusiasm. "You too. A nice day, ain't so?"

"The best, now that you're here." Titus offered to unhitch the horse and lead it to the stable for water. "Mamm's waitin' for ya on the back porch," he said, giving Sylvia a quick peck on the cheek after checking to make sure no one was looking. "She has a surprise."

"Do I get a little hint?"

Titus smiled mischievously. "It's somethin' you'll love. And that's all the hint ya get."

Even more curious now, Sylvia made her way the short distance around the walkway, where Spanish bluebells bloomed on the side closest to the house. Reaching the porch, she called a hullo to round-cheeked Eva, then asked, "*Wie geht's?*"

"*Gut*, Sylvia. It's so nice to have ya with us. *Kumme* join me." Eva motioned her near, sitting there barefoot in her purple dress and black apron. She even wore her white organdy *Kapp*, which, like most women, she primarily donned on Sundays for Preaching or for going visiting, and its long white ties hung down the front of her dress bodice. "How was the ride over?"

"Just fine." Sylvia sat next to her on one of the several wooden porch chairs.

"Did ya notice our new baby ducklings?" Eva asked. "They hatched just yesterday."

"Not yet. I'd love to see the fuzzy wee critters . . . and to go walkin' along the perty path near the pond sometime."

Eva nodded and beamed. "Maybe you an' Titus can go together today."

Sylvia shouldn't have been surprised at how talkative and welcoming Eva Kauffman was. After all, being a preacher's wife meant that she spent a lot of time with womenfolk in the church, as well as counseling couples with her minister husband. Eva was a natural at it.

Eva reached into her quilted carryall, which hung on the back of the rocking chair. "I've been working on a little something for your hope chest." She reached in and brought out an embroidered dresser runner. "Titus says you like tulips." Eva handed it to her.

My favorite flowers. Sylvia's heart beat a little faster, realizing that Eva surely knew before today that her son's interest in her was serious. She ran her pointer finger over the stitching. "It's so lovely. *Denki.*"

"I chose different colors for the clusters on each end of the doily." Eva described how she'd worked on it evenings a little bit at a time while the girls redded up the kitchen. She offered Sylvia the carryall, too, for the runner's safekeeping.

"How thoughtful," Sylvia said, accepting the gift and folding it carefully before placing it back in the carryall.

"Been wantin' to do something special." Eva began to rock again. "Titus thinks the world of ya."

Sylvia felt embarrassed. "He's a truly *wunnerbaar* fella," she said, catching the delicious scent of barbequed chicken. The tantalizing smells coming from the nearby kitchen prompted her manners, and she offered to help with food preparation.

"Everything's nearly ready—Lavina, Connie, and I made the potato salad this mornin', and the baked beans, too." Eva smiled. "Hope ya like chocolate cake."

"*Ach*, who doesn't?"

Together, they laughed softly, and when Titus came back from the stable, he leaped up the porch steps and stood there, fanning his face with his straw hat, his bangs fluttering in the breeze. "Sounds like yous are getting better acquainted," he said, hazel eyes shining.

Without skipping a beat, Eva suggested he take Sylvia down to the pond while she got the table set up "out yonder." She bobbed her head toward the white gazebo.

"Oh, why don't we help ya?" Sylvia proposed, eager to assist yet also wanting some time with just Titus.

But Eva insisted they let her and her daughters get everything ready, so Titus motioned for Sylvia to follow him. Eva nodded and smiled approvingly as she rose and headed inside.

"Mamm has spoken," Titus whispered with a smile.

"Well, I like her," Sylvia said as she and Titus walked down the sloping lane.

"What a coincidence." He chuckled. "I do, too!"

Sylvia suppressed a laugh.

"It was her idea to have ya come over for part of the day. Mamm thought we needed time to talk." He paused a moment. "I would've come to get ya, but I knew I'd be hauling and stackin' hay in the barn with Dat this mornin'. I hope ya understand."

So, today was his Mamm's idea, she thought, feeling a twinge of disappointment before brightening again. Of course, the important thing was that she was here with her beau.

Sylvia nodded, enjoying the fragrance of the nearby redbud bushes and the sun glistening on the pond. "There's always farm work to be done," she answered.

His fingers brushed against hers, and she sensed he wanted to reach for her hand, though she guessed that would have to wait till they were out riding in his courting buggy after Singing tomorrow evening.

Leisurely, they walked halfway around the pond before coming upon the downy ducklings Eva had talked about. Crouching on the path, Titus talked softly in *Deitsch* to the tiny creatures pecking at seeds in the grass. The ducklings' parents stood guard nearby, the mother particularly watchful.

"See that?" Titus whispered, glancing up at Sylvia. "You'll be just like her . . . a caring and kind Mamma to our children one day."

Sylvia's heart beat faster at the thought as he rose to his feet.

"I love you," he said, his face full of affection. "And more than anything, I want ya for my bride, Sylvie."

Prior to talking with his mother on the porch, she'd wondered what Titus might have in mind today, but she hadn't imagined he would propose here, where the pond lapped against its grassy bank and the trees swayed so gracefully, as if nodding in approval. The moment nearly took her breath away.

She accepted his extended hand. "I love ya, too, Titus."

"Whew!" Titus exclaimed, pretending relief as he stepped closer. He didn't kiss her, but his eyes were fixed on her mouth. "You'll make me the happiest fella ever," he said as they fell into step again.

She could scarcely speak. It had been one thing to dream about this moment, but it was quite another to hear Titus's words just now.

"Would ya like to talk with your parents to see what day in November suits for our wedding?" he asked as they strolled along, a light breeze coming off the pond.

She agreed and couldn't help but smile as he stopped walking and lifted her hand to his lips. "As far as where we'll stay at first, I realize your room would be available to us, but maybe we should talk things over with my Mamm first. She has some other ideas."

"Other ideas? Like what?"

"Well, to give us more privacy, Mamm thinks we should stay *here* after the wedding, during the first few weeks," Titus said, "when our kinfolk drop by with wedding presents an' all."

Sylvia briefly wondered if Titus had cleared *everything* with his Mamm, but she dismissed that. *It's good to marry a man who loves his mother,* she thought. After all, every bride had to make adjustments when leaving her family and childhood home. *I'm willing to do this for our love.*

Just then the dinner bell sounded, and Titus quickened his steps. Sylvia matched his pace as they headed up toward the house and the gazebo, though she was somewhat reluctant to leave the beautiful pond and pebbled path where she and her beloved had just agreed to wed. She felt so fortunate to be marrying into such a devout family—Amos Kauffman's reputation amongst the People had few equals.

We'll be uniting two well-respected Hickory Hollow families, she thought happily.

CHAPTER

Four

*R*hoda noticed an extra carriage parked outside her sister Hannah's house as she walked up the lane. "Wonder who's here," she murmured, realizing now that it might not suit Hannah for her to stop by, after all. On the other hand, if one of their other sisters was visiting, they could all enjoy a delicious treat together. Through the years, Rhoda had come to learn that a soft snickerdoodle had a way of lifting one's spirits. The taste might not last long, but for those brief moments, people tended to forget their hurt. *A piece of chocolate works wonders, too,* she thought, smiling as she knocked on the screen door.

Standing there, she could see the kitchen shades were pulled down to the windowsills, and she could hear soft talking coming from within. Rhoda didn't want to listen too closely, but it sounded like Ella Mae Zook might be with Hannah, and if so, what ideal company. The Wise Woman of Hickory Hollow had a true gift for bringing cheer to any gathering, large or small.

Not wanting to simply walk in, Rhoda knocked a bit harder. And soon here came Ella Mae herself to the door, as straight and tall as if she were decades younger. "Hullo, Ella Mae," Rhoda said as the older woman let her in. "Hope I'm not interrupting."

"*Ach*, your sister will be glad to see ya, dearie," Ella Mae said, a smile stretching across her heavily wrinkled face. "And so am I."

Rhoda offered her arm to Ella as they walked into the large kitchen, where Hannah sat holding a pretty floral teacup over its matching saucer. "I brewed some of my homemade peppermint tea," Ella Mae said as she took a seat at the table across from Hannah. "Would ya care for some, too?" she asked.

"*Denki*, but I'm a bit warm from the walk here." Rhoda set down her basket of snickerdoodles and patted her sister's shoulder before sitting next to her. "I've been thinking 'bout ya," Rhoda said quietly, relieved to see Hannah drinking some tea when she'd had so little appetite. "Prayin' too."

Hannah glanced at her. "Honestly, I've felt quite ill," she said in a near whisper. "I'm a little better today . . . but it's so hard."

Ella Mae folded her thin hands on the table, her skin speckled with age. Her pure white hair was pulled into a tidy bun beneath an organdy *Kapp*. "Why, sure it's hard," Ella Mae said to Hannah. "Your wee babe was a part of you and always will be."

"I fear I'll never carry a baby to term," Hannah said, stopping to wipe her eyes. "And if not, what then? My husband will have no sons to help him around the farm, and I'll have no daughters to—"

"Hannah, dear," said Ella Mae, "let's take things one day at a time."

Sighing, Hannah gave in to tears.

Rhoda moved near to comfort her sister, slipping an arm around her waist. And for the longest time, the two of them sat there like that while Ella Mae closed her eyes as though she was praying.

When Hannah finally did speak, she admitted that she was holed up in the house not only out of sadness, but because there would be mothers with babies everywhere she might go. "And little ones trailin' along." She shook her head. "Not sure how I can get past this, not this time."

Ella Mae's small eyes glistened. "Your heart's broken wide open. . . . I know the feelin' all too well." She began to reveal slowly that she, too, had lost a baby to miscarriage. "'Twas ever so long ago, but even now not a day goes by that I don't think of him." Here she managed a faint smile. "I was never told, but I feel sure that my little one was a boy. I think of him a-waitin' for me in Gloryland, up there with his Dat."

Having never struggled with her own pregnancies, Rhoda could only imagine what her precious sister was going through, and she was thankful for Ella Mae's willingness to share about her own past heartache.

Hannah glanced toward the ceiling, her chest rising and falling. "After ya lost him, did ya feel like you couldn't put one foot in front of the other?"

"For months, I did," Ella Mae said. "It was one of the most difficult times in my life, quite honestly."

Hannah nodded. "And I can't understand it . . . but my arms hurt terribly, too. It makes no sense."

"Maybe this'll give ya hope," Ella Mae said. "In time, I delivered healthy, full-term babies, and I believe you will, too." She glanced at Rhoda. "Your sister and I will pray the Lord gives you the desire of your heart, won't we, Rhoda?"

Agreeing, Rhoda offered a small smile.

"In fact, let's do that together right now," Ella Mae said, folding her wrinkled hands and bowing her head, leading out in a prayer. It was quite irregular to do so, but the prayer appeared to bring some calm to Hannah.

Afterward, Rhoda reached to open her basket and placed the plate of snickerdoodles near Hannah, who still looked pale. But it was obvious that her sister wasn't interested in a cookie, though she did glance at them. Then, unexpectedly, she excused herself to leave for the small bathroom around the corner from the kitchen.

"What more can we do for her?" Rhoda asked Ella Mae quietly.

Ella Mae rubbed her high forehead. "Her body and her emotions seem to be in equal turmoil . . . only time and God's compassion will comfort her. She'll need time to fully grieve, just as any of us must mourn a dear one's passing."

Rhoda believed that, as well, but she wished her sister didn't have such a long road to travel. "Perhaps you already know that Hannah wants to keep mum about what happened," she told Ella Mae.

"'Tis understandable." The Wise Woman looked toward the window, where thick, gnarled vines of blooming wisteria pushed so close they almost looked like they were anxious to come inside. Ella Mae turned back to regard Rhoda. "Do any of your children still have a teddy bear?" she asked.

Curious about the sudden turn in conversation, Rhoda said, "Let's see, I think Calvin and Tommy still have the one they shared. Why do you ask?"

"Hannah said her arms ache . . . makes me wonder if holding something the size of a baby might help ease her pain."

Rhoda was dumbfounded at this notion, though she thought the idea worth a try. "I'll go an' buy her one if need be," she promised.

Anything for my poor sister!

Sylvia was engrossed in Titus's talk about his preacher father, a born farmer. She and Titus were enjoying their picnic beneath the shelter of the gazebo, just the two of them. Mistakenly, Sylvia had assumed Titus's family would be joining them—*or perhaps just his Mamm,* she thought humorously—but everyone else remained in the house.

Titus set down his tall glass of iced tea. "Like many men round here, my father loves the hard work of farmin', especially harvesting the reward for his labor. Even in his early teens, Dat knew he wanted to be a crop farmer and also raise chickens, not run a dairy operation. He's always known that farmin's his calling in life."

Sylvia smiled. "It's helpful for a man to know how he wants to earn a livin'," she agreed, "even though it seems some of *die Youngie* don't know till close to when they join church." She shared that her own father had come to Amish farmland in search of a different sort of life. "He was real happy to find an apprenticeship as a clockmaker, but I suppose you know that already, ain't?"

Finishing his barbequed chicken, Titus nodded. "My Dat remembers the week yours showed up here," he said with a grin. "I guess it was quite a time. The ministerial brethren were scratching their heads that a Yankee fella wanted nothin' to do with the world he was brought up in. Joked that he must be runnin' from something."

Sylvia laughed. To hear Titus tell it, it was like her father had dropped out of the sky.

"Your Dat's an inspiration to me," Titus added. "I've always enjoyed workin' alongside him, haying and loading the bales into the hayloft each summer."

Sylvia smiled as they finished their private meal, and it was almost as though his Mamm knew they were ready for dessert, because in a few minutes, she came marching up the steps of the gazebo with a large piece of cake for each of them. "S'pose you're ready for something sweet," Eva said cheerfully, her eyes shining with love for Titus and fondness for Sylvia, too. Smiling and waiting, Eva stepped back and watched them take a first bite.

"Oh, it's so moist and light," Sylvia exclaimed. "It's *wunnerbaar-gut!*"

"Say, we should have this cake for the youth Ascension Day picnic," Titus suggested. "What do ya think, Sylvie?"

"Well, if your Mamm's willing to share her secret for making a cake this light, I'd be glad to bake a couple, sure."

Eva was already nodding her head, a sparkle still in her pretty blue eyes. "I'll jot down the recipe if you'd like."

"Would I ever!" Sylvia thanked her, and Eva scurried back down the gazebo steps and toward the house to do just that.

Titus waited till his mother was out of earshot. "Mamm suspects this is more than just a date."

Surely she knows what happened down at the pond. . . .

Sylvia felt humbled that both Titus and Eva treated her like one of them. To think that she, the daughter of a former outsider, was so welcomed by this pious family!

CHAPTER
Five

*O*nce Sylvia returned home and realized Mamma must still be visiting Aunt Hannah, she decided to make good use of her time and go over to dust Dat's shop, especially his work area. With her father away from the house, too—the spring wagon was still gone from the carriage shed—now seemed to be the perfect opportunity. *I won't be in his way.*

She took a clean dust cloth from the kitchen pantry and made her way across the back porch, thinking of the momentous events of the day. *I'm engaged to marry Titus Kauffman!* she thought, not even trying to hide her smile.

Slipping inside the shop, she heard the gentle ticking of a new grandfather clock and several pretty mantel chime clocks—a pleasant backdrop. She breathed in the familiar scent, something her father jokingly referred to as "the aroma of time."

She opened the door to his workspace and began to dust, being careful to lift and replace things right back where she found them. It would never do to misplace one of her father's special tools.

Then, glancing at the shelves, she brought the sturdy wood chair over and stood on that to reach the top shelf with the tinderbox, going lightly over her father's one and only heirloom.

As she dusted, a tiny key flew off the shelf and fell to the floor. "*Ach*," she murmured, displeased with herself. Then, wondering if it might be the key to the old tinderbox, she stared at the floor where the tiny key lay, her head in a whirl.

Moments passed as she looked now at the brass box, passed down through generations of Dat's family. She remembered the times she'd yearned to see its contents—a mere child then. Now she was engaged to marry, a young woman who had put away childish things. So why did she still long to lift the lid and peek inside? *If only for a second . . .*

She argued with herself. *Dat keeps it locked for a reason.*

But her curiosity was like a boiling caldron threatening to spill over into action.

Walk away, she told herself. Even so, she wondered why the key was in plain sight today, when she'd never seen it before.

"No one has to know," she whispered, still standing on the chair, as she reached to bring the tinderbox down from the shelf, wondering if it might already be unlocked.

Cautiously, she tried the lid, lifting it a fraction of an inch before she stopped. Struggling with the memory of Dat's warning never to snoop inside, she closed the lid, staring at the box all the while.

Then, losing the battle, she pulled the lid open again, this time completely. To her surprise, she found a boy's-size Yankees ball cap, and feeling emboldened, she stepped down from the chair and set the box on the worktable. Carefully, she unrolled the fabric behind the cap's bill and found what looked like a plastic-coated ball game ticket. She removed the cap and ticket and placed them beside the tinderbox, surprised to find still more items—a keychain with an hourglass dangling from it, a high school diploma, a crocheted red Christmas ornament, and letters and photographs of people she did not recognize. She took the time to look at each picture, pausing at the sight of a young girl with a heart-shaped face who somewhat resembled her father.

Who's this? she wondered.

Setting the photos aside, she looked in the very bottom of the tinderbox and found something wound in soft cotton cloths—something quite hard, by the feel of it. She glanced over her shoulder, suddenly afraid Dat might walk in and find her snooping, something she'd never dreamed of doing since that long-ago day.

Her heart pounding, she lifted the lump out of the tinderbox and unwrapped the cloths. Again, she looked behind her. What would Dat say if he caught her? She was intruding on his privacy, yet her curiosity continued to pull hard.

The cloth fell away to reveal a sparkling gold timepiece. It was the most attractive pocket watch she had ever seen. Where had it come from?

Still fearful of being discovered, she quickly lifted the large watch out of its padded nest and stared at the exquisite face, its black numerals crisp and clear and the background as spotless as new-fallen snow.

Why doesn't Dat use this? It's a bit fancy, but he could carry it in his pocket like some of the other menfolk.

Turning it around to look at the back, she found an inscription. *To Earnest, with all my love, Rosalind.*

"Rosalind?" she murmured.

Sylvia pondered this, wondering if it might have been a special gift from her Dat's only sister. She recalled hearing that she had died as a young teen. If so, could a girl that age have afforded a remarkable timepiece like this? Or could it have been purchased by her father's parents on behalf of his dying sister?

"*Ach*," Sylvia groaned, wishing she'd paid closer attention to the few instances Dat had talked about his sole sibling—one of the only relatives he'd mentioned. *Did he ever mention her name?* Sylvia tried to remember. *Was it Rosalind?*

She thought it strange that her father rarely spoke of his family. She recalled that it was Mamma who'd told her and the boys that Dat's parents had passed away years ago.

I certainly can't ask Dat 'bout this, or he'll know I was prying.

The neigh of a horse startled her. And, realizing that her father might appear at any moment, she quickly rewrapped the pocket watch and placed it back in the tinderbox, with the other items on top, the way she'd found them.

Then, closing the lid, Sylvia stood on the chair again to return the tinderbox to its rightful spot on the shelf. She hopped down, picked up the dustcloth, and finished redding up the lower shelves.

Surely Mamma would remember Dat's sister's name, she thought. Yet how to bring it up without letting on what she'd done?

Going out on the porch, Sylvia gave the dustcloth several slaps against the rail, her mind still fixated on the inscription. If it was from his sister, why inscribe the words *all my love*?

Once back inside the house, Sylvia ran upstairs and hurried to her parents' bedroom. For a moment, she stood in the doorway, scanning the room, her gaze falling on the beautiful blanket chest Dat had given Mamma years ago, a piece made by Preacher Mahlon Zook . . . and the beautiful three-chime clock on the bureau, too. Dat loved to give Mamma extravagant gifts around this time of year to mark their engagement, something she'd never heard of other husbands doing amongst the People.

She drew in a long breath and pondered again the strange contents of the tinderbox, especially the timepiece. Someone must have loved her father very much to give him such an expensive gift.

Nagging questions rolled through Sylvia's mind while she started supper for Mamma and Tommy went out to milk Flossie. Later, when the family gathered to eat the evening meal, she felt so preoccupied she could scarcely focus when Dat talked about having gone earlier to help Preacher Zook by doing his barn chores.

Sylvia studied his face; he seemed ever so worried about his friend. But the way he spoke seemed different somehow . . . or was it just the way *she* felt that colored everything?

For the life of her, Sylvia wanted to ask right out who the mysterious Rosalind was. And why on earth was Dat hiding such an expensive watch and all the other interesting items?

After Rhoda cut Earnest's and Tommy's hair outside, and they'd had family prayers, Earnest headed upstairs to bed. Rhoda didn't let the early hour bother her, since he'd mentioned feeling tuckered out and not to worry.

She and Sylvia dished up homemade ice cream for the boys

and washed up again before Sylvia took herself out for a walk, leaving Rhoda to finish redding up the kitchen.

She recalled how Hannah had eventually reached for a snickerdoodle prior to Rhoda's departure today. Ella Mae had also enjoyed a cookie or two, remarking that sometimes a little dose of sugar was helpful. *I couldn't have said it better myself,* Rhoda thought before breathing a prayer for her sister.

She again considered Ella Mae's suggestion of a teddy bear for Hannah to hold and rock. So, when the boys went to the barn to do their chores, she headed upstairs to look in Calvin and Tommy's shared bedroom closet. On the shelf above the hanging clothes, she found the soft brown bear she'd purchased a few years ago. Reaching for it, she held it near, walking around her youngest sons' room and remembering when her own youngsters were just infants. The reality of Hannah's plight hit hard. She could not imagine the loss of any one of them!

Rhoda hoped that the cuddly bear might bring not only solace to Hannah but healing, too, in time.

I'll just borrow this bear for a while, she thought, taking it downstairs and placing it on the wooden bench next to the kitchen table.

Rhoda sat down and began to add her thoughts to a long circle letter from four other women named Rhoda, all with the same October twentieth birthdate. Several years ago, a woman named Rhoda Kinsinger from Somerset, Pennsylvania—the second oldest of all Amish settlements in the United States— had announced an invitation in an Amish newspaper to start up a circle letter amongst other Rhodas who shared her birthday. Three other women responded, including one from Maryland, the state where Earnest's mother's parents had lived decades ago. Earnest had told her how much he had always enjoyed his Old Order Mennonite grandparents, whom he'd spent time with a few summers as a youth, and one wintry week during Christmas vacation. Over the years, they'd even taught him to speak some Pennsylvania Dutch, which had helped him pass his Proving time here more quickly. Even though both Papa and Grammy Zimmerman were deceased years before he came to Hickory Hollow, Earnest had insisted that they had been a big influence on his becoming a convert to the Amish church.

She fiddled with her pen and thought back on the early days of their marriage, back when Earnest had first talked so glowingly of his mother's parents. Rhoda had often wondered why he seemed so closely linked to them, perhaps even closer than to his parents, but she'd never asked. *It's been years since he's mentioned them at all,* she thought, hearing the tread of footsteps moving from one end of the upstairs bedroom to the other, and then back again.

Is Earnest pacing? She stopped writing to listen. Soon, she heard the steady creak of the rocking chair against the floor. Her husband certainly seemed restless. *Should I go up to him?*

Keeping an ear out in case Earnest called to her, she continued to write, sharing with the other Rhodas a little about her past week, the kinds of ordinary things one might share with a neighbor.

She was close to signing off when Sylvia wandered into the kitchen, her face red and perspiring. "Well, goodness, were you out runnin'?"

Sylvia shook her head. "Just walkin' fast."

"Are you all right?"

Her daughter frowned momentarily, then seemingly shrugged

off the question and went to get a tumbler down from the cupboard. Without turning around, she reached for the faucet and ran cold water. "Dat's sister died real young, *jah*?" Sylvia asked abruptly.

Rhoda wondered what had prompted this question. "Well, she was only thirteen . . . your brother Adam's age. A rare form of cancer took her." Rhoda found it surprising that Sylvia had asked about Earnest's only sibling. "It was the saddest thing. It wasn't long after that their mother developed a heart condition."

"Dat doesn't talk much 'bout his family, does he?" Sylvia stood at the sink, letting the water run.

"Well, he used to every now and then, but that was back before you and your brothers were born. Guess maybe it's hard for him . . . sometimes a loss does that to a person."

Sylvie turned off the water. "What was his sister's name?" she asked, still at the sink. "I've forgotten."

Rhoda placed stamps on her envelopes. "Charlene, but she went by Charlie."

Suddenly, Sylvia's tumbler dropped onto the floor, splattering water everywhere. "*Ach*, I'm sorry, Mamma."

"Ain't breakable—no need to fret," Rhoda said, wondering just what had come over Sylvia.

CHAPTER

Six

*E*arly the next morning, Earnest slipped over to his shop after he and Ernie watered the livestock and let them out to pasture. His sleep had been sporadic, and he required solace before this Lord's Day breakfast with the family. His clock shop was the best place for that.

He was wishing there was time to visit Mahlon before the Preaching service when a glint of light caught his eye. He looked closer and noticed a small key lying on the floor back near the workbench, nearly invisible.

A sudden rush of panic blew through him. *Get ahold of yourself,* he thought, shaking his head and trying to think rationally. He must have dropped it while looking inside his grandfather's tinderbox recently. *Simple as that.*

Even so, a deep groan echoed within him. *I've never been so careless. . . .*

He picked up the key and placed it on his worktable. Then, reaching for the tinderbox, he lifted it down from the shelf, looked inside, and found the prized remnants from his modern life all in place. He removed everything to get to the bottom item and noticed the cloth wrapping had been done up differently than before.

His heart dropped, and fearing the worst, he removed the pocket watch. Finger smudges clearly marked the clock's face.

Sylvia was excited, this being the start of baptismal classes for her and the eight other candidates. Today's instruction was scheduled to take place upstairs at Elam and Annie Lapp's farmhouse, the hosting family for the Lord's Day Preaching service. During the time of congregational singing downstairs, Sylvia and the other candidates followed the ministers to the *Abrot*, the counsel room—usually Annie's big sewing room. Sylvia was happy to see Titus among the young men present.

As they gathered, the bishop greeted each one and encouraged them in their decision to follow the Lord in holy baptism at the end of the weeks of studying the eighteen articles from the Dordrecht Confession of Faith. Bishop Beiler, Preacher Kauffman, and Deacon Peachey took turns admonishing them to be diligent in searching the Scriptures that were the basis for the articles.

All the while, Sylvia listened attentively, taking in the teaching with an open heart.

Earnest listened as Preacher Amos Kauffman stood tall for the morning's opening sermon, like a statue in black, except for his crisp white shirt. As was his custom, Amos rarely made eye contact with the congregation, largely staring at the back wall as he spoke. Their older minister, Mahlon Zook, had always paced while delivering his sermons, his tone as solemn and reverent as Amos's. Years ago, Mahlon had confided in Earnest that, while preaching without notes or an outline made him nervous, it also made him rely all the more on the Holy Spirit. Earnest had never envied his friend's ordination as a minister, knowing all too well from Mahlon the burden he carried for the flock . . . and earning the trust of the People, too. *His cross to bear for these many years now,* thought Earnest of his dying friend.

Amos Kauffman continued, his demeanor increasingly serious. "Never forget that we're pilgrims just a-passin' through on this earthly journey," he said, emphasizing the importance of adhering to the *Ordnung* during one's life. "At all costs, we must avoid the world, the flesh, and the devil and keep our eyes fixed on the Lord *Gott* and what is right in His eyes," he said. "Do not yield to temptation."

To think this man's eldest son is courting my daughter. Earnest recalled how Sylvia had told him.

Struggling to refocus on the sermon, Earnest shifted his weight on the wooden bench, where he sat next to Mahlon's brother Edwin and Edwin's two married sons, James and Caleb. The bishop's married sons, Hickory John, Levi, and Jacob, sat nearby. Oddly, this sermon seemed longer than its usual thirty minutes, and Earnest found himself fidgeting even more. He tuned out Amos's admonitions, brooding until a cool sweat broke out on his upper lip.

In due time, Amos finished and the People knelt for silent prayer. Afterward, while Deacon Luke read the twelfth chapter of Romans, Earnest stood with the congregation.

"'Be of the same mind one toward another. Mind not high things, but condescend to men of low estate,'" Luke read in

German from the large black *Biewel*. "'Be not wise in your own conceits.'"

I am a dreadful man, thought Earnest, wishing to exit the service as quickly as possible.

Before the fellowship meal of homemade bread with various spreads, pickles and cheese, celery and carrot sticks, pies and cookies and plenty of coffee, Sylvia helped her mother put out the dishes and silverware, enjoying the process. To Sylvia's delight, Eva Kauffman was also one of the helpers, which made it especially fun.

At the seating for *die Youngie*, Sylvia joined five of her girl cousins, happy to see her very closest ones, Alma and Jessie Yoder, ages nineteen and seventeen respectively, and to hear about the brunettes' busy week.

Soon, though, her mind wandered to Dat's deceased sister, Charlie, and she wished she'd had the chance to meet her. Sylvia felt the same about her father's parents, both taken from him within the space of months around his sophomore year of college.

Sylvia was tempted to ponder the pocket watch and its inscription, but she pushed it out of her mind and glanced toward the fellows at the opposite table. She caught Titus's eye, her heart speeding up at the thought of riding with him in his open carriage later tonight, after Singing.

Our first date as an engaged couple, she thought, wondering if Titus would kiss her for the first time. Or would he wait till their wedding day?

The late-afternoon sun filtered in through Sylvia's bedroom windows, casting shadows on the floor and on her bed quilt—the Heart and Nine Patch pattern she so admired. Amongst happy chatter, she and Mamma and aunts Hannah and Ruthann, along with Alma and Jessie, had all helped to stitch it up on her sixteenth birthday. They hadn't been able to completely finish the quilt in one session, but it had been a memorable day just the same. When her father had seen the nearly finished quilt, he'd remarked on the striking colors—reds, yellows, and greens. *"It's perfect,"* he'd said. *"Like you, Sylvie."*

She glanced around the room, thinking what it might be like to share it with Titus in the early days of their coming marriage, but Titus's mother had other plans, which was probably all right, considering Sylvia's room was bookended on either side by her brothers'.

Eager to attend the evening's Singing, Sylvia took great care to undo her hair bun and brush many strokes before putting it back in the tidiest bun possible, prior to leaving with Ernie. Next year, Ernie would be attending Singings, too, but for now he seemed glad to give her a ride there, making it possible for her beau to bring her home later that night.

"You seem mighty happy, sister," Ernie said as they rode together in Dat's gray buggy.

"Do I, now?" she said, not letting on why. *Too soon to tell him about my engagement,* she thought, enjoying the ride and taking in the masses of apricot rhododendron blossoms near the shady stream banks. *I should tell Dat and Mamma first,* she decided.

"I've been thinking a lot 'bout Preacher Zook, hoping he might surprise everyone and rally to recovery." Ernie glanced at her. "I hate the thought of losin' him."

"I know how ya feel, Ernie. He's such a kindhearted man."

"And Dat . . . what'll *he* do without his friend? The man's nearly like a father to him."

"We can pray that God will heal him," Sylvia suggested.

"Sick as he is, I don't see how that's possible. The cancer's in its final stage, Dat says."

"The Lord's ways are not ours" was all she could think to reply.

"You sound like Mamma," Ernie said with a grin, the driving lines slack in his hands.

She smiled, but he didn't look her way. "Preacher's illness is hard on all of us," she assured him. "I couldn't help but notice the anxious expressions durin' Preaching this morning."

"*Jah.*" Ernie nodded. "Preacher Zook hasn't been at church for months now."

"I miss his sermons," Sylvia said, wishing her brother was old enough to accompany her to the Singing tonight. The fellowship and happy blend of voices and refreshments would surely lift his spirits.

That evening, Rhoda and Earnest and the boys went over to visit her parents once Ernie returned from taking Sylvia to Singing. The dairy farm where Rhoda had grown up was one of the largest around—so large that Rhoda's father had divided up portions of the land amongst his four married sons, leaving eighty acres of his own for grazing and cropland.

Looking out past the hayfield, Rhoda could see the neighbor's small herd of beef cows grazing in the meadow across the road. On this side, the field steepened to the north, where it ran up to a wooded area her father and Earnest had used for turkey hunting nearly every November since Earnest's arrival in Lancaster County. She remembered their first Thanksgiving together as man and wife; at the time, she'd been stunned by the impressive size of the bird he'd bagged.

Today, while Adam, Calvin, and Tommy played outside on the two tire swings their *Dawdi* kept for their frequent visits, Rhoda talked with her mother in the kitchen. Earnest and her father and Ernie sat in the front room on the cane-backed sofa, waiting for popcorn and meadow tea to be served.

"I've been over to see Hannah quite a lot here lately," Rhoda's Mamm said quietly. "Honestly, I'd hoped she and Curtis might stop by today."

Rhoda nodded as she poured cold meadow tea into tumblers while her mother finished popping the corn. "Not surprised, really."

"Well, I wondered if Curtis might be able to get her out of the house for a short time." Mamm sighed and looked serious. "At some point, she'll have to push herself to be around people again."

"Could be she thought there'd be little ones here today. She's real sensitive to that now."

Mamm frowned. "Surely not when they're her own nephews and nieces."

"Well, just think 'bout it. It's only been a little more than a week."

Mamm rubbed the back of her neck. "I do hope an' pray something can be done to cheer her up. She's yearnin' so for a baby."

Rhoda shared that she had taken a teddy bear over to Hannah early that morning, before Preaching. It had been a chance to look in on her sister, as well. "The bear's a poor replacement, but Hannah's arms ache somethin' awful for her baby." She went on to say that Ella Mae had thought it worth a try. "Apparently some *Englischers* sell special bears made for that very purpose."

"Never heard of that." Mamm shook her head. "But who am I to argue with the Wise Woman?"

This brought a smile to both of them, and they carried the refreshments into the front room. Then Rhoda briefly stepped onto the porch and called for the boys to come inside. She stood there a moment, watching Calvin and Tommy untangle themselves from the tire swing they shared, laughing as they did so. Adam had been swinging alone on the other one and leaped off quickly, glancing back at the younger boys as he made a beeline for the house.

"I'm mighty thirsty," Adam said as he ran up the porch steps to Rhoda.

"There's plenty of cold tea waitin'," she said. "Nice an' sweet, too."

"*Wunnerbaar*," Adam said, dashing inside.

Once Calvin and Tommy were also indoors and had washed their hands at their *Mammi's* request, all of them were seated in a semicircle, talking and laughing while munching on popcorn. Tommy tossed his high into the air at Ernie, who caught each one in his mouth, never missing.

Rhoda's mother wagged her head. "How does he do that?"

Rhoda laughed. "Lots of practice," she said, and Ernie grinned.

"If only he could put that talent to *gut* use," Dawdi joked, glancing at Earnest, who stared at the floor as if in a daze.

When he must have sensed Rhoda's eyes on him, Earnest met her gaze and gave her a reassuring smile.

In spite of the way he could warm her heart, Rhoda had noticed his distraction more than a few times today. He was uncharacteristically quiet and withdrawn; doubtless his thoughts were consumed with Mahlon. Maybe she and the boys should have come here on their own and let Earnest go and sit at his friend's bedside again. *Might be his last chance,* she thought sorrowfully.

But since Earnest *was* here, she hoped he might try to enter into the conversation, at least for her parents' sake. They'd always appreciated his jovial spirit.

My husband's just not himself. . . .

CHAPTER
Seven

*A*fter a short time of fellowship, the barn Singing started with the hymn "Savior, Like a Shepherd Lead Us," one of Sylvia's favorites. The tempo was slower than that of some of the songs they frequently sang, but after a few more hymns and gospel songs, one young man requested they sing "Keep on the Sunny Side," the perfect tune to promote an upbeat mood. How could anyone feel glum when singing that song?

As was usual, *die Youngie* sang in unison, though now and then several broke out into parts, something not allowed in Preaching services. Their bishop didn't mind if they occasionally sang in harmony at Singings, but in church, it called attention to those who were better singers and put the emphasis on the harmony instead of the words.

During the time for refreshments, Titus came over to sit with Sylvia at her table. "We've been invited to go to my uncle's to play Ping-Pong later," he said softly. "Would ya like that?"

She nodded and guessed that it meant another couple

would be joining them, but she didn't ask, knowing it was proper for him to plan everything.

After forty-five more minutes of singing, the gathering became more informal, with couples pairing up to head outside to courting carriages while others lingered in the hayloft talking. She and Titus took time to greet their respective cousins and friends before quietly exiting to his gleaming black courting buggy. Beneath the light of the full moon, she could see that Titus had cleaned and oiled the harness and groomed his striking horse. The sleek black mane was perfectly smooth, as was the long tail. "Your mare looks 'specially beautiful tonight," she commented as he helped her up.

Titus bobbed his head as if to thank her. "It's *you* who's beautiful, Sylvie."

Her face warmed, and she had to glance away. Something had changed between them since his proposal yesterday, something new and powerful . . . she felt as if she were being pulled toward a magnet. This sense of yearning made her heart beat fast, and she imagined Titus taking her into his arms.

They rode straight to his uncle and aunt's house, where it appeared that Titus's close cousin Mel Kauffman and his date, Emily Swarey, had already arrived. The game of doubles Ping-Pong turned into a full-blown match, with Titus keeping careful track of the score.

We're winning too easily, thought Sylvia, wondering if they shouldn't let Mel and Emily win a couple games, although that was not the way most fellows would want to play. Titus, though, didn't seem as competitive as some.

When they had won two games in a row, Titus suggested they stop for the ice cream and cookies provided by his uncle and aunt. Mel and Emily quickly agreed, and Titus and Mel seemed to enjoy talking between bites as Sylvia and Emily discussed all the asparagus they had been putting up lately. Then Mel brought up the Ascension Day picnic, and Emily brightened when Sylvia mentioned the chocolate cakes she wanted to bake.

"Titus's mother's recipe is delicious," Sylvia told her. "So light it melts in your mouth."

"Is that right?" Emily said with a glance at Titus. "You must've visited Titus's home recently."

Sylvia's face warmed, but she didn't admit to it.

"It'll be a fun day," Mel added, mentioning all the volleyball the youth would be playing.

"Hopefully one with pleasant weather," Sylvia said as she spooned up her ice cream.

"Well, we've played volleyball in the rain before," Titus said, smiling at Sylvia. "It adds a little somethin' when the ground's muddy."

Both Emily and Mel laughed outright.

"If it rains, we can always play Dutch Blitz in the barn," Mel said. "And maybe have a spur-of-the-moment Singing, if everyone agrees."

"What about addin' a barn dance, too?" Emily suggested with a grin.

This surprised Sylvia, who wasn't entirely sure Emily was joking, and Titus said nothing as Mel quickly changed the subject.

In time they resumed their Ping-Pong match, and Sylvia could see that Mel and Emily were beginning to play better as a team. They won the next game . . . and the next. Each couple now had claimed two games apiece.

"Ready?" Titus asked Sylvia as she prepared to serve to start the fifth game.

"Sure!" Sylvia said, her paddle poised.

The game play moved faster than before, and she and Titus had to be quick on their feet and speedy in returning the tiny ball. Sylvia gave it her all, as did Mel and Emily. Late in the game, however, Titus seemed to be backing off, and she wondered if he was letting them win.

Emily squealed with glee when she and Mel managed to score the final point, clinching the game. "I can't believe it!" she exclaimed, patting her hand against the paddle. "It's the first time I've ever played doubles. And to think we won the match!"

After they'd all thanked Titus's uncle and aunt, who'd politely remained upstairs in the front room, Titus and Sylvia said their good-byes to Mel and Emily.

During the ride home, Titus asked what Sylvia thought of possibly spending more time with Mel and Emily.

"Are they a regular couple?" Sylvia wasn't sure, since she'd never seen them together before.

"Mel's hopin' so. But it takes two to agree," Titus said with a chuckle.

"Well, if you want to, I don't mind double-dating." She liked Mel and Emily but hoped to be alone with Titus sometimes, too—get to know each other better. After all, they were going to be married in six short months.

Titus slowed the horse. "And if not with Mel and Emily, then another couple."

"All right with me," she said, wondering why he was suggesting this; they'd never made a habit of going out with other couples before.

Titus smiled and reached to give her hand a squeeze. "I'm glad ya feel that way. My Dat says bein' alone too much ain't wise for unmarried couples," he admitted.

She found it a bit surprising that his preacher father had spoken to him about that. Suddenly a bit shy about this topic of conversation, she asked, "Did you go visiting after Preaching today?"

"Headed home after the shared meal," he said. "How 'bout you?"

"I mostly spent time readin'," she told him. "It was fairly quiet round the house, like usual on Sundays. But Mamma and I did sit out on the back porch for a little while and talk before it was time to get ready for Singing."

Titus listened, nodded a bit. "You and your Mamma work closely together, *jah*?"

"We're *gut* partners in the kitchen, for sure."

He seemed to think on that, then said, "By the way, my Mamm was real impressed with you, Sylvie. She wants you to become better acquainted with our family before the weddin'."

Sylvia smiled at the thought. "I'd like that."

"Just so ya know, she's not the only one. . . . Lavina and Connie were dyin' to join us in the gazebo yesterday. Dat told me Lavina pleaded for Mamm to let her bring the cake out."

"She's fifteen, right?"

"Same age as your brother Ernie," Titus said. "Maybe they'll get to know each other next year at Singing, if Dat lets her start goin' when she turns sixteen."

Sylvia was surprised. "Ya mean he might not?"

"Well, she has some growin' up to do before Mamm will feel comfortable with her goin' out with a fella. S'pose Mamm knows best on that."

Sylvia had heard something like this about one of her cousins a couple of years ago, but as far as she knew, that cousin had still attended Singings at sixteen. It was rare for a parent to keep a youth of that age from going.

Their conversation flowed from one subject to another as Titus told how his fourteen-year-old sister, Connie, was learning to sew head coverings—and having a rough time of it—before moving on to discuss the upcoming horse auction at a nearby sales barn.

Sylvia mentioned all the fun she and her younger brothers, Calvin and Tommy, had while planting beans and putting out the pepper plants last Wednesday afternoon. "And the schoolboys are itchin' for summer break," she added. "'Specially Tommy."

Eventually, they began to talk about how difficult it had to be for Preacher Zook's family since his diagnosis, seeing the once-robust man slowly lose his strength.

"Dat's been over to sit with him often lately," Sylvia shared softly. "To be honest, he's worryin' himself nearly sick over Preacher Zook."

"So's my father." Titus paused a moment before reaching for her hand. "You just made me think how I want us always to be truthful with each other, Sylvie. Okay?"

She nodded. "Honesty is one of life's important virtues, Mamma always says."

"She's right." Titus nodded and slipped his arm around her shoulders, something he'd never done before. "It's a little chilly out," he said, as though making a perfectly logical excuse.

She smiled, enjoying the closeness as they rode that way for several minutes, discussing how often they would see each other now that they were engaged. They decided that, while a couple times a week would be nice, once a week was more realistic for Titus, considering the demands of the coming months of work on his father's farm.

The night air was still and the moon so bright, Sylvia could hardly contain her happiness.

"I love ya so," Titus whispered, leaning his head against her *Kapp*. "I wish we could be married sooner. . . ."

Oh, she felt the exact same way! But just then she recalled the inscribed pocket watch in her father's tinderbox, and the puzzling thought nagged at her. Without realizing it, she must have stiffened.

"What is it?"

Not wanting to spoil their time together, she shrugged. "I'm all right."

Quickly, he directed the mare to the shoulder, beneath a large oak tree, and halted. Then, turning, he looked at Sylvia for the longest time, his eyes searching hers as well as they could in the moonlight. "Are ya sure?"

She nodded, feeling shy.

"My dear Sylvie . . ." He pulled her so close that she could feel the steady *thump-thump* of his heart.

"I love you, too," she said as he reached to touch her face. "Ever so much."

He leaned closer still, and she was surprised when he sweetly kissed her cheek, more gently this time than the sudden peck he'd given her after she said yes to his proposal.

Titus moved back enough to look at her with tender eyes. "*Ach*, Sylvie . . . I'll take care of you and cherish you all my life."

It almost seemed as if he was making a vow, and she'd never known such joy or felt such love. Truly, it was hard to think of being apart from her beloved for even one day.

CHAPTER
Eight

*T*he next morning, *Weschdaag*, having finished pinning the washing to the line, Rhoda was working alongside Sylvia in the kitchen when a knock came at the back door. Quickly, Rhoda went to see who was knocking instead of just walking in, as family and Amish neighbors were accustomed to doing.

There, she discovered Preacher Zook's twenty-year-old grandson Andy, his straw hat held in front of him and his blond hair unkempt like he'd been up all night. The expression on his handsome face was mighty serious.

"Dawdi Zook passed away a little while ago," he relayed in a low voice.

"Oh, Andy, I'm awful sorry," Rhoda said, leaning on the doorjamb. "I'll come over with food for your Mammi and family real soon."

"Will ya let Earnest know?" Andy asked.

Nodding, Rhoda glanced toward her husband's shop. "I'll go right over an' tell him."

"*Denki.* My family would like him to help spread the word on this side of Hickory Hollow. . . . The funeral's this Wednesday." Andy nearly stuttered as he tried to get the words out. "Dawdi Zook loved Earnest . . . told me as much last night, when he was strugglin' so. . . ." Andy rubbed the stubble on his chin and looked at the sky for a moment. "It was one of the last things he said before passing."

This touched her deeply, and she held her breath to keep from tearing up. "You can be sure that Earnest will let all the neighbors over here know."

Andy gave a weak smile and inched backward, still holding Rhoda's gaze, before slowly turning to head down the porch steps, straw hat still in hand.

Dear Lord, be with him and his family, she prayed, opening the screen door and stepping out to give poor Earnest the news.

Mahlon was my second father, Earnest thought, distressed to learn of his death. While this day hadn't been unexpected, the reality hit him hard, and he reached for Rhoda and held her near, gritting his teeth to keep his emotions in check. She was the one and only person who could comfort him at a time like this.

"You'll miss him terribly, I know," Rhoda whispered as he clung to her.

Earnest was relieved that she had been the one to tell him.

Slowly, he released her, reaching now for her hands, searching her lovely face. "I'd better be on my way," he said quietly. "The People must be told." He kissed her before she left to return to the house.

Quickly, he moved to his workroom and put out the gas

lamp, then went to remove his straw hat from one of the three wooden pegs near the door. He closed the door behind him and made his way to the carriage shed for the spring wagon, leaving the family buggy for Rhoda in case she needed it.

In something of a daze, Earnest trudged up to the stable to get Lily, his older driving horse, then led her out to the wagon and hitched up. The burden of loss weighed heavily upon him, and it was a relief to have this time alone to absorb the news. *Not something one can prepare for,* he thought, *losing such a friend.*

The People, too, would bear the loss. They embraced the belief that death, no matter when it came, was God's sovereign will . . . no questions asked. If the truth were known, Earnest was still coming to terms with that—he'd never quite accepted his young sister's death years ago, the first-ever loss in his life.

But he wouldn't contemplate that now. It was Mahlon whom he must honor with his thoughts. After all, the man had lived to serve others long before he was ordained as preacher.

Earnest reached for the driving lines, and considering the painful absence of his friend, he traveled the east side of Hickory Hollow from farmhouse to farmhouse to share the sad news.

Sylvia felt the silence in the kitchen where she sat mending a hem on one of her work dresses, acutely aware of her mother's serious demeanor. It occurred to her that sharing about her engagement might help to lift a bit of the solemnness, at least for a while. After last night's romantic ride with Titus, she could scarcely contain her happiness even now.

"Mamma," she said, putting down her sewing needle. "I have some *gut* news . . . if it's all right to share."

Her mother's head jerked up as she stood at the counter slicing potatoes for the noon meal. "*Gut* news is surely welcome."

"Well, Titus Kauffman asked me to marry him come November," Sylvia said, her face warming at the memory of his affection. "I wondered if you might have put it together Saturday, when I headed out for the picnic." It felt so good to tell her mother.

Mamma set the knife down near the cutting board and came over to Sylvia, smiling sweetly. She took a seat in Dat's chair right there at the head of the table. "A preacher's son?"

"Not just any preacher's son. Titus is really *wunnerbaar* . . . and you'll think so, too, once you get to know him better." She knew her face must be alight with the joy she was feeling.

"I kinda thought there was somethin' going on, Sylvie. You'd been actin' a little off beam. I should've guessed you were preoccupied with a beau." Mamma reached for her hand, her eyes soft. "Your father will be as pleased as I am. Or have ya already told him?"

"*Nee* . . . wanted to tell ya first."

Mamma asked when in November they were thinking about tying the knot.

"Well, Titus wants me to talk it over with you and Dat. He thinks so much of Dat, by the way."

Mamma beamed. "And we'll have the wedding here."

"Of course," Sylvia said. But it was then she realized she didn't know when she would tell Dat of the engagement. Better for Mamma to do that. Because ever since learning that the gold pocket watch had *not* come from Dat's sister, she'd felt leery approaching him about much of anything.

The worldly past he'd seemed to avoid discussing was more concerning now that she knew he was keeping a box of items locked away, including a pocket watch with a puzzling inscription.

"Sylvie?" Mamma asked. "What's a-matter?"

"*Ach*, sorry." She put on a quick smile.

I must never tell Mamma what I found, she promised herself. *Some things are better left unknown.*

Despite her earlier reluctance to speak with him, Sylvia was sitting on the back porch waiting for Dat when he arrived home. Even though it wasn't long before the noon meal, she hoped she might talk to him and quickly rose from the willow rocker to walk toward the shop.

Her father's face was drawn, and if she wasn't mistaken, he was limping a bit.

"Did ya hurt yourself?" she asked.

"Oh, just stumbled getting out of the wagon at the last house," he told her. "Clumsy today."

"Need some ice?"

He offered what appeared to be a halfhearted smile, yet she read the tenderness in his eyes, mingled with obvious grief. "You're a gift to me, Sylvie. Always so kind and helpful." Then he shook his head. "But don't fret over me." Dat slipped past her and into the shop. "I'll be okay."

She hesitated to follow him when he seemed so down. Standing there, she stared into the workroom, where the tinderbox loomed large on the shelf.

"A penny for your thoughts?" His tone was conciliatory

yet strained as he limped toward the door leading to his shop and took a seat.

"Never mind, we can talk another time," she said, turning to go.

She made it to the outer door before he called to her. "Sylvie? We can talk if you want to."

Every fiber in her tensed, and she felt guilty. "Honestly, it can wait."

But Dat turned in his seat, his hands open in a supplicating manner. "You seem . . . troubled."

Coming toward him, she felt downright *ferhoodled*. She feared that what she had to say might set something in motion that she could not stop. Dare she take that risk?

Dat folded his arms and gave her the look she'd seen her whole life. Never impatient, always ready to hear what was on her mind.

Not if he knew what I have to say, she thought.

"What is it, daughter?"

"I'm sure it was awful hard havin' to spread the word 'bout Preacher Zook," she said. "I feel for ya, Dat."

He bowed his head and inhaled slowly. "I've had better days. I'll be goin' over to Zooks' to help Mahlon's family after we eat." Slowly, almost as if it pained him, he raised his head to look at her. "I know you well, Sylvie . . . somethin's bothering you, and it's not that."

She studied him, the dearest father ever. "*Ach*, if I knew it would upset ya, I'd hightail it out of here."

He leaned forward now, his chair moving on its rollers. "We've never had trouble talking before." He smiled faintly but seemed to be on edge, as if he somehow sensed what she was about to say.

Sylvia hoped she was doing the right thing, as distressed as he was. As for herself, she knew she had to clear the air and own up to what she'd done, or she wouldn't sleep again tonight. "I did something I shouldn't have, Dat."

His smile faded, and strangely, he glanced at the tinderbox.

He knows, she thought, heart sinking. For a terrible moment, the room was absolutely soundless.

"So you're the one," he said at last.

This pronouncement startled her no end. "I wish I'd never looked inside."

He scrutinized her, his dark hair glimmering in the sunlight from the high window nearby. "Now that you've seen those items, you must have questions," he said, his voice more gentle now.

The fact that he hadn't scolded her was a jolt. She bit her lip. Did she dare say? "*Jah,* mostly questions 'bout the pocket watch." She decided not to mention the inscription.

He ran his fingers through his untrimmed beard. "I kept that . . . uh, well, as a reminder to myself."

"A reminder of what?" she said, the confusion in her heart increasing.

Abruptly, her father rose and walked to the other door, where he closed it and pulled down the green shade on its window. "This really isn't your concern, Sylvia Ann."

Sylvia Ann? she thought, taken aback by his unfamiliar tone.

Misery and frustration rushed over her. "Well, you won't tell Mamma, will ya?" Sylvia began to plead. "And I won't breathe a word, either. Just keep it a secret, like before." Surely her father would see the sense in that.

Dat's eyes widened as if in surprise. "What are you saying?"

"Don't tell Mamma 'bout any of this if you know it might hurt her." Sylvia bit her lip, realizing she'd crossed a line. "She thinks she's the only woman you've ever loved."

Their eyes locked, and a chill passed through her as grim recognition settled on her father's face. Neither said a word, but in that moment, he had to realize that she'd seen the inscription.

Nine

*R*hoda tied on her white half apron after the noon meal and got busy making a chicken and noodle casserole to take over to Mamie Zook. Other womenfolk would be doing much the same, as well as assuming the tasks of cleaning the house and tending to Mamie's vegetable garden.

What she must be going through! Rhoda thought sadly, praying silently for comfort and peace.

"Would ya like to go with me to Mamie's?" Rhoda asked Sylvia, who looked too glum for being newly engaged. The sparkle and excitement of this morning had seemingly disappeared.

"Oh, I'll just stay here and take the clothes off the line for ya. Fold them, too," Sylvia said, her voice wavering. "Someone should be here when the younger boys get home from school, too, since Ernie's over at Zooks', helpin' out. That way you can visit with Mamie for a while."

"That's a help," Rhoda said, wondering if Sylvia was feeling affected by her father's grief. Earnest had been so subdued at the dinner table. *Like a man in shock . . .*

When Rhoda was ready to leave with the food, Earnest went out to hitch Lily to the family carriage for the short ride, then he solemnly kissed Rhoda and turned to head back to his shop. She was thankful for his help; she'd felt all in since Mahlon's grandson had come with the news. Perhaps, too, it was the realization that Mamie Zook was not only a widow now but also living alone, considering that all of her children were married.

Rhoda looked across the field at the tall house Earnest had frequently trekked back and forth to over the years. Now she would be the one going to the preacher's house till other plans were made for Mamie. It was certain Earnest would also be over there helping for at least the next few weeks. Ernie too.

Will the family sell the farm? she wondered as she drove to Mamie's with the food she'd prepared, hoping one of Mamie's sons might take it over. She prayed again for her friend, as well as for Hannah, whose home she passed on the left. She wondered if the stuffed bear had given Hannah any measure of comfort, or if her sister had thought the gesture silly. Sometimes it wasn't easy to know what Hannah thought.

Just then, Rhoda noticed Henry Zook, one of Ella Mae's grandsons, coming this way in his buggy with Ella Mae herself, who smiled and waved. Rhoda waved back, glad to see them, and watched in her side mirror after they passed and were turning into Curtis and Hannah's lane. *Gut,* she thought, wondering if Ella Mae might end up over at Mamie's later, as many womenfolk would.

Both Hannah and Mamie are in sore need of a soothing balm.

Rhoda found Mamie on the back porch in her wooden glider, a daughter on either side of her, waiting for the local mortician to return Preacher Zook's body. *Bless her heart*, thought Rhoda, knowing there was much to do to prepare for Wednesday's funeral. Because Mahlon Zook was so well-known in the area, there could be as many as six hundred mourners, including English neighbors.

Rhoda carried the chicken and noodle casserole into the kitchen and placed it in the fridge next to the dishes brought over by others in the district. Then she set to work helping four church women plan the meal for invited guests and family, following the burial. Rhoda had helped in the past with a number of funeral meals, but there was something rather sacred about working in the home of the deceased man of God.

She glanced out the nearby window, hoping to spot Earnest, who'd surely arrived by now to help plan and set up the house and the barn for the two simultaneous funeral services. Due to the anticipated crowd, one would be conducted by the bishop, and the other by Preacher Kauffman.

A short time later, Henry Zook arrived with Ella Mae. The Wise Woman walked with him up the steps and straight to Mamie, where she sat on a rocking chair near her and her daughters and bowed her head to pray. Witnessing Ella Mae take Mamie's hands after the prayer and talk quietly with her, Rhoda struggled with a lump in her throat. *Just what's needed,* she thought, grateful for Ella Mae's deep faith and compassionate spirit. Most of the womenfolk in the church were like worker bees, but Ella Mae always took time to tend to a person's heart.

More women arrived, some with their teenage daughters, all bringing groceries and hot meals. Rhoda wished now that she'd insisted on Sylvia's coming, too, especially when Rhoda's nieces Alma and Jessie arrived with Rhoda's sister Ruthann Yoder.

"Where's Sylvie?" Jessie asked, and Rhoda explained that she was doing chores at home.

"Maybe we can drop by an' say hullo later," Alma suggested, and both girls looked at their Mamm.

"It'll be a busy enough day, girls, so not this time," Ruthann said, touching Rhoda's arm and motioning for her to walk toward the far end of the porch. Clearly something was up.

"I ran into Hannah at the general store this mornin'," Ruthann whispered once they reached the end. "She looks like she hasn't eaten in days."

Rhoda merely nodded and wished Hannah would tell Ruthann and their other sisters about the miscarriage.

"Is she ill?" Ruthann pressed.

"Well, I know she'd enjoy a visit from you," Rhoda said quickly, glancing back at the girls waiting for their Mamm. "Maybe go by an' see her tomorrow?"

Ruthann nodded. "I'll do that."

Rhoda sighed and hoped she'd said the right thing. Hannah, delicate as she was, needed loving care, not to be peppered with questions. *Surely she'll open up and tell Ruthann about her loss. . . .*

Earnest arrived with a group of men to clean out the barn and haul away the manure. They tended to the livestock and swept the upper level, where the overflow funeral service would take place, then decided on the best plan for setting up the benches there and in the house, where visitation would begin this afternoon and run through the early evening hours tomorrow.

He flinched when the local mortician returned with Mahlon's body in a modest pine coffin ready-made by one of the Amish carpenters in the district. Three of Mahlon's brothers had requested that Earnest be present with them to help dress the body for the visitation and the coming funeral.

Earnest wasn't entirely surprised to be asked, and he regarded the invitation as an honor. Although in his tormented state, he hardly felt worthy. Yet how could he refuse without causing confusion? The family knew how close he and Mahlon had always been.

In his mind, he replayed his conversation with Sylvia. The dear girl had pleaded with him, *"Don't tell Mamma. . . ."*

She's been ensnared by my deceit, he thought, recalling the uneasy look in her eyes.

Following Judah, Edwin, and Matthew Zook into the brick farmhouse, Earnest realized now he had no other choice.

Rhoda and Ruthann and her girls were carefully preparing the house for the visitation and viewing that afternoon. Rhoda helped the women sweep and wash the floors in each of Mamie's rooms, conscious of the closed door to the spare bedroom where the body lay.

Earlier Rhoda had seen Earnest go in with Mahlon's brothers, but her husband had never once glanced her way, although he had to know she was there. His strange manner had taken her off guard—and not only now, but also earlier at the dinner table, when he remained silent after Sylvia had seemed quite aloof toward him.

With all of her heart, Rhoda wanted to show her husband understanding, since Mahlon's passing was so heavy on his heart. All the same, something more seemed to be troubling Earnest, something completely separate from his friend's death. Yet she hadn't the slightest idea what.

That evening, while Rhoda was preparing for bed, Earnest entered their bedroom and went straight to his favorite chair. Instead of reaching for one of the Amish newspapers, he folded his hands on his chest and said, "I need to talk to you, Rhoda."

She reached for her cotton duster and put it on. "Ah, it must be about what Sylvie shared with me this mornin'."

Earnest's face turned sheet white. "Sh-she *told* you?" he stammered, looking terribly alarmed.

"Well, *jah*." Momentarily, Rhoda wondered at his reaction; then she nodded her head and smiled. "Isn't it just *wunnerbaar*, Titus Kauffman asking her to marry him?"

Her husband's shoulders sagged with apparent relief. "Oh, I didn't know." Sighing, he appeared to force a smile. "She did say the other day that he was courting her. And I was going to tell you, but I was in a fog over Mahlon."

"So . . . she didn't share with you about the engagement?" Rhoda asked, perplexed at this, not to mention his odd reaction.

"*Nee*." Glancing now toward the windows, Earnest stared out at the deepening twilight. "To think that our daughter's marrying a preacher's son." He seemed somehow relieved.

"I said nearly the same thing when she told me," Rhoda said, chuckling a little in an effort to lighten things up.

Earnest rose just then and went to get his pajamas out of the dresser. When he was finished getting ready for bed, he ambled across the room. He sat on the bed, his hands on his head now. "Honestly, this feels like the longest day of my life," he said as he pulled back the quilt and sheet.

Rhoda tried to comprehend the reason for his odd, even lukewarm response to their daughter's exciting news. Earnest had always loved connecting with Sylvia and rejoicing in her happiness. *But not today,* Rhoda thought, taking down her hair and brushing it many times before finally turning out the gaslight and slipping into bed. Lying there, she stretched her hand across the sheet, not quite touching her husband's bare back, and realized he was knotted up in a ball, practically hugging his side of the bed.

She recalled what he'd first said when coming into the room, and it struck her that Earnest must have had something on his mind unrelated to Sylvia's engagement. *Something I interrupted,* she thought, sliding her hand back across the sheet to her own side. Staring blindly into the dim room, she finally closed her eyes and prayed her silent nighttime prayer.

CHAPTER
Ten

*J*ust after dawn the next morning, Earnest rolled over in bed and saw that Rhoda was still sleeping soundly, both hands tucked beneath her pillow. As she sighed in her sleep, he couldn't help gazing at her, his heart full of love.

He hoped she wasn't feeling poorly—he'd heard her get up in the night. Had his lackluster acknowledgment of Sylvia's engagement been the cause?

Without a doubt, he had botched his attempt to talk with her last evening . . . to reveal some of his past decisions. *Hopefully without devastating her.* And then Rhoda had taken the conversation in an entirely different direction, and he hadn't attempted to get it back on track. *I was caught off guard,* he thought as he reached over to carefully move a golden strand of hair from across her cheek.

Oh, Rhoda, my darling. How he wished to spare her what he must lay bare. Yet with both Rhoda's and his involvement in funeral preparations, neither today nor tomorrow was a good time to open such a can of worms.

79

Earnest cringed at the thought of their once-happy marriage coming under such a strain. Even worse, the possibility of Rhoda sending him away. The latter prospect was the very reason he had kept his secret under wraps.

He contemplated the maze of the next two days and, in so doing, felt drained of all emotion. Sylvia's opening the tinderbox had altered everything.

Yet I have no one to blame but myself.

Ernie and the younger boys were still hauling water for the troughs in the stable when Earnest entered the kitchen for breakfast. Going immediately to the sink, he washed his hands and then went to sit at the table without a word to Rhoda, who was frying German sausage at the stove.

Sylvia removed a container of orange juice from the fridge and began to pour the juice into glasses. "I understand Mamma told ya 'bout Titus's marriage proposal," she said unexpectedly.

Earnest bobbed his head and sat up straight. "*Jah,* and we're so happy for you." In that instant, as he looked across the room at Sylvia, he felt as if his only daughter was growing away from him, a little girl no longer.

"We're *very* happy," Rhoda added with a glance at Earnest.

Sylvia carried the full juice glasses on a tray to the table and set it down. "By the way, Eva Kauffman has some ideas about where Titus and I will stay for the first few weeks after we're married, till we get our own place."

Puzzled, Earnest looked at Rhoda before replying to his daughter. "Not here, in keeping with tradition?"

Sylvia explained what Eva had said about them having more privacy over there.

"So, Eva's making the decisions?"

"Dat, for pity's sake," Sylvia said, her face bright pink.

"Excuse me—I need some air." Earnest heaved a sigh and got up to go out to the back porch. From where he leaned on the rail, he could see not only the boys outside, washing up at the well pump, but also through the screen door, Rhoda standing at the gas stove.

He could hear his wife trying to smooth things over with Sylvia. "Your father's obviously upset," she was saying. "He's suffering, ya know, with Mahlon's funeral tomorrow."

Sylvia nodded and sniffed. "I don't blame Dat, really. Titus's Mamm can be rather . . ."

"Self-assured?" Rhoda volunteered.

Sylvia shrugged and laughed a little.

Rhoda nodded and removed the black skillet from the stove and put the lid on. Then, surprising Earnest, she came to the screen door and stood there looking out at him. "Sylvie's pretty upset." She stepped outside.

Earnest felt terrible. He was wrong to take out his anger at himself on anyone else. "I'm sorry," he said, shaking his head apologetically. "Things are just off-kilter."

Rhoda looked at him with tender eyes. "Anything besides Mahlon's passin'?"

Earnest knew full well what was eating at him. Fumbling for a response, he whispered, "Grief is just plain hard." Not wishing to trouble her further, he chose to do what he'd done for years—sweep it under the rug.

His wife nodded meekly, studying him.

"I love you, Rhoda," he said finally. "Never forget that." He turned, feeling suddenly like an old man, and called for the boys to come in and eat.

After Earnest had bowed his head for the silent blessing, he stated that they would be going to Preacher Zook's visitation that afternoon. "You boys will have to wash up and change into Sunday clothes right quick after school . . . once chores are done, of course. You, too, Ernie and Adam."

Tommy exchanged a worried glance with Calvin. "Must I look at Preacher Zook in his coffin, Dat?" Tommy asked timidly.

Earnest pressed his lips together. "Well, he was *your* minister, too, son." He nodded then at all of his stair-step sons. "It's a way to show respect and love to Preacher Zook's family."

Rhoda agreed. "And that we care for them, and always will."

Tommy picked up his fork and began to eat slowly, his small shoulders tucked in tight.

Earnest felt sorry for him. "Listen, Tommy . . . why don't you stand next to me during the viewing?"

"*Denki*, Dat." His shoulders relaxed, and he resumed eating with a little more enthusiasm.

Calvin seemed to sigh, as if perhaps wishing that he were still the youngest. But Earnest would be mindful of both boys during the difficult viewing.

All during breakfast, Sylvia had minded her manners, not wanting to say anything she would later regret. The last place she wanted to be was in close proximity to her father, so she again declined going with her parents to help Mamie Zook. The way she felt this morning, keeping Dat's secret, it was enough work to get the younger boys off to school and then redd up and make the noon meal. She would put her energy into making one of her favorite recipes—creamed chipped beef—to keep her hands busy and her thoughts from straying to the contents of that wretched tinderbox!

Dat and Mamma had already left for Mamie's, and it was time for the boys to head out the door, when Adam began to complain about a small hole in the front of his shirt, near a button. *"Puh!* Look at this," he said, trying to tuck it farther in.

"I'll patch it after school," Sylvia offered, looking at the wall clock.

"That won't help me *now.*" Adam shook his head.

"Jah, his girlfriend might see it durin' reading class," teased Calvin.

Sylvia squelched a smile. "Just ya wait two years till you're Adam's age."

"Puh! I'll never look at a girl frog-eyed!" Calvin insisted.

Sylvia ignored that. "There's no time to change your shirt, Adam, unless you want to risk bein' late for school," she said. "I wouldn't advise it."

Adam, almost as tall as Ernie, was trying to hide the hole by shoving his shirt into his pants. Frowning, he finally got it to his satisfaction.

"By the time ya walk to school, your shirt'll prob'ly be out again," Ernie said.

Red-faced Adam just ignored all of them, then dashed out the back door ahead of his brothers.

"Be kind to each other," Sylvia called as Tommy ran after poor Adam.

Calvin, however, glanced back at Sylvia. "I'll look after him," he reassured her.

Sylvia nodded, thankful for Calvin, and went to the front window to peer out.

Earnest felt the wind rise as he walked out to the carriage house. He had been at Zooks' most of the day and then rushed home to clean up, donning his best black trousers and white shirt. Squinting into the afternoon sunshine, he considered how Mahlon's dying had altered everything for Mamie and the family. True, they'd had some time to get accustomed to the possibility of his passing, but the reality of death was certainly far different, he knew all too well. *Mahlon was everything to Mamie,* Earnest thought, recalling the grief he'd experienced when his sister and then father died. His mother, too, later that year. The intense finality of those losses continued to this day.

Later, in the crowded carriage, Calvin and Tommy sat on their older brothers' knees, as they did whenever the whole family rode together. The children were talking quietly, except for Sylvia, who sat next to Rhoda in the front, the extension seat protruding slightly outside the buggy.

Earnest noticed Rhoda reach over and place her hand on their daughter's, leaning over to say, "These visitations are hard, I know, dear."

Sylvia's upset about more than just the viewing, Earnest sensed, concerned about his daughter's frame of mind.

When they arrived at the Zook farmhouse, other Plain folk had already arrived to pay their respects. Like everyone else, Earnest parked on the wide strip of lawn on the south side of the lane, where at least ten teen boys worked to unhitch each horse and lead it to water near the stable. One of the fellows was Titus Kauffman, who smiled when he glanced their way.

As Earnest and Rhoda headed inside, Earnest motioned for Tommy, who hurried to catch up with him. In the front room, over near the open door, Mahlon was laid out in the hand-built coffin. Taking a seat with his family, Earnest recalled his first encounter with Mahlon—the man had been surprisingly cordial to a young outsider. He had quickly taken an interest in Earnest and gone out of his way to introduce him to Isaac Smucker, Hickory Hollow's elderly clockmaker.

Such a gracious, tolerant man, Earnest remembered fondly.

He glanced to his left, where his children sat reverent and still, and his heart filled with pride. *Dad and mom and my grandparents would be impressed by them if they were alive today*, he thought.

When it was time, Earnest rose and walked with Tommy to the front of the room to file into the line. Two of Mahlon's nephews joined them and offered handshakes before speaking with Earnest in hushed tones.

Shortly thereafter, Rhoda and the rest of the family joined him, and slowly, as Tommy gripped his hand, Earnest filed past the coffin containing the body of his friend. *My final good-bye*, he thought, aware of Tommy's hesitancy . . . and eagerness to move along.

After the visitation, he and Rhoda and the children greeted each person present, including Samuel and Rebecca Lapp, and Mary Beiler, the bishop's wife. Mamie Zook caught up with them, as well, and Earnest noticed how drawn her face was, as though she hadn't slept the past two nights.

"I'll be here for the service tomorrow," Earnest assured her. "If there's anything more you need done before then, have Judah send one of his boys over."

Mamie thanked him, and they left the house.

On the ride home, Earnest's family was silent, and he wondered how the viewing had affected his children. He hadn't forgotten how numb he'd felt at his young sister's funeral, as well as those of his parents.

Life is surely a vapor, he thought, clenching his jaw.

CHAPTER
Eleven

S ylvia wanted nothing more than to go for a walk alone as her father pulled into their long driveway after the viewing. "Do ya mind, Mamma?" she asked as they got out of the buggy.

"Take your time, dear. I'll put together some sandwiches for supper . . . something light."

Sylvia hurried to her room to change clothes. Carefully, she removed her best white head covering and hung it on one of the wooden pegs near the dresser. Then she did the same with her black dress and apron, looking through her everyday dresses, touching the sleeves lightly, trying to decide which color was most appropriate. It wasn't like she was a member of the Mahlon Zook family and should be wearing black for months on end. But she did feel as though she'd lost a family member.

She chose her brown dress, black apron, and a brown bandanna before making her way downstairs.

"Will ya bring in the mail on the way back?" Mamma asked as Sylvia headed toward the rear door.

"Sure, Mamma."

Glancing at the sky, Sylvia noticed rain clouds gathering on the horizon. She'd gotten caught in rainstorms before and didn't mind getting a little wet. Not like Calvin and Tommy, who seemed to relish getting sopping wet, especially when they were younger, stomping in mud puddles. She smiled, recalling her brothers' antics. *Preacher Zook liked to have the boys go over to help water his many rosebushes,* she remembered. There were times in the heat of summer when the boys ended up spritzing each other with the preacher's yard hoses, forgetting about watering the prized roses. On occasion even Preacher Zook would join in, making them all the wetter, laughing and having himself a wonderful-good time.

Like one of our Dawdis might . . .

Those pleasant memories lingered as Sylvia walked through the meadow, soon to be knee-deep with tall grass, ideal for their grazing livestock. As she went, she let her mind wander back to her lovely date with Titus last Sunday evening, while his buggy was parked beneath the sprawling oak tree. The breeze had been welcoming then, too.

She still couldn't believe he'd kissed her cheek so tenderly, his lips lingering there. Always before in the carriage, Titus had only held her hand.

Remembering how it felt to be so close to him, wrapped in his strong arms, she could hardly wait to see her fiancé again. Would he ask her to go riding this weekend, even though the next Singing was more than a week away? Her heart had lifted when he'd noticed her at the viewing today. He'd given her a spontaneous smile, not seeming to mind that he was observed by others. *He truly loves me,* she thought, *and doesn't care who knows it.*

She raised her face to the sky and realized that her relationship with Titus was really the only thing that had lifted her spirits since her uncomfortable talk with Dat. *Did I make a mistake urging him to keep the pocket watch from Mamma?* she thought. Sylvia was still uncertain what she'd actually stumbled upon. But the unknowns surrounding the inscription in particular haunted her.

Later, when heading toward the house, Sylvia checked the mailbox as promised, and was pleased to find a letter from Titus. She opened it and began to read as she walked.

> *My dear Sylvie,*
> *How are you?*
> *I've been thinking about when we might see each other again, missing you already. Does Saturday evening suit you?*
> *If it does, meet me down the road from your uncle Curtis and aunt Hannah's house, and I'll pick you up there. I invited another couple to join us for a double date. We'll go into town for some dessert and good fellowship. Maybe we'll see other couples there, too.*
>
> *With love,*
> *Titus*

She laughed under her breath, because she had just been thinking about wanting to see him, and here was an invitation for this very weekend. Oh, the happy thought of spending time with Titus again!

At four o'clock the next morning, Earnest quietly got out of bed and pulled on his work trousers and an old shirt, then tiptoed downstairs and over to his shop to do some work prior to dressing for the funeral.

He worked for an hour on a beautiful wall clock, an eight-day key-wound Westminster chime clock, occasionally glancing at the tinderbox on the top shelf, letting his mind wander back to the bitter-cold morning Papa Zimmerman had given him the box. *More than three decades ago . . .*

It was the day before Christmas, and ten-year-old Earnest and his parents and sister had traveled from their home in Fredericksburg, Virginia, to just a few miles outside of Loveville, Maryland, where his mother's parents resided. Because of the cold temperatures, the back roads leading to the old homestead—a large truck farm—had deep wagon tracks from all the carriage wheels of Amish and Old Order Mennonites alike. Occasional crystalline snowflakes seemed to float through the air, and his sister, Charlie, said it looked like a fairyland.

After getting unpacked, Earnest had gone with Papa Zimmerman to level out the rutted road with two mares hitched to a homemade road drag made of two bridge planks. Papa liked to do things the old way—or the hard way, some people said. At any rate, he ignored the fact that most farmers used a spike-tooth harrow to drag the roads around their farms.

When Earnest and Papa returned home, their teeth chattering, Grammy had hot cocoa ready for them, and Dad had built a roaring fire in the fireplace. Earnest and Papa went to sit in the front room on the hearth, shivering till their backs eventually became too hot, clear through their flannel shirts. Earnest's parents and sister were out talking with Grammy in the kitchen. *"Christmas secrets,"* Mom had said, eyes alight.

After warming themselves, Papa said, "Say, Ernie, would

ya like to have a look at the tinderbox my old pappy gave me
when I was just a boy?"

"Sure would," Earnest said, anxious to touch the shiny box,
which had been in Papa's family for generations.

Papa got up and reached for the brass box that had sat high
on the mantel for as long as Earnest could remember. Sitting
back down, Papa set the box in Earnest's lap. "Here, young
man. I've been wantin' you to have this."

Earnest was shocked. "For *me*?"

Papa nodded his head, brown eyes shining. "Consider it an
early Christmas gift."

Astonished, Earnest ran his hand over the smooth, gleaming surface. Papa was giving it to him! "Wow . . . thank you!"

"Listen, if you take good care, it'll be worth somethin' by
the time you're married and have children of your own."

Earnest looked up at his papa there next to him. "Are you
sure I should have it?"

Grinning, Papa leaned his shoulder against Earnest's. "I'm
mighty sure."

The large German clock nearby cuckooed twelve times,
and Grammy came in to refill their cocoa mugs. "The noon
meal's almost ready," she said, ruffling Earnest's hair. Then,
stepping back, she put one hand on her hip. "Are you two up to
something?" she asked, eyeing the tinderbox in Earnest's lap.

Papa shrugged comically. "Santa just came a little early,"
he said, winking at her.

Grammy blew a kiss to them. "Well, if you're hungry, come
to the kitchen in a few minutes."

Earnest smiled, but his appetite had vanished. All he
wanted to do was sit there and hold Papa's wonderful tinderbox . . . now his.

Moved by the memory, Earnest cleared his throat and stared at the gift that had brought him such pleasure that long-ago Christmas Eve day and so many days following. *Till recently.*

But he knew better. The trouble wasn't Papa's box; it was the inscription on the pocket watch . . . and the fact that Earnest had saved Rosalind's gift all these years. He forced air out through his lips and ran his hands through his beard, embarrassed by his behavior toward Sylvia. *All she did was find me out.*

He turned to look at the oak storage cupboards to the right of his work space and opened the one closest to the floor, where he kept small boxes of clock replacement parts. Removing all the little boxes, he pushed the tinderbox out of his sight— and anyone else's. As honored as he had been to receive such a treasure, Earnest feared that its most valuable item might destroy what he cherished most.

Rubbing his jaw, he returned to his chair and double-checked his work on the wall clock, dreading the funeral and the rest of the week stretching before him like a long black tunnel.

Earnest directed the horse into the Zooks' lane, missing Mahlon already. The man who had made him feel so welcome initially, the man who had reminded him of his papa Zimmerman's peaceful, uncomplicated way of life. The man without whom Earnest would never have become Amish . . .

The Zooks' farmhouse and bank barn were packed with people, some of whom had arrived more than an hour before the start of the service. Earnest parted ways with Rhoda and the children and headed for the house, pausing to shake hands with dozens of black-clad mourners waiting to be ushered into the front room.

Mahlon's young grandson Andy spotted him and came back to greet him, indicating that Earnest was to sit up close to the front, in the row behind the pallbearers—four of Mahlon's married grandsons.

The Amish usher nodded, and Earnest followed Andy, feeling conspicuous and thankful the service would last only two and a half hours, instead of the more than three typical of a Preaching service.

He noticed Judah and Edwin Zook sitting with bowed heads as they awaited the start of the service. Their brother Matthew reached over to shake Earnest's hand and motioned for him to take a spot beside him on the long bench with all of Mahlon's brothers. The ministerial brethren, including their longtime bishop, sixty-year-old John Beiler, were two rows up. On the opposite side of the room, the women sat facing the men, every one of them somberly clothed in a black cape dress and black apron.

At the stroke of nine o'clock, the funeral service began with the reading of a hymn from the *Ausbund*, followed by several Scripture verses and a written prayer. Then Bishop John Beiler rose and took his place. Slowly, deliberately, he began his sermon at the same time as Amos Kauffman started to preach to the overflow crowd in the barn.

Earnest listened to the bishop's sobering words in the stillness of the packed house, the air so very warm and stuffy.

"Mahlon Zook's death comes to us as an alarm bell—an important warning," Bishop stated, his black leather Bible in his callused hand. "Ofttimes the end of life catches us by surprise."

At the word *warning*, Earnest had to remind himself to breathe. *Mahlon would have entrusted me with his life*, he thought. *Yet I didn't trust him with the truth.*

"A year ago, Mahlon would never have thought he'd be gone from us today." Bishop John paused for a moment, his gaze scanning both sides of the crowd as a holy hush continued over the room. "Without a doubt, the Lord God has spoken through the death of our brother Mahlon, who desired that each of us live a life pleasing to our heavenly Father in word, deed, and thought."

Just then, Earnest recalled his effort to start the conversation with Rhoda—a conversation it was imperative they have. Yet since Monday night, he hadn't tried to pick it up again and follow through with his plan to confess, using the distraction of Mahlon's funeral as a sort of excuse. This failing annoyed him, and as this understanding merged with Bishop John's words, he felt all the more frustrated.

"Those of you who have not yet followed the Lord in holy baptism, I urge you not to put it off," the bishop said, now directing his remarks to the young people in attendance.

Earnest thought of his own children, especially Sylvia, who planned to be baptized this September, before her marriage. As far as he knew, she had never wanted to do otherwise, even prior to her engagement to Titus. The same held true for Ernie Jr., who was an obedient and loving son. While the day of Ernie's baptism was still a ways off, Earnest fully expected him to take the kneeling vow at the first opportunity.

Shortly thereafter, the second sermon began, this one given by an Amish minister from Bird-in-Hand who'd known Mahlon since childhood. The Gospel of John, chapter five, verses twenty-eight through thirty was the focus. "'Marvel not at this: for the hour is coming, in the which all that are in the graves shall hear his voice, and shall come forth; they that have done good, unto the resurrection of life; and they that have done evil, unto the resurrection of damnation. I can of mine own self do nothing: as I hear, I judge: and my judgment is just; because I seek not mine own will, but the will of the Father which hath sent me,'" the preacher read.

Sitting there, Earnest imagined almighty God requiring an account of his life, fiery eyes penetrating into his very soul. Bowing his head, he shook off the image.

Yes, he regretted things from his past, but he also felt soul-sick at the rupture in his relationship with his only daughter . . . and knew he risked the same with his darling wife. *Yet I owe Rhoda the truth.*

After the funeral, as the viewing recommenced, Earnest hung back with the non-relatives. Some folk, like Ella Mae Zook, paused a bit longer, and when Samuel Lapp and his married sons stood before the coffin, Ben, the youngest, pulled out a white handkerchief and wiped his eyes.

As for himself, Earnest doubted he would ever see his friend on the other side of the grave. That was the worst of it. But here and now, he doubted that Rhoda could ever forgive him.

"*Der Graabhof* is such a perty place. S'pose that sounds strange," Sylvia's cousin Alma said quietly as she and Jessie and Sylvia walked up the hill toward the cemetery. It was a place not just of repose but of peace; the age-old trees created a shimmering green shelter over the fenced-in sanctuary, its familiar landscape linked to grief.

Sylvia agreed. "Mamma says that the more of our loved ones are buried here, the less difficult it will be for us to visit."

"Why's that?" Alma asked, reaching for Sylvia's hand.

"Maybe because, as we grow older, there'll be more people we love over in Glory than alive here on earth," Sylvia said, looking at her cousins.

Jessie nodded her head. "It'll make us want to join them, too, one day."

Farther up the hill, Sylvia saw her mother with her own Mamm and with Aendi Ruthann, as well. Hannah was noticeably missing, as was *Onkel* Curtis, and Sylvia wondered what was wrong that Hannah had been homebound for so long.

Sylvia saw Eva Kauffman with her daughters. Eva was helping her oldest sister walk over the uneven areas on the ground. Sylvia couldn't keep her eyes off Eva, curious about her opinionated yet caring ways. What sort of *Schwermudder* would she be?

Sylvia realized she hadn't spotted Titus today, although she assumed he had been in the Zook barn with his brothers, since his father had preached the first sermon out there. She really hadn't expected to run into him anyway, since the young men usually stayed together at such gatherings. Even so, she had hoped at least for a glimpse of him.

At the graveside service, new mourners arrived, including English neighbors who hadn't gone to the funeral. Amongst such a throng of people, it was hard for Sylvia to hear the minister as he read a hymn while the coffin was lowered into the grave and family members shoveled dirt onto it.

Standing now on tiptoes, Sylvia spotted her father with

Judah and Edwin Zook, their heads bowed before everyone present recited the Lord's Prayer. At the words "Thy will be done," a shiver went through Sylvia as she surrendered anew her will to the heavenly Father.

When the prayer was finished, Dat shook hands with Mahlon's brothers, his eyes glittering with tears. The Zook grandsons who had been pallbearers came over to shake her father's hand, as well.

They're his family, too.

Will things ever be normal again? Sylvia thought as she and her mother and brothers gathered in the front room for Bible reading and prayer hours later. The sun would be setting in another hour or so, yet Dat was still at work in his shop. Seeing Mamma's serious expression as she gave the Bible to Ernie, Sylvia didn't dare inquire as to why.

It wasn't the first time Ernie had read in Dat's stead. There had been two other times that Sylvia remembered—once when Dat was sick with influenza, and another when he was out of town on business.

Ernie picked up where Dat had left off last evening, reading from Psalm one hundred and thirty. "'Out of the depths have I cried unto thee, O Lord. Lord, hear my voice: let thine ears be attentive to the voice of my supplications. If thou, Lord, shouldest mark iniquities, O Lord, who shall stand?'"

Muted footsteps came into the sitting room, and Sylvia looked up to see Dat standing in the doorway. He was still wearing his for-good black trousers and best white shirt and black suspenders. But he looked downright miserable.

"Keep reading, son," he said, leaning against the casing.

Ernie continued. "'But there is forgiveness with thee, that thou mayest be feared. I wait for the Lord, my soul doth wait, and in his word do I hope.'" Ernie glanced up at Dat and frowned a bit, perhaps, like Sylvia, wondering why he wasn't sitting down with them. "'My soul waiteth for the Lord more than they that watch for the morning: I say, more than they that watch for the morning,'" he continued.

Ernie read clear to the end of the psalm; then they all turned around in their seats and prayed the silent evening prayer, her father kneeling in his usual place next to Mamma.

When they had finished, Sylvia waited to speak, curious whether her father might say anything to the family, as he often did, but he only mentioned having more work to do before he left the room.

Ernie and Adam went out, as well, heading to the stable to clean the horse stalls, and Mamma sat back on the settee, fanning herself with the hem of her work apron.

"Are ya hungry?" Sylvia asked.

Mamma shook her head, looking ever so weary. "Not a speck," she murmured.

Certain her mother sensed something amiss, Sylvia felt uneasy.

CHAPTER
Twelve

*L*ate that night, Rhoda awakened, feeling overheated. She leaned up to push back the lightweight quilt and realized Earnest was missing. Shaking off her sleepy stupor, she slid her legs over the side of the bed and fumbled around on the floor for her slippers.

Downstairs, she saw no sign of him, not even in the spare room, where he sometimes had his forty winks after the noon meal. She hurried out the back door and across the porch to Earnest's workshop door. There, peeking in the screen door, she saw her husband sound asleep, his head resting on his hands on the worktable, the gas lamp alight. He still wore his church clothes from the funeral, minus the black frock coat and vest.

"For pity's sake," she whispered, going inside and inching her way over to him. With all the windows wide open and the screen door letting in the night air, the shop was cooler than their upstairs bedroom.

Earnest's breathing was shallow and held its familiar snuffle.

Standing near, she wanted to touch his dark hair, stroke his neck, and coax him to bed, but he was clearly exhausted.

Stepping back, she sighed, deciding to let him be. *Sleep restores the mind and the body,* she thought, feeling certain that Earnest was very much in need of that just now.

Taken aback by the sight of her husband slumped in such an uncomfortable position, her gaze rose to the shelves above, the wood gleaming in the gaslight. *Sylvia's kept up with the dusting and cleaning here,* she thought, then noticed a vacant spot on the very top shelf.

Looking around, it crossed her mind that Sylvia might have moved Earnest's family heirloom while dusting and then forgotten to put it back in its esteemed spot. *Earnest placed the tinderbox there the day he set up shop,* she thought, frowning. *Never once has it moved.*

She went to put out the gas lamp, deciding to ask Earnest about it tomorrow.

In the wee hours, Rhoda turned over in bed and stretched out her hand. Earnest was asleep right beside her. Knowing this made her feel more relaxed, and she fell back into slumber.

Later, when sunlight seeped beneath the green window shades, she awakened to birds chirping near the eaves. Earnest must have gotten up earlier and dressed, leaving his bureau drawer partway open and his pajamas folded on the back of his favorite chair.

In a hurry, she mused, picking them up and adding more laundry from the hamper around the corner from the dresser. Then she walked to the laundry chute in the hallway and dropped in the dirty clothes.

I really need to sit down with Earnest, she thought, perplexed at his strange behavior the last few days.

Sylvia washed up and dressed, relieved that Preacher Zook's funeral was behind them. Then, heading downstairs and out the back door, she heard Uncle Curtis's watchdog barking loudly and looked across the field. She didn't see anything unusual, though she did spot her brothers out harvesting radishes and onions, no doubt talking in *Deitsch* as they worked in the early morning sunshine.

When she crept into the barn, she was conscious of the sweet smell of new hay and the familiar scent of the road horses in their stalls. But Sylvia hadn't expected to see her father washing down the cow's udder, preparing to milk by hand. Quickly, she turned to leave, darting straight back to the house to make breakfast, hoping her father hadn't noticed her.

Rhoda rushed downstairs, where she found Sylvia already washing newly picked asparagus. "*Guder Mariye,*" she greeted her daughter.

"Good mornin' to you, too, Mamma. Dat's out milkin' Flossie, so I thought I'd come in an' help you," Sylvia said as she placed the asparagus spears on a paper towel to dry. "Oh, and the younger boys are still out pickin' radishes," she said. "Thankfully they were up early enough that they'll have plenty-a time to clean up for school."

"Last day of school's the thirteenth, the day before Ascension Day. How 'bout that?" Rhoda said, making small talk.

Sylvia glanced at the calendar on the back of the cellar

door. "That reminds me, I promised Titus I'd bake a couple chocolate sheet cakes for the gathering with *die Youngie.*"

"Oh, they'll like that." Rhoda reached to grab her work apron from the hook. "Say, when are Alma and Jessie picking ya up for the jam-making frolic?"

"Around seven-thirty."

"You'll have a real *gut* time putting up rhubarb jam together." Glancing toward the back door, Rhoda said, "Listen, I'll be right back." She wanted to catch Earnest alone in the barn, hoping Ernie was over in the stable just now.

Hurrying across the yard, Rhoda hoped this would be a good time to talk. She slid the barn door open and closed it behind her as two gray cats scurried out of sight and the cow mooed. "*Ach,* hope I didn't startle Flossie," she said when Earnest glanced over at her.

"She's a little skittish today." He frowned. "Everything all right?"

"Do ya have a minute?"

Earnest continued milking, the fresh milk squirting hard against the side of the bucket. "I always have time for you, dear."

Forging ahead, Rhoda began to say how worried she'd been about him, especially in the night. "When I found you asleep at your worktable, I felt awful sorry for ya." She paused a moment. "And while I was there, I noticed your tinderbox missing. The spot where ya kept it was—"

"I put it away," Earnest said.

His voice sounded so pinched, she hardly knew how to respond.

"It's a long story," Earnest went on, the cow's stream of milk beginning to slow. "And complicated, too. I started to tell you about it Monday evening."

"*Ach*, sorry I interrupted." She'd regretted it later that very night.

"Wasn't your fault, Rhoda." He shook his head, his voice so soft she could scarcely hear him now. "None of this is your fault." He fell silent.

"You're not yourself, love." She stepped forward. "Anything I can do?"

Earnest shook his head again, and his solemn expression pained her. "Once the boys leave for school and Ernie heads to the Zooks', we can talk more," he said quietly.

"Well, and Sylvie's goin' with Ruthann's girls to make jam pretty soon," she added.

Earnest held her gaze. "Judah Zook and I are going to Bird-in-Hand, but not till this afternoon."

"Whenever it suits ya, then," she offered, feeling strangely tense talking to her own husband. "I'll be here."

"*Jah*, it's best not to put this off."

The urgency of his words gave her goose pimples. "You're not . . ." Her breath caught in her throat. "You're not ill, are ya?" Solemn as he looked, the thought had just crossed her mind.

Earnest shook his head. "Fit as a horse."

Rhoda sighed heavily. Then just what was gnawing at him?

Sylvia enjoyed working alongside the other young women her age in the assembly line at the jam–making bee. Anytime she was invited to a work frolic, she jumped at the chance. Unlike most of the girls present here today, she'd missed out on having a sister.

Currently, she and Alma were washing rhubarb stalks in the deep sink while Alma and Jessie's cousin on their father's side, Anna Sue, was over at the table chopping with another young woman from the district. All the while, there was chatter about next week's Singing.

Sylvia perked up her ears when she heard that the host family was including another small group of *Youngie*.

"From Smoketown," Anna Sue was telling Jessie, but all of the girls seemed to be paying close attention.

"That'll be fun," Alma said, her big brown eyes bright.

"*Jah*, some new fellas," one of the girls said, which was followed by a peal of laughter all around.

Sylvia smiled, glad she was settled with a beau. *A fiancé!* she thought, eager to see Titus again this Saturday.

After a time, Alma brought up the fact that there had been over six hundred mourners at the funeral yesterday. "My Dat and his brother counted heads," she was saying. "And when the People from other communities kept comin', there was some talk that they might need a *third* location to accommodate everyone." She glanced at Sylvia. "Did ya hear that, too?"

Sylvia shook her head. "But I'm not surprised. There were so many inside the Zooks' house." The bench she'd sat on had been overly crowded, with scarcely space to turn to kneel and pray when it was time.

"If I was a church member, I know who I'd want to nominate for preacher next October," Cousin Alma said right out, looking straight at Sylvia.

Bewildered, Sylvia said nothing. Besides, it was too soon to talk like this—Preacher Zook hadn't been laid to rest for even twenty-four hours—and the nomination process wouldn't begin until St. Michael's Day, October eleventh.

Fortunately, Alma changed the subject and started talking

about another canning bee to be held over at Lois Peachey's. "Next Tuesday," Alma stated. "So if you can go, let me know."

"It'll be another *gut* day," Sylvia said.

"*Wunnerbaar.*" Alma smiled.

Maybe Mamma will come, too, Sylvia thought as she continued washing the rhubarb.

Refusing to surrender to the fear that lurked in her mind, Rhoda kept busy in the kitchen, even making time for an extra load of laundry. While the clothes were drying on the line, she baked an apple cobbler, one of Earnest's favorite desserts.

Around midmorning, her husband came inside and went to sit at the head of the table. He had removed his straw hat and sat with his hands in his lap. "I closed down the shop for the day," he stated matter-of-factly. "The sign's in the window."

Closed for the whole day? Rhoda had to wonder. She took coffee over and set it down in front of him, resting her hand on his shoulder. Earnest thanked her, put a cube of sugar in it, and stirred. "Do ya want a sticky bun, too?" she asked. "Curtis brought a dozen over this mornin' from Hannah."

Shaking his head, Earnest raised his coffee mug to his lips, then glanced back toward the dim hallway leading to the utility room door. He set down his coffee and rose suddenly to close the back door.

Rhoda tried to be calm, because Earnest's actions startled her. "Why must the door be closed?" she asked quietly.

Returning to the table, Earnest patted the chair on his right, where she always sat for meals. "Honestly, Rhoda, I'm not sure how to say this . . . but I must."

"Sounds awful serious," she murmured, taking her seat.

Earnest reached over for her hand. "It is." His brown eyes, usually bright, looked murky, and his countenance was resigned. "And no matter what you may think of me afterward, please know that I sincerely love you . . . with every beat of my heart."

A sigh escaped as she braced herself.

Earnest released her hand. "Earlier you asked about the whereabouts of the tinderbox," he said, adding that Sylvia had admitted to looking inside several days ago. "Unthinking, I had left it unlocked." Sighing, he went on. "But perhaps I wanted someone to find me out." Crinkles she had never noticed before appeared at the corners of his eyes.

"Aren't there just matches and whatnot inside?" she asked, baffled.

"*Nee*," he said. "I hid away certain items from my past as an *Englischer*. That's part of what I want to share with you."

"And Sylvia saw those items?"

He nodded. "Among other things, there's a gold pocket watch with an inscription." He glanced at the ceiling for a moment. "But while Sylvia saw that, she knows nothing of what I'm about to tell you." He drew a labored breath, his face almost ashen. "*Ach*, Rhoda, I've kept this a secret far too long."

She shivered. They'd never kept secrets from each other or anyone. Oh, but the pain registered on her husband's dear face made her listen with an open heart.

"There's no easy way to tell you," he said.

"Go on, dear."

Nodding, Earnest said at last, "It's best that I start at the beginning, leaving no stone unturned. . . ."

Thirteen

*I*n the autumn of his sophomore year of college, Earnest met an attractive young woman, well dressed and witty. From their first meeting, Rosalind Ellison engaged him as if she had known him for a long time. Though she had grown up in South Carolina in Hilton Head's Sea Pines community, Rosalind wasn't at all smug about it. She just stated it, and with an adorable southern accent, too.

Earnest wasn't about to ask if this had been her first choice for college, or her parents' choice. *Like mine*, he thought. His father had graduated from Georgia Tech with a degree in mechanical engineering, and Earnest's parents were pleased he was following in his father's footsteps.

Rosalind looked at Earnest with a sparkling smile and tilted her pretty head, her shoulder-length blond hair brushing against her chin. "Why did you pick this school?" she asked, sitting next to him.

"That," he said, "is debatable."

"Ah . . . so you didn't have much say, either?" She laughed softly.

"Don't misunderstand; I'm glad to be here. . . . A scholarship always helps," Earnest told her, lowering his voice at the latter.

"I've always liked a humble guy." She got up to walk, and Earnest fell in step with her.

That first encounter made him want to see Rosalind again—her breezy, casual style fascinated him. And after only a few dates, Earnest realized he was falling for her.

During Thanksgiving break, he took her home to meet his parents, who seemed surprised at how quickly they had become serious. Earnest's mom admitted she liked Rosalind's southern charm, but one evening after Rosalind had gone to the guest room, she also pointed out to Earnest that the young woman seemed very materialistic. "That worries me."

Later, Earnest's father privately encouraged him to take his time getting to know Rosalind. "And be sure to talk to God about your relationship," he added, his expression serious.

Earnest merely listened, preferring to make his own path in life. Talking to God was the last thing he wanted to do. What possible reason was there to second-guess a relationship with a fun-loving young woman like Rosalind Ellison?

"Bear in mind that you're both very young," his father also stated. He hadn't said *"and naïve,"* but it was certainly implied.

One week before Christmas, Earnest and Rosalind decided to elope. She surprised him with a gold pocket watch with an inscription on the back: *To Earnest, with all my love, Rosalind.*

Earnest's gift to her was a heart necklace with tiny diamond chips. Like Rosalind, he hadn't waited until Christmas to present it, anxious to solidify his devotion and love. Despite the fact that the pair had skipped over a formal engagement, moving straight into marriage, Rosalind seemed deliriously happy and wore her heart necklace every day . . . just as Earnest carried his pocket watch to classes and to his part-time job. Though the schedule could be challenging, his new goal in life was to give his bride a lifestyle comparable to what she was accustomed to.

Rhoda trembled as she sat at the kitchen table, her eyes fixed on Earnest's face—this man she so loved. The unexpected revelation was nearly impossible to comprehend and equally hard to stomach. "You were *married* before we met?" she asked quietly.

Earnest reached across the table for her hand, but she pulled away. "I was wrong not to tell you—or the People."

"Well, what happened to her?" Rhoda asked, trying to understand why Earnest hadn't told her till now. "Did she . . . did she die?"

"There's more to tell." His voice grew soft. "But . . . are you really sure you want to hear it?" He paused and looked somber. "This must be terribly hard on you."

Determined, she nodded. "I have to know."

Earnest and Rosalind's first winter together brought sorrow when Earnest's father succumbed to a massive stroke. The shocking loss left Earnest feeling strangely unmoored; it was inconceivable that the man who'd always sought to direct and guide him was no longer there. Rosalind did her best to raise his spirits, but Earnest was in no mood for consolation.

Spring break of that year, she pleaded with him to take her home to visit her parents.

"Sure, we can do that," Earnest agreed, thinking how down he had been since his father's death. "A trip to see your parents and have some fun might be good for both of us. But not for too long. I have some coursework to finish up over break, unfortunately."

She hesitated. "Maybe it would be better if I just go alone."

It was as if a dart had pierced his heart.

"At least for a while," she added hastily, reaching to gently touch his cheek. "That will give you time to study. You don't mind, do you, Earnest? It's just what I need right now."

Her voice sounded tired, and Earnest pulled her near. "You know how much I love to be with you," he said as she rested her head on his shoulder.

She breathed in deeply, letting it out with a long sigh. "All right, I guess . . . this time we'll go together."

Relieved, he said, "We'll leave first thing in the morning."

The drive to Hilton Head was spectacular—the salt-marsh landscape and lush, tall trees, including palm trees, the Harbour Town Lighthouse, the pristine golf courses, and the mansion-like homes. Everything seemed exceptionally beautiful, if not perfect, when Rosalind was by his side. Earnest truly did enjoy being with her, in spite of her growing tendency to indulge in shopping sprees, especially for clothes. And shoes, too—"a pair for every outfit," she liked to joke.

"You're going to outgrow our closet," he teased in reply.

"No question about that, darlin'," she agreed, laughing.

The day after their arrival, Rosalind left to go shopping, leaving Earnest at the beach house with her parents. Earnest took the opportunity to offer a reimbursement check of sorts to his father-in-law for many of Rosalind's expenditures during the past months.

"Oh, we don't mind taking care of our little girl," her father said dismissively.

Our little girl . . .

Earnest bristled.

"Rosalind is always welcome to use my credit cards."

Earnest bit his lip, sitting there in the man's luxurious cherrywood-paneled home office. *Does he realize he's undermining me?*

As it turned out, Rosalind's shopping expedition spilled into the evening, and after an awkward dinner with his in-laws, Earnest took himself off to the beach for a walk and a chance to clear his head. For reasons he couldn't fathom, it seemed that Rosalind's parents were actively working against his young marriage.

Emotionally weary, he headed back to the house and to bed, awakening hours later, when Rosalind tiptoed into the guest suite. She must have realized he was awake as she slipped to his side of the bed, because she said she'd lost track of time while out with a few friends. As was her way, she kissed him and apologized, saying she hadn't meant to abandon him.

Ready to forgive, he opened his arms to her.

As they packed to return to Georgia, Rosalind asked if she could stay behind for a few more days. "Would you mind terribly, hon?"

Earnest didn't let on how taken aback he was.

"Just for a little while?" she pleaded.

Realizing that it might make sense for a short time, Earnest agreed.

What Rosalind wants, Rosalind gets, he thought wryly.

The requested few days turned into a week, and then another. At the end of their daily phone conversations, Rosalind was often in tears, saying things like, *"I don't feel up to classes right now, and I miss living here on the beach,"* before tossing in a laugh. Earnest wasn't sure what was going on. All he knew was that he couldn't understand why she wasn't ready yet to come home to him.

Finally, when March had turned to April and it appeared that Rosalind wanted to stay even longer, Earnest put his foot down. "You've been gone long enough."

For a moment, Rosalind was silent; then she dropped a bombshell. "You know, Earnest, I'm leaning toward just staying here."

Something inside of him had suspected this, but he hadn't wanted to give it credence. "Why, Rosalind?" he asked. "We're married. We belong *together.*"

"I know . . . but these things happen to the best of couples," she replied.

What things? he wondered, afraid his marriage was already crumbling.

Filled with sorrow, Earnest said good-bye and hung up the phone.

Rhoda sat there feeling numb. It was hard to even glance at her husband when her heart was surely breaking.

The kitchen was no longer her happy domain, where she'd lovingly cooked and baked and brought her family together three times each day. The room was a prison now, trapping her at this beloved table, across from this man whose eyes and countenance were Earnest's, but who did not, at this moment, resemble her adoring, joyful husband. She wanted to rush outside and stop up her ears, because everything in her was telling her she must.

"Are you all right, dear?" Earnest asked, touching her elbow.

She winced. A myriad of feelings flowed through her as she sat there, studying him—disbelief, sadness, and anger. Most of all, shock that Earnest had never confided in her about this.

"I should have come clean to you long before now," Earnest said, "but I was so broken up when Rosalind divorced me. . . . I guess I wanted to pretend our short marriage never happened." He shook his head and grimaced. "There were years when I almost convinced myself that it hadn't. . . ."

She listened, struggling to understand.

"Since my early teens, I've admired the kind of life my Plain grandparents lived. And I found it here in Hickory Hollow with you, Rhoda darling." He pulled his blue paisley handkerchief out and wiped his eyes.

"We really need to keep this quiet," Rhoda said suddenly. "Just between us."

Earnest looked momentarily stunned but began to nod his head. "Are you sure?"

"It's an awful secret, Earnest—one that would shake up the whole community, not to mention our children. . . . *Nee*, you must not tell a soul." Slowly, she made herself rise from the chair. "Excuse me . . . I have to go upstairs to rest."

Earnest stood when she did, eyes pleading, but she turned away.

"Please give me some space right now."

"I dreaded the thought of telling you, Rhoda. I didn't want to hurt you like this," he said, following her through the next room. "And now I have."

She turned to face him, her lower lip quivering. "Under God, are we even married?"

A sad expression rolled over his face. "Rosalind divorced me early that summer to marry another man," he said, explaining that he believed he was permitted to remarry according to Matthew chapter nineteen. "But I never intended to marry again, not after what I went through. I couldn't bear the thought. And then I was falling in love with you, believing with all my heart that you would be true to your marriage vow. It was wrong, but by then, I'd already shoved my past life and marriage out of my mind. . . ."

Rhoda had no strength left and forced herself to trudge toward the stairs. Reaching for the bannister, she felt as if she'd aged twenty years in a single morning.

Fourteen

*E*arnest waited until Rhoda had made her way up to their room before he plodded to the spare room near the front of the house. There, he sat on the bed, sick at heart, knowing he should have insisted on telling Rhoda the truth when they were getting to know each other, back when he'd offered to discuss his past with her. But Rhoda had claimed that knowing any of that wouldn't have changed how she felt.

She never imagined I was divorced, though!

Too distraught to pray, Earnest recalled one of the many verses Papa Zimmerman had helped him memorize years ago. *He brought me up also out of an horrible pit, out of the miry clay, and set my feet upon a rock, and established my goings.*

"For me, that rock was Amish life," Earnest murmured. *Coming to Hickory Hollow at Mahlon's invitation gave me the fresh start I desperately needed—meeting and falling in love with Rhoda was the best part,* he thought, concerned for his wife. *Yet how can we recover from this?*

He closed his eyes and slipped his suspenders off his shoulders, letting his thoughts drift back to his first encounter with Rhoda Riehl.

In the May that completed Earnest's sophomore year, he moved to Ephrata, Pennsylvania, for a summer internship. Relocating also proved a way to keep his sanity as his marriage crumbled around him—and after the death of his father that past winter. Earnest spent his weekends in Amish country. On his first trip to Lancaster, he stopped in at the historic Central Market at Penn Square for a snack and discovered handmade soft pretzels, sauerkraut, and delicious spaetzle. There was also glasswork, pottery, and hand-painted wood signs. Most impressive of all, however, had been a display of hand-crafted clocks.

The vibrant marketplace had reminded Earnest of his Plain grandparents and their values of humility, community, and a more traditional way of life. Being around the Amish and Mennonite vendors stirred up a yearning to start a new chapter in his own life. One Amishman in particular, Mahlon Zook, extended the hand of friendship, and Earnest quickly came to appreciate how similar in personality he was to Papa Zimmerman.

Days after that first memorable visit, tragedy struck Earnest yet again as word reached him of his mother's sudden death—struck down by a heart attack mere months after his father's stroke. *Her heart couldn't take the loss,* he thought sadly. He'd never felt so alone as at her funeral, standing beside her casket without anyone to comfort him. It was as if his very world had ceased to exist.

Still numb and hurting, Earnest returned to Pennsylvania to complete his internship. By then Rosalind had expressed her intent to remarry as soon as their divorce was final, this time to a young man she'd known since her childhood on Hilton Head. Earnest could hardly process this thought. Now more than ever, there seemed little reason to rush back to Georgia.

In midsummer, Mahlon introduced him to an elderly clock-maker, Isaac Smucker, who was looking to sell his lifelong business in Hickory Hollow. In part because of his friendship with Mahlon, but also due to Earnest's own Plain family heritage, Isaac took a liking to him.

"Must I be Amish to apprentice for Isaac?" Earnest asked Mahlon one evening while they sat on Mahlon's back porch drinking iced meadow tea.

"If you're an honest man, that'll do for Ol' Isaac."

Meanwhile, Mahlon and his wife, Mamie, continued to encourage Earnest with their kindness and moral support. And while Earnest never admitted what he was running from, they seemed to sense that he was a broken man in need of a surrogate family. When his internship in Ephrata came to an end, Earnest was only too relieved to accept the invitation to rent their spare bedroom, opting not to return to college but to work instead for Isaac Smucker, the esteemed Amish clockmaker.

Long talks with Mahlon spurred Earnest to consider a radical idea. What if *he* could embrace the Plain life for himself? Would escaping into this cloistered world bury his painful past—assuming, that is, that he could put his modern customs behind him? After all, that was his biggest worry: Could he do it?

Earnest asked what it would mean to join the Amish church—what things he would have to give up, and what he would have to accomplish during his Proving time. Once he fully understood the ministers' expectations, Earnest went with Mahlon to meet with Bishop John Beiler, still uncertain he'd ever make it as a full-fledged Amishman.

One afternoon while driving on Cattail Road, he stopped at a farm to purchase some homemade bottled Amish root beer. A young woman with golden hair and the kindest eyes he'd ever seen was tending the stand, and as the two made conversation, he felt comfortable enough to tell her of his interest in becoming Amish.

She took one look at his bright red vehicle and his modern attire, and joked, "So far, ya ain't doin' so *gut, jah?*"

They laughed, and she offered him some Amish peanut butter spread on a cracker. He was struck by the extraordinary sweetness and asked about the ingredients.

She smiled and shook her head a bit flirtatiously. "Well now, I'm afraid ya have to be Amish through and through before I can tell a Riehl family secret."

The young woman captivated his imagination in the time it took to purchase the root beer and a pint jar of the fantastic peanut butter spread. But in spite of having asked around about her, curious to know her first name, it was another week before he saw her again, across the room at a Preaching service.

Later, after the shared meal, Earnest helped with the driving horses, hitching them up for various families. As it turned out, one of the horses belonged to the young woman's father, and Earnest smiled and said hello to Rhoda when he spotted her. She had brightened, then looked away, appearing surprised that he'd managed to learn her name.

It didn't take Isaac long to figure out that Earnest had noticed the lovely young woman, and he declared Rhoda Riehl to be one of the most devout young women he'd ever known. "If you're honestly thinkin' of going forward with the Old

Ways, you oughta get to know her," Isaac encouraged Earnest. "But you'll need to follow the rules: There'll be no courtin' till *after* ya join church."

Without explanation, Earnest agreed, knowing he would never remarry anyway. The gold pocket watch was a reminder of his mistakes, he thought, drawn to embrace this new sense of contentment and to keep the memories of his depressing past locked deep within.

During his Proving, Earnest worked alongside Isaac to learn the art of clock making, and when Isaac felt he was ready, he offered to turn over his business to Earnest for a modest down payment. Instead of a promissory note, Earnest gave his word with a gentleman's handshake to pay off the remaining balance over time, something that likely wouldn't take many years with Isaac's existing customers and notable clock inventory.

The following year, Deacon Peachey invited Earnest to take baptismal classes with the other candidates, all younger than he—and all of them born Amish.

It was mid-September when Earnest knelt before Bishop John Beiler and the membership and was baptized at the age of twenty-one, having adapted to gaslight and broadfall trousers and a bowl-shaped haircut. He did secretly miss his car, and wondered if any other Amishmen ever longed to travel faster than a horse and carriage would permit. But it was only a matter of convenience—with no close family to return to in the outside world, and Rosalind remarried, Earnest was content to make his home with the People.

Settled in his singleness, Earnest did not attend the Sunday Singings and other activities for the area's young people. His heart had been shattered, and besides, since divorce amongst the People was absolutely forbidden, he wasn't suitable for any Amishwoman who might look his way.

But when he again encountered sweet-spirited Rhoda Riehl at the General Store, he was taken aback by how pleased he was to know she was still single. Guarding his heart against his attraction to her and still burdened by his past, Earnest was tempted to pursue a friendship with such a wonderful young woman.

Waking up still inconsolable even after her deep sleep, Rhoda lifted herself out of bed and went to the dresser, where she peered at her mussed hair in the small hand mirror. She wondered if Earnest had ever struggled to look at his reflection these past more than twenty years. Had he felt guilty while regarding himself in the small mirror that hung over the sink in the bathroom downstairs, where he shaved his upper lip each morning? It boggled her mind to think that he'd somehow dismissed his past and not bothered to tell a soul. *Not even Mahlon Zook.*

Truth be told, she understood why Earnest hadn't revealed his former marriage ahead of their courtship, but why not sometime before their engagement? These and other serious questions pestered her as she tried to straighten her hair enough to tie on a blue bandanna.

Someone rapped at the door, and she cringed, not ready to see Earnest, least of all there in the room where they had been so intimate.

"Rhoda?" he called softly.

She looked at the three-chime clock on her bureau and realized it was close to the noon meal. Reluctantly, she crept to the door, opening it only slightly. "I'm really not up to cookin'."

"That's not why I'm here." His face was haggard, his hair rumpled.

She opened the door a bit wider.

"I wanted to check on you."

"Just resting, is all," she whispered.

"All right . . . I won't bother you, then." He turned toward the stairs.

"Earnest," she managed to say, "why did ya keep the pocket watch?"

He faced her and took a few steps back, eyes blinking. "It was a strange thing to do, I realize. But I saw it as a reminder of what I did wrong . . . I never wanted to be that impulsive again." He went on to explain that, in those early days, he'd also kept it as something he might be able to sell if he needed to keep afloat financially. "I went out on a limb not finishing my college degree, and I knew the watch was valuable enough that it could provide me with some extra cash in a pinch. Of course, that was before I was sure that I could make a go of Isaac Smucker's clock-making business."

"Around the time you and I were starting to be friendly," she said, the memory of those seemingly innocent days nearly overwhelming her now.

A brief smile flitted across his face, then disappeared.

"I didn't keep the watch because it was special to me. If anything, it reminds me of the way my former life was ripped apart . . . so many broken dreams." He looked like a lost soul as his arms hung limply at his sides. "Maybe I needed to feel that pain, to punish myself for ignoring my parents' concerns about Rosalind, and our being so very young. We didn't care what anyone thought—we just rushed into marriage."

She was conscious of the sadness in his eyes.

"I'm willing to sell the timepiece. That was actually the reason I unlocked the tinderbox the day Sylvie looked inside." He paused. "If I had followed through and sold it immediately, she never would have seen it. . . ." He sighed.

Rhoda shook her head, surprised. "Well, and then I might never have known the truth," she said matter-of-factly, almost wishing that were so. "But it ain't my place to say what to do with it."

"I mean it, Rhoda. I'm happy to sell it."

Rhoda didn't want to talk about it anymore—not just now. "*Ach*, it's all so troubling, my head hurts." *And my heart all the more.*

He was silent for a time, glancing toward the seat near the window where he'd often sat and read the Good Book aloud to her. "Maybe I could give the money to the alms fund."

"Are ya suggestin' you can *buy* your forgiveness?"

He shook his head.

"Well, it might seem that way," she said softly, wanting so much for this conversation to end.

"Everything comes down to what's right and wrong," he said. "And I've wronged you and our family—I know that much."

Feeling weak again, she went to sit in her chair near the window.

Earnest stepped into the room and was about to close the door when they heard something downstairs. Had Sylvia come home early? Their eyes met, and Rhoda's breath caught. "*Ach*, Earnest . . ."

It seemed as if they both realized the same thing in that moment: Revealing the truth about Earnest's past was not only damaging to her and Earnest's marriage, but it could ruin

Sylvia's relationship with Titus, too. Truth be told, it could hurt the whole family!

"Oh, Earnest," she murmured, tears welling up. "What are we to do?"

"Can we work through this . . . together?" he asked, his palms outstretched. "I'll do whatever it takes."

"Together?" He must think I'll leave him. Rhoda's stomach lurched as she looked across the room at Earnest. He appeared as desperate as he sounded. "All I know this minute is that I best be fasting," she said.

"I understand." He mentioned making a sandwich for himself. "I can see to Ernie, too. But is there anything I can do for you, dear? Anything at all?"

She shook her head, hardly able to stand the sight of him in their bedroom.

Earnest turned to leave, and she soon heard his tread upon the stairs. Staring out the window, Rhoda was thankful that Sylvia was gone for the day—it didn't sound as if she had returned early, as Rhoda and Earnest had feared. And of course with school, the younger boys would not be home till midafternoon.

How can I possibly display a cheerful spirit around all my children every day this summer? she thought then, knowing she must for their sakes. *Dear Lord, how?*

CHAPTER
Fifteen

*O*utside at the rhubarb jam–making bee that noon, Sylvia looked up from the well pump in the side yard just as Titus and his brother, eighteen-year-old Jonah, rode by in their father's spring wagon.

She was pleased when Titus called to her, and she waved back, so glad she'd come out for a drink. Oh, she wished she could tell him right then how she looked forward to seeing him again, and to thank him for his nice letter. But she simply watched the wagon move down the road, her heart wishing the hours away till Saturday.

That afternoon, when Sylvia's cousins dropped her off at the house, she found Adam and Calvin sitting on the back-porch steps talking about one of the younger schoolboys who had caused trouble at recess.

Calvin, rather vexed, said he wished the teacher would do

something drastic to punish the offender. "'Cause I'd like to punch him real *gut!*"

"*Ach, Bruder*, you know better'n to say that," Adam said. "We don't fight back. It's not our way."

Calvin scrunched up his face. "Well, the least the boy could do is buy two new lunch buckets with his own money, ain't?"

"True, but stop an' think how you'd be if you was an only child, like he is," Adam said, looking serious.

"*Were*," Calvin corrected. "*Were* an only child."

Adam shrugged. "I'm gonna be a farmer, not a professor or whatnot. What do I care how I talk?"

"*Puh!* Who's gonna be a professor . . . sure ain't me!"

Adam laughed. "*Now* you sound just fine. *Jah*, much better." He grinned. "You were startin' to sound like Dat sometimes."

"Like an *Englischer*, ya mean?" Calvin asked.

Adam nodded. "*Jah*, sometimes."

"Maybe that's 'cause he *was* one." Calvin dried his hands on his pants and went into the house.

Sylvia walked across the yard to Adam. "Did I overhear that someone's getting under Calvin's skin?"

"*Jah*, but school's nearly out for the year, so Calvin can quit complaining and let the teacher an' the parents work it out." Adam looked at her questioningly. "If you was the teacher, I mean *were*"—he glanced toward the house—"what would ya do to a boy with no respect for others' belongings?"

Sylvia's interest was heightened. "I'd think of somethin', but what would *you* do?"

"Prob'ly make him go and fish two lunch buckets out of the hole in the outhouse."

"*Was in der Welt?*" She screwed up her face. "For goodness' sake, how awful! What's the teacher doing 'bout it?"

Adam was trying not to grin. "That's just it, she seemed too *ferhoodled* to do anything. She should at least call in his parents to set him right if she can't do it herself." And with that, he walked away to do his barn chores.

Sylvia stood there, shaking her head. *Sure glad I'm not the teacher!*

She headed for the house, wondering if she should tell Mamma that, while riding home with her cousins, she had seen Hannah out sitting on the front porch. *She was just rocking and staring at the sky*

In the kitchen, Mamma was washing asparagus spears, murmuring under her breath.

"What can I do to help get supper on the table?" Sylvia asked.

"Ah, *gut*, you're home," Mamma said, her gaze still on her task. "Roast beef is bakin'—did ya smell it when you came in?"

"I do now ya mention it," Sylvia said. "Guess I was deep in thought."

Mamma looked up, eyes puffy and her hair askew. "Oh?"

Sylvia stared at her, alarmed. "Are you all right? Ya look—"

"It's been a different sort of day." Mamma shrugged and went back to rinsing soil off the asparagus, clearly unwilling to talk about it. "What were ya thinking 'bout, dear, when ya came in?" she asked.

"Just something Adam and Calvin said happened at school." Sylvia took a white work apron out of the bottom drawer, curious why Mamma looked as disheveled as if she'd just crawled out of bed.

Her mother kept working, not inquiring further about what Sylvia meant, which was not like her at all. That being the case, Sylvia decided not to mention the lunch boxes that had been thrown down the outhouse, not now. *Better to wait till we aren't in the kitchen, anyway!*

After bowing heads for the silent blessing at the supper table that evening, Sylvia realized that not a single one of them was talking about their day. She was aware only of the sounds of utensils on the plates and tumblers being set down on the table. Dat and Mamma seemed especially preoccupied with their own thoughts. In fact, the depressing silence continued till Mamma got up and brought over the rhubarb pie and ice cream. This brought spontaneous applause from her three younger brothers, but Ernie and Dat didn't join in like they typically might. When Sylvia looked at Mamma to see if she noticed, too, she spotted her frown and quivering chin.

A jolt passed through her, and she was filled with foreboding. Had Dat told her about the contents of the tinderbox?

The possibility rattled her. And with everything in her, Sylvia hoped not.

Rhoda was relieved when, after supper, Earnest went with the boys to freshen the livestock's straw bedding. She found it easier to breathe when her husband was absent from the room. This stark realization shook her; in just a few hours' time, everything about her life had been turned topsy-turvy. Why, she had been tricked into marriage to a man who'd once been wed to another! *Snookered,* she thought, still traumatized by Earnest's disclosure.

Standing at the kitchen sink, she put some dish soap in the water and absentmindedly swished the suds around. Then, reaching for the stack of dirty plates, most of them chipped from use over the years, she gently lowered them into the deep sink.

Sylvia dried each plate as she worked alongside Rhoda, doing what she had been trained to do since age five, when she had stood on a chair to dry dishes, chattering all the while. This evening, though, her daughter was strangely silent, even though she surely had thoughts of Titus to share.

Occasionally, during the course of washing and drying the dishes, Rhoda's hands lightly brushed against Sylvia's. The ordinary gesture triggered something profoundly maternal within her. She thought again how Earnest's deceit would likely affect their precious children, rippling out like a stone tossed into a lake.

Reaching now for the utensils and placing them in the dishwater, she wondered how she and Earnest could possibly keep such a secret. Was it even possible to continue the charade that all was well? From the children's concerned glances around the table, she doubted they were even succeeding. It was hard to disguise her aloof behavior toward her husband, the sudden sense of distance between them.

These things Rhoda pondered long after the kitchen was cleaned up and Sylvia had left the room.

When Earnest and the family met for Bible reading and prayers, Rhoda could tell that his heart was not in their devotional time. His voice sounded so flat, she wondered if perhaps he had been acting a part all of these years. Was it possible that their relationship wasn't the only thing built on a false foundation?

Yet everyone amongst the People thought Earnest to be

an upstanding Amishman, herself included. *And now only I know the truth.* . . . The weight of it was so heavy that, just now, she didn't see how their marriage could survive. It crossed her mind that they might simply part ways, not divorce but separate. *Earnest can return to his English roots, if he wishes. After all, it seems faith wasn't what drew him to become Amish,* she thought sadly.

Rhoda noticed just then that Ernie and Adam were trading glances, though aside from that, they had seemed to be paying attention. Calvin and Tommy, however, appeared to be daydreaming, and considering their father's mind-numbing monotone while reading the Good Book, who could blame them? Why, even poor Sylvia looked nearly as pained as Rhoda felt.

She gave a sigh of relief when they all turned to kneel at their seats. As was their norm, Rhoda prayed the silent rote prayer, tonight adding a fervent request for almighty God's intervention. *If it be Thy will, O Lord, help us through this difficult dilemma. I pray this in Jesus' holy name.*

Earnest was wary while lying beside Rhoda when they retired for the night—mere inches felt like yards away. Even so, he didn't want to cause her further anxiety by calling attention to his presence in their room . . . or bed. He wished there were a way to offer her some comfort. He had yet to get a real grasp on what she had been thinking these past few hours since they'd talked. Was she planning to ask him to leave? He'd almost detected as much at the supper table. She had been so dreadfully quiet, even leaning away from him.

He yearned to turn back the clock and do things differently.

Yet the thought of never having known and loved Rhoda caused his eyes to sting.

"Have ya kept in touch with Rosalind?" Rhoda asked sleepily, startling him.

"Not once, after the divorce was final."

That was all Rhoda asked before falling into a long and painful silence again.

Peering into the darkness of the room, Earnest mentally recited the psalm he'd pondered earlier that morning. *He brought me up also out of an horrible pit, out of the miry clay, and set my feet upon a rock, and established my goings.*

After a time, Earnest lifted the sheet, reached for his bathrobe, and got out of bed. *My faith is so weak,* he thought. *Can I expect God to lift me out of this mess . . . my own doing?* Then, making his way across the room, he headed downstairs to sit at the table where he'd always sat since marrying his dearest Rhoda. Bowing his head there, he thought of beseeching God to forgive him but felt too unworthy.

Eventually Earnest rose and walked to the utility room and lit a small lantern. Carrying it outside, he felt the slight chill of the night but welcomed the quiet, the closest thing he knew right now to peace. If Rhoda changed her mind about staying mum and confided in Mamie Zook or any of the other womenfolk about Earnest's former marriage and divorce, only the Lord above knew what their future might hold. He shuddered to think of losing his family, but things were on the brink of that, he knew. *How could I endure such a loss?*

Restless and in need of a friend, Earnest realized he had not allowed himself to fully grieve Mahlon's passing. And now this breach between Rhoda and himself felt like a death, too. *She must think we've lived a lie for twenty years!*

While he understood her turning away from him and not wanting him physically near, he could not imagine sharing their bed and not reaching for her as he had all during their happy marriage.

I brought all this on myself, he thought, taking a seat on a nearby rocking chair and staring at the night sky, the lantern casting a ghastly glow around him.

Awful as it is, at least we're unified in keeping my secret.

CHAPTER

Sixteen

Sylvia heard footsteps on the stairs, and recognizing that Dat was up, she crawled out of bed, put on her long summer duster, and tiptoed down to the kitchen. One of the floorboards creaked, and the smell of lantern oil came in through the rear screen door. Glancing at the table, she recalled how painful it had been to sit there during supper as something terrible overtook her family. Exactly what, she did not know. But she knew that even her brothers had sensed the sudden divide between their parents.

Barefoot, Sylvia went to the back door and saw her father sitting with his head bowed low. A good many moths dipped and wheeled near his lantern as Sylvia hung back, waiting.

The longer she waited, the more she wondered at his rigid stillness. Was he breathing? She opened the screen door to step forward, and just then, his head came up and he yawned. He folded his arms across his chest and leaned back in the rocking chair.

"Dat?" she said softly, not wanting to alarm him.

He turned to look. "*Ach*, you're awake?"

"Heard your footsteps on the stairs earlier," she said, wondering why he was down here instead of in bed with Mamma.

She sat on the rocking chair next to him, crossing her legs and pulling her long duster down over them. She felt as if a wall had descended between them. *Ever since I opened the tinderbox,* she thought. As a little girl, she'd often sat in this very spot to watch the moon rise with Dat. He'd never been a big talker, but he listened real good, and his silences were comfortable, if not comforting. Truth be known, words hadn't mattered, because she and Dat had always been able to enjoy just being together.

Yet she had still wished that he would oblige her now and then and tell her more about his own childhood . . . not only about his family, but also his hopes, if not his fears. But then again, Dat hadn't been one to reveal his feelings. At least not to her.

I have so many memories. She thought of all the years Dat and she had been close. *And they're good ones. Yet sometimes it seems like I hardly know my own father.*

She sighed softly, trying to work up her nerve. "Is Mamma all right? I was sure something was wrong while we were makin' supper." She took the chance that just maybe this might open things up between them.

"Sylvie," her father said, his voice sterner than she expected. "You mustn't get caught up in this."

"Well, I already am," she protested, wanting to get all of this out in the open. "Dat, please, can't we talk?"

"It's late."

"Just for a minute?"

He looked her way, the muscles in his face softening a bit.

She squeezed her hands together and took the plunge.

"Does Mamma know what I found in the tinderbox—that gold pocket watch?"

He looked away, then nodded. "*Jah*, we talked for a long time this morning about that . . . and many other things."

What's he gone and done? she worried. Sylvia looked out toward the barn, where the waning three-quarter moon's silvery beams made the steel roof gleam. The night enveloped them, still lovely despite the tension between them.

She swallowed hard and tried to resist the growing frustration she felt. *The pocket watch was surely from an old girlfriend,* she thought. *Why bother Mamma with it?*

She recalled Mamma's quiet listlessness, even sadness, so out of character for her.

Dat did not volunteer more, and the refrain of crickets took over. He looked like a man in need of consoling, but with poor Preacher Mahlon dead and in the ground, no one was close to her father anymore. Except Mamma, but she seemed to be in equal need of consolation.

"S'pose I ought to return to bed," Sylvia said at last, the rocking chair stirring back and forth as she rose.

Heading for the back door, her heart broke for the breach between Dat and herself—and between her father and mother, too. And a thought plagued her. *If Rosalind was Dat's former girlfriend, why is Mamma so upset?*

As Sylvia awoke the next morning, fresh, fragrant breezes wafted in through her open windows from the purple redbud bushes and pink and white dogwoods in full bloom. Stretching out as she sat up, she noticed the way the sunlight shone on her pretty bed quilt. Just one more day, and she would see her beloved Titus. If only that could eliminate her worries over Mamma. And Dat, too.

She didn't dare let herself imagine the things her father must have shared with Mamma yesterday. But by the look on his face—and Mamma's behavior—something disconcerting had happened. And Sylvia was very sure the mysterious Rosalind's inscription had everything to do with it.

She pulled on her bathrobe to head downstairs to shower, looking forward to working the soil in the garden, and weeding and hoeing, doubtless a good idea since Mamma could maybe use some time alone in the house to think. *Or pray.*

Back upstairs after her shower, Sylvia sat on the edge of the bed and read from the Good Book, thinking she might need to paste a smile on her face to make it through the day without drawing questions from her brothers. *They're bound to have enough of those already!*

Rhoda poured cold water in the teakettle, wishing she could talk privately with Ella Mae over a cup of warm peppermint tea. She planned to brew some presently. Aside from talking to the Lord above, though, there was no substitute for exposing one's soul to the Wise Woman. Yet Rhoda had been the one to insist Earnest *not* tell a soul about his past. Earnest's future as a church member was at stake, and they alone held the power to safeguard that.

Despite all of that, she believed that God must be frowning on her for uniting with Earnest in his deceit. *Frowning on us both,* she thought, wondering how long she could live with this knowledge tearing at her.

What would happen if Earnest was nominated for preacher

come October, and *then* it was found out? Or if Sylvia married and *then* Titus learned the truth about his father-in-law's past?

In dire need of some sunshine and fresh air, Rhoda decided to visit Hannah, not Ella Mae, after the breakfast of eggs and scrapple . . . once morning chores were done.

Earnest had gotten up very early again to work on his most recent custom clock order, doing the meticulous work he was credited with. For the years he'd lived and worked here, the People valued a fast worker as a good worker, but he had always been one to work methodically, especially when it came to the art of clock making. Not so carefully, though, when it came to hauling manure or chopping wood. For everyday chores, Earnest was as speedy as the next Amishman.

If I can still consider myself such a man, he thought while hitching up Lily to head over to help Judah and Edwin Zook take stock of some farm equipment and tools in preparation for the auction they were planning across the field at Mahlon's. They would decide on which Amish auctioneer to hire, place an ad in the local newspaper, and create sale bills to distribute to various businesses around the county to get the word out. The family was leaning toward not selling the farmhouse immediately, instead wanting to rent out the cropland once the autumn harvest was in. Along with the farm items up for auction, they hoped to sell some of the house furnishings, since Mamie would be the only one living there for the time being. One of Matthew's unmarried daughters was spending nights with her and lending a hand around the house for now, and in the fall, they would sit down with Mamie and let her decide whose home she would like to move to.

She's fortunate to have so many options, Earnest thought, glancing at the back porch, where he'd seen Rhoda shaking out rugs earlier. The sight of her made him sad, aching as he was to set things right with her.

He signaled Lily to pull out of the driveway onto the main road, feeling drained by the worrisome thoughts that crossed his mind. *Today will be a test of Rhoda's and my relationship—an indication of how things might look going forward,* he thought, feeling even more wretched.

Before he'd left the house, Rhoda had mentioned her plans to go over to see her ailing sister. At the time, he'd felt the urge to say something, wishing she wouldn't put herself in the position of being observed by someone as close to her as Hannah—his wife had seemed so dejected as she'd talked with him in the kitchen before the children came down. Somehow, though, she'd forced herself to take on a cheerful facade at breakfast, and for that he was thankful.

Earnest slapped the reins and clicked his tongue to urge Lily into a trot, and her head dipped, thick mane flying, as the spring wagon moved along. Last night's short talk with Sylvia came to mind—he'd purposely kept her in the dark, much as he'd done with Rhoda all these years. Yet it wasn't his place to tell Sylvia the truth, not when Rhoda had decided it wiser to keep silent on the matter. Undoubtedly, though, his only daughter was questioning why something as small as a pocket watch was causing such agitation.

Rhoda walked along the driveway and out to the road, then moved to the left shoulder, where she could better see the teams of horses and buggies coming around the bend up ahead. She swung her right arm to appear to be on a mission, which she was. The basket of goodies on her left arm held not only raisin bread but a fresh batch of fudge, too.

The soaring shade trees created interesting shadows on Hickory Lane as one buggy after another rode by. She walked alongside her brother-in-law's white horse fence that lined the meadow where Curtis turned out his frisky colts each spring.

Just then, she saw Annie Fisher Lapp headed this way in her gray family carriage, which glinted in the sunlight. Annie waved, smiling broadly as her horse clip-clopped past. Rhoda recalled the day Annie had married Elam Lapp, shunned Katie's older brother. She remembered it clearly because she was to have been one of Annie's wedding attendants until she had contracted a bad case of bronchitis. Truth be known, until yesterday, that had been the most disappointing day of Rhoda's life.

When Rhoda turned into the narrow lane, she noticed Curtis walking across the side yard from the springhouse, his straw hat pushed back on his head. He broke into a grin when he saw her, raising his hand high in welcome.

"Hullo," she called to him as she neared. "Is Hannah around?"

"Sorry to say, ya just missed her." Curtis pointed over yonder. "She's gone to Ella Mae's."

"Okay, then," Rhoda said, somewhat astonished that Hannah had felt up to leaving the house. "I'll just drop this off with ya." She offered the basket to him.

Curtis shook his head. "Why not take it to her at Ella Mae's? Surprise her." He chuckled. "The three of yous can have yourselves a nice long chat, and some goodies." Smiling, he added, "If that's what ya brought, that is."

"*Jah*, plenty of sweets."

Curtis adjusted his straw hat. "Give my best to Earnest."

"I'll do that," she said, slipping the basket handle back on her arm.

"Say, before ya go, how's he doin', since Mahlon's passing?"

"I doubt it's sunk in yet."

Curtis glanced over his shoulder in the direction of the Zook farm. "Mamie's one strong woman, isn't she? At least she was the day of the funeral."

"Once the day-to-day sets in, it'll be ever so hard."

Rhoda said good-bye to Curtis, feeling an even greater determination to spend as much time with the new widow as possible.

Something precious has died in me, too, Rhoda thought, then chided herself for comparing her own predicament to Mamie's.

Rhoda slowed her stride as she walked toward Mattie and David Beiler's farm, where Ella Mae's little *Dawdi Haus* was connected to her daughter and son-in-law's ivy-covered farmhouse. There was no need to rush, since she didn't want to interrupt Hannah's time with the Wise Woman. Truth be told, she felt nearly too tired to engage in much conversation.

There *had* been many times, though, when Rhoda was eager to arrive at Ella Mae's sunny kitchen and loath to leave the warmth of acceptance and understanding the kindhearted woman radiated. One such time, more than twenty years ago, had been right after Earnest invited her on their first date, on the heels of the bishop having lifted his Proving and inviting Earnest to join church.

Earnest seemed somewhat shy in those days. Hesitant to mention anything to her own Mamm about Earnest Miller's interest in her, Rhoda had confided in Ella Mae instead, asking for wisdom.

She remembered it as clearly as yesterday. . . .

CHAPTER
Seventeen

*A*s usual, the Wise Woman's renowned teapot was simmering on the back burner of the wood stove as a young nineteen-year-old Rhoda was welcomed into the cozy *Dawdi Haus.*

"I have some peppermint tea right here, just waitin'," Ella Mae said, her blue eyes bright at seeing her. And Rhoda was happy to be seated at the table graced by two place mats embroidered with yellow roses.

"Sugar cubes are in that buttercup bowl near the window," Ella Mae said from the other side of the small kitchen. "But you're mighty sweet already, so maybe ya don't take it in your tea."

She gave her familiar laugh, setting Rhoda at ease, who was glad since this was only the second time she'd come here. First for solace, and now for advice.

"I've been thinking 'bout ya, dearie," Ella Mae said, interrupting young Rhoda's own thoughts. She carried a tray with two rose teacups set on matching saucers. "If I may say so, ain't very much I miss round here."

Rhoda was grateful for this teatime, glad that Ella Mae was available to talk—the dimple-cheeked woman was in such high demand. "Then ya must have an idea why I'm here."

"Well, I've heard there's a certain brown-eyed young man spendin' his money at your roadside stand."

A flush of warmth spread over Rhoda's cheeks. "Did Mamm tell ya?"

Ella Mae reached for the bowl of sugar cubes and dropped one into her tea. "'Twas a little birdie, let's say."

"Those birdies seem to be everywhere lately."

Nodding, Ella Mae said, "Birds are known to fly, ain't so?"

Rhoda laughed, enjoying her visit. "I s'pose it's all right to come right out an' ask ya what I'm wonderin'."

"Well, I daresay the day it ain't all right will be the day I'm dead and gone." Ella Mae sipped her tea and looked over the top of her cup at Rhoda, her little glasses steaming up. "If ya speak your mind, honey-girl, I promise to listen. All right?"

Stopping to pick up her own pretty cup of tea, Rhoda felt ever so cared for. "*Denki* for bein' willing to listen with your heart like ya do."

"Is there any other way?"

Rhoda began to talk about Earnest Miller, explaining that they'd met last summer while she was tending the family vegetable stand, but that she hadn't talked with him much during his Proving.

Ella Mae nodded.

"I saw him at the General Store, and we talked a little again." Rhoda admitted that initially she'd thought he might be too bashful to ask her out, so she was surprised when he invited her to go with him to meet his clockmaker friend, Isaac Smucker. "Do ya know Ol' Isaac?"

Ella Mae's eyes lit up unexpectedly. "Truth be told, I do— well, I *did*—but that's a whole 'nother story. Go on, dearie."

"Anyway, I was so *ferhoodled*, I didn't know how to answer. So I said I'd have to think 'bout it."

A big grin smoothed out Ella Mae's wrinkled face for a moment. "A girl after my own heart." She set down her teacup and rested her chin on her hands. "And what *have* ya thought?"

Rhoda paused. "Honestly, it seems strange to consider goin' with someone from the outside world."

"Someone who wasn't born Amish, ya mean?"

"*Jah*, and he just doesn't talk about his family, 'cept that his parents died not so long ago." Rhoda sighed. "Maybe it's because his people are all fancy folk. I really don't know."

"Does it make any difference to ya that the bishop has given him the right hand of fellowship?"

Rhoda considered that.

"You do trust Bishop John, don't ya? God ordained him to oversee the flock here in Hickory Hollow."

Rhoda was quick to say she did.

"So, I s'pect the next thing to consider is what your heart's tellin' you . . . and not only that, but your noggin, too. The Good Lord gave us brains to use and hearts to be wide open to His will."

Taking this in, Rhoda realized something and was surprised she hadn't thought of it before. "Ya know, I could just tell Earnest I'll go with him once . . . give myself a chance to decide if I want to again."

"See? Now you're usin' your noggin. And if this fella's the right one, the Good Lord will prompt your heart. You'll know."

Ella Mae reached for her teacup again and took a longer sip. Then, setting it down again, she added, "God's will doesn't just drop into our laps when we're sittin' still. *Nee*, He guides us when we're walking in His steps, moving forward. That way, He can stop us or nudge us onward."

This made sense to Rhoda, and after accepting a second cup, she thanked Ella Mae for the delicious tea—and the heartfelt advice.

Presently, Rhoda shifted the basket on her arm, realizing she had been smiling during her reverie. *Why haven't I visited Ella Mae more often?* she wondered, already knowing the answer. Once she'd married Earnest, her life had become a happy whirl of tending the house and cooking and spending time with him. And once the babies started coming, things had gone smoothly enough that there was no need to seek counsel from the Wise Woman. Rhoda's Mamm assisted her whenever needed, and she had no reason for solace, because her life seemed to be altogether joyful.

Just then she spotted David Beiler's white clapboard farmhouse and headed down the driveway. At the flower-lined walkway, she made her way around to the back of the house, where the *Dawdi Haus* was connected, and the small square back porch came into view. It had changed little over the years, what with fresh white paint and the same clay pots with new red geraniums each springtime. Something else was new, though—a delicate silver metal wind chime that hung on the far side, away from the door.

The thought of Ella Mae's delicious peppermint tea made Rhoda's mouth water. But today the celebrated tea would not be enough to lift her spirits. Truly, even if Rhoda were visiting for her own sake rather than for her sister's, nothing short of a miracle could solve the mess she and Earnest found themselves in. *Keeping his awful secret . . .*

Rhoda knocked and Hannah came to the door, her face tear stained. She reached to hug her, then stepped past to set down the basket on the kitchen counter, pulling back the tea towel that covered the goodies. "See what I brought," she said, mentioning that Curtis had encouraged her to drop by. "Since I missed ya back at your place."

Ella Mae rose from the table to peer into the basket. "I don't know 'bout yous, but my taste buds are doin' the two-step."

Hannah laughed. "Well now, how do ya know 'bout that?"

"Don't forget that I was young once." Ella Mae's smile was mischievous. "Could've gotten myself put off church."

"Truly?" Hannah said with a glance at Rhoda, who was lifting the lid from the pan of fudge.

"Oh, let's just say I came to my senses in the nick of time." Ella Mae motioned them both toward the table.

Hannah and Rhoda giggled at that.

"Would ya like to put the goodies out so we can see what ya brought?" Ella Mae asked as she sat back down.

Rhoda and Hannah carried over the fudge and the raisin bread and placed them in the middle of the table, alongside a sharp knife for each pan.

After she had unwrapped the bread, Hannah pointed to the stuffed bear near the door with her things. "I've been carrying him around now and then, but talking regularly to Ella Mae has helped me even more. Prayer too."

"Oh, sister, I'm awful glad to hear that," Rhoda said, offering her a piece of fudge.

"I do cradle the bear sometimes, though, when I can't sleep at night . . . and I'm up walkin' around the house." A tear trickled down her face, and Hannah wiped her face with a hankie. "These ain't sad tears, in case ya wondered," she told Rhoda.

Ella Mae spoke up. "Tears can be mighty healing." Her eyes were on the moist raisin bread, so Rhoda cut her a thick slice.

"Well, it looks like I came at the right time," Rhoda said. "Wasn't sure if I'd be interrupting yous."

Hannah shook her head. "Not at all."

Going to the fridge, Ella Mae poured some iced peppermint tea into a tumbler for Rhoda. "Goodness, I think we might just ask a blessing for this unexpected treat." And she did, right out loud, and Rhoda bowed her head and respected Ella Mae's way.

Sylvia poured her energy into uprooting the pesky little weeds in the family vegetable garden that had sprouted in just the last couple of days. She was anxious for her younger brothers to finish up their school year so they could help more in the garden, too. With five of them weeding and harvesting, Mamma wouldn't need to tend to it. And, thinking of Mamma, Sylvia was glad to have seen her head over on foot to Hannah's after breakfast. *Maybe they'll cheer each other up,* she thought, unsure if her aunt was still ailing.

Hoeing harder, Sylvia recalled sitting with Dat on the back porch last night, and with everything in her, she wanted to help fix whatever was happening between her parents. Though it wasn't her place to be their peacemaker, it bothered her to sit idly by and watch them fall apart. And from the continuing silence and stiffness at breakfast, they certainly seemed to be.

Hearing a horse and wagon pull into the lane, she looked up to see Mamie Zook's grandson Andy, who waved as he halted the horse. "Lookin' for my Dat?" she called to him, leaning on the hoe.

Andy nodded, his white blond hair blowing in the wind as he removed his straw hat. "Is he around?"

She pointed in the direction of his grandparents' farm. "Jah, over at your Mammi Zook's."

At that, Andy laughed a little. "Ya know, I had a feelin' he might be helpin' prepare for the auction. It's awful hard thinkin' of Dawdi Zook's things bein' sorted through already. 'Specially his lifetime farm tools." Andy sighed, a faraway look in his eyes. "If I had a bushelful of money, I'd buy up most of it."

"Well, I can't blame ya," she was quick to say.

"So, are you the only one home?" Andy asked, still sitting there in his wagon.

Sylvia wondered why he was asking. "For now. I don't mind keeping the home fires burnin'."

"I stopped by to look at some of your father's chiming clocks, if he has any in his inventory."

"Sure, I can show ya what's available," she said, always happy to look after Dat's customers, though most weren't quite as handsome as Andy.

With a smile, Andy hopped down from his wagon and tied the horse to the hitching post. She carried the hoe with her and propped it against a tree near the back walkway to her father's shop.

"You won't say anything, will ya?" Andy said, walking with her. "It's a surprise for my sister." His blue eyes were questioning.

"Oh, trust me, I can keep a secret," she said opening the

door to the showroom. "Here we are," she said, eager to make a sale for her father. "Dat's the best clockmaker around, as ya know. . . ."

Rhoda, Hannah, and Ella Mae were still nibbling on treats and drinking their iced tea when Ella Mae turned her attention to Rhoda. "Are ya feelin' all right, dear?"

Surprised, Rhoda drew in a quick breath.

From where she sat beside her, Hannah turned to glance at her now, too. "Ya looked a bit peaked when ya came in." She lifted a piece of fudge out of the pan and handed it to Rhoda. "Maybe more goodies will help? That's what you always tell me." She smiled.

Ella Mae was quiet now, observing.

Rhoda peered out the window. "I wish it were that easy," she said, reminding herself that this was Hannah and Ella Mae. Neither of them was known to gossip.

Hannah slipped her arm around Rhoda's shoulders. "We're here for ya, sister. Whatever 'tis."

All this kindness was going to bring her raw emotions to the surface, and Rhoda couldn't have that. "I appreciate bein' here . . . for each other," Rhoda managed to say, hoping for a change of topic.

"Preacher Zook's death has caused lots of sadness in the Hollow," said Hannah, reaching for her teacup. "Curtis is feelin' glum, an' so are a lot of other folks, too."

"I'll say." Ella Mae looked longingly at the little bit of fudge left on her paper napkin. "Mahlon Zook was a true man of God, one with a servant's heart."

"Curtis has been draggin' around like one of his own kin

passed on," Hannah told them as she patted Rhoda's arm. "So I understand, dear sister."

Nodding, Rhoda was thankful their conversation had redirected into safer territory. Even so, she promised herself she would be more careful in the future. *No need to stir up even a chance of tittle-tattle.*

Before they parted ways, Ella Mae looked right into Rhoda's eyes and said softly, "Remember, we're connected to our heavenly Father by threads of love we can't always see."

Rhoda carried that wisdom in her heart as she walked toward home, thankful she'd gone to Ella Mae's and hoping against hope that neither of them would think twice about her awkward hesitation earlier.

CHAPTER
Eighteen

That evening Rhoda spent time in her room embroidering a doily while the children did their outdoor chores and Earnest worked in his shop. He'd seemed quite pleased that another chime clock had been sold, thanks to Sylvia minding the store while they were gone.

Rhoda glanced at Earnest's bedroom slippers on the floor, peeking out from beneath the bureau across the room, and recalled how peculiar last night had been. They had shared the bed and not even kissed each other good-night. *'Tis best,* she thought, looking out the window as a group of birds flew high over the meadow. Earnest had picked up on her unspoken desire that he not embrace or touch her in any way. When she thought now of lying in his arms, or even of simply hugging him, hurtful thoughts of Earnest's former marriage and divorce pushed into her mind.

Rhoda shivered as a sudden gust blew in through the open windows, and she set her jaw, uncertain of her future.

If anyone noticed Sylvia hurrying along Hickory Lane, they might have guessed she was on her way to meet a beau early that Saturday evening. As she walked, she spotted two yellow tulips gleaming against the dark tree trunk where she and Alma had planted them last fall during a Sisters Day event hosted by Mamma. All of Sylvia's girl cousins and her mother's sisters had come for the day, and one of the activities had been to plant tulip bulbs in a secret place, going two by two . . . a floral hide-and-seek of sorts. Mamma had joked that the best fertilizer was the planter's shadow, so Sylvia had made sure her shadow fell on the ground every other day or so after planting the bulbs, which also gave her a chance to make sure that no critters had dug them up for a snack.

Looking forward to seeing Titus, she wondered what he had planned tonight, since she rarely knew ahead of time. *Who will we double-date with?* she pondered as she watched for his father's gray enclosed carriage to appear.

Rhoda was content to wash and dry the supper dishes on her own, quite sure Sylvia had rushed off to meet Titus. She hoped that her daughter would be able to have fun on her date. *Considering the tension in this house,* Rhoda thought, going over to wipe off the green-and-white-checked oilcloth on the big table. She prayed silently that all would go well tonight with Titus . . . and continuing forward to the November wedding.

The minute she was finished in the kitchen, Rhoda took off walking through Curtis's field to Mamie's with a batch of cookies she'd baked, hoping Mamie didn't already have more food than she knew what to do with. Of course, with her granddaughter now spending the nights, Mamie might be glad for extra sweets.

Looking back at her own house, Rhoda wondered if Earnest would feel slighted that she hadn't said where she was going. He hadn't done so either the last few times he'd left for errands or whatnot, so she guessed it didn't really matter. *O Lord in heaven, be ever near us and our family during this wretched time,* she prayed as she hurried along.

She glanced toward Hickory Lane just then and noticed a gray carriage stop. A young man jumped down to greet a young woman, who was hoisted up in a flash . . . and they were off.

Must surely be Titus coming for Sylvia.

Seeing them together, Rhoda hoped with all of her heart that her daughter's relationship might be spared.

"It's *wunnerbaar* to be with ya again," Titus said as he winked at Sylvia before picking up the driving lines. She was impressed to see he wore the attire normally reserved for Sundays— black broadfall trousers and black vest, his long-sleeved white shirt crisp and pressed. "I've sure missed ya this week, Sylvie."

She smiled to hear it. "I missed ya, too. Your letter was a nice surprise."

The horse turned the corner, and they headed up a back road. As they approached Preacher Zook's former home, Sylvia spotted her mother walking briskly, a basket over her arm. "Looks like Mamma's goin' to see Mamie."

Titus glanced over with a nod. "No one's friendlier than Mamie, ain't?" he said. "And I've heard my Mamm say she can work rings around her daughters and granddaughters, even at her age."

"Seventy-six ain't so old," Sylvia countered. "Lots of folk round here live well into their nineties and older."

"True, but losin' a spouse can take the wind out of a person." Titus mentioned that he'd observed this happen to his own Dawdi Kauffman.

"*Jah*, people in love are bonded to each other," she said softly. *Or should be* . . . She sniffled a little and looked away.

He reached for her hand. "Say there . . . are ya all right, Sylvie?"

She wasn't feeling so good at the moment, but she didn't dare spoil the evening by acknowledging it. "I just don't want anything to come between us," she said, thinking of Dat and Mamma and whatever hardship they were going through. It was all so perplexing—and frustrating, too.

Titus jerked his head back. "*Puh!* How could that ever happen to us?"

"I don't know." *Sometimes people fall out of love.* . . .

Titus adamantly shook his head. "Nothin' short of death will separate us," he assured her, squeezing her hand. "I'll always love ya . . . be right by your side if you become sick or whatever as we grow old together. But that's a long, long time away."

That wasn't at all what she meant, but Titus's comments were ever so dear, and she loved him all the more for them.

Riding alongside him in his father's gray carriage, she felt as if they were alone in the world, just the two of them, her hand in his. *Is it true that we'll never part?* She tried not to think of the sadness that had so recently claimed Mamma's face.

They passed the pond on the far side of Zooks' property; the way the sun shone against it, the pond looked like a mirror, glossy and bright. She pointed it out to Titus, who nodded. "I can't wait till winter to take ya skatin' there," he said. "It'll be fun playin' crack the whip with the other *Youngie*."

"Just so I'm not at the tail end, like the time I went flyin' and landed against the bank."

"When was this?" Titus asked.

"Oh, before we were dating."

"Who were ya seein' then?" he asked with a grin.

"No one special."

He chuckled. "Glad to hear it."

Everyone before you is hazy, she thought fondly.

They talked about several couples who'd just begun pairing up after Singings—couples Titus seemed to know of—and she wondered if any of them might be tonight's mystery couple.

"Is it a secret who's doubling with us?" she finally asked. "Any hints?"

His hazel eyes twinkled. "Well, let's see . . . she's kin to you."

"Could it be Cousin Alma?" Sylvia hoped her guess was right.

Titus nodded. "You're a *gut* guesser."

"But who's *her* date?"

"Uh, that you'll *never* guess," Titus said, keeping a straight face now.

She wondered if word of Alma's crush had somehow found its way to Titus's ears. "Could it be Danny Lapp, maybe?"

Titus turned to look at her, eyes wide. "How in the world did ya know?"

"Well, she *is* my close cousin. But how'd *you* know Alma likes him?"

"Her big brother thought they'd make a *gut* match, so I talked to Danny, and he was all for it."

Alma must be beside herself with happiness, thought Sylvia. "I wonder what Alma thought when Danny invited her to double with us."

"Can't say." He grinned at her. "I wasn't there."

Now she was giggling. "*Ach,* I should've known you'd say that!"

Titus bobbed his head. "We'll have lots of fun tonight."

"You can say that again." Sylvia could hardly wait to see Cousin Alma with tall, golden-haired Danny.

After picking up first Danny Lapp and then Alma—Alma and her date settling into the carriage's second bench seat, behind Titus and Sylvia—Danny let it slip that they were headed to the Lapp Valley Farm in New Holland for some ice cream.

No wonder Titus said it'll be fun, Sylvia thought, delighted Cousin Alma was along. Sylvia could only imagine how excited Alma was, spending time with Danny, and by the perpetual smile on her face, Sylvia was certain her cousin would not forget this evening.

When they arrived at Lapp Valley Farm Dairy and Ice Cream, there were a few buggies at the hitching posts and mostly cars in the parking lot. Titus came around to offer to help Sylvia down, while Danny did the same for Alma.

Inside the dairy section, the familiar red benches lent a festive flair, and Titus led the way to the line-up of ice cream flavors. Both Titus and Sylvia ordered chocolate almond ice cream in a homemade waffle cone, still warm from the press.

Sylvia had to smile at that, and Cousin Alma whispered and laughed, "Yous are twins."

Sylvia was still smiling as they all headed for the wrap-around porch, where several very friendly cats were eating cat chow nearby. In the front yard, they could see a peacock spreading its feathers. "Lookee there," Alma said, glancing at Sylvia, dark eyebrows raised.

"Real perty, ain't?" Titus said with a smile at Sylvia.

Alma was quiet as she ate her butter brickle ice cream next to Sylvia while Titus and Danny sat across from them. From there, they could see the Jersey cows in the distance, and Alma commented how neat and tidy everything looked.

Danny mentioned that he had worked there in the summer to keep things redded up in the barn and the grounds. "Really great people to work for."

They enjoyed their ice cream, grinning when the cats came over to lick up any crumbs from the cones that fell to the porch floor.

Suddenly, the peacock let out a shrill shriek, and Alma jumped, startled.

"This must be your first time here," Sylvia said.

Alma admitted that it was.

"Well, now you'll know if ya come here again," Danny observed, eyes squinting nearly shut as he grinned. Throughout the evening, Sylvia had noticed Danny paying close attention to Alma, thoughtfully responding to her comments and purchasing her cone. *I think he likes her!*

After finishing their ice cream, they sat and talked, Danny sharing about a handful of true-life situations he'd read about in *The Budget*, and Titus hamming it up, too. "S'pose ya heard 'bout the Amish fella in Colon, Michigan, who calls himself an Uber driver," Danny was saying. "Five bucks for a horse-drawn buggy ride into town or wherever."

"I wonder how that guy gets by with it," Titus said, shaking his head and glancing at Sylvia.

"Their bishop must be more tolerant than ours," Danny said, then looked a bit chagrined for having said so.

Later, during a pause in conversation, Danny mentioned that he'd seen Sylvia's father and Ernie working with Preacher Zook's sons at his farm. "They've been sorting out some of the farm equipment," Danny said. "Made me wonder if there's gonna be an auction soon."

"There is," Sylvia replied, "but I'm not sure just when."

"Are ya goin' to bid on some items?" Titus asked Danny, and the two of them starting talking about that.

Sylvia exchanged smiles with Cousin Alma, asking how Jessie and her other siblings were doing.

"Well, 'tween you and me, Jessie's out with a fella tonight, too," Alma said quietly, tucking a strand of dark brown hair beneath her white head covering. "Her first date ever."

"Anyone I know?"

Alma nodded. "*Jah.*"

"Who?" Sylvia said it so loudly that both Titus and Danny turned simultaneously and glanced her way.

"Tell ya later," Alma mouthed to Sylvia.

"Okay." Sylvia nodded. "Just don't forget."

She glanced at Titus, who caught her eye and winked. *He planned the best evening,* she thought, blushing.

At the end of the evening, Titus dropped Alma off at her house before taking Danny home. Repeatedly Danny thanked

Titus. "Let's do this again sometime," he suggested, and Titus agreed.

On the drive back to Sylvia's, Titus slipped his arm around her. She couldn't help but smile in the dark as they rode snuggled up that way, Titus doing most of the talking. Being alone with her beloved again was just what she'd hoped for.

Yet as they rode, she began to feel downhearted at the thought of returning home. *Our once happy house . . .*

A mile or so before the turn to Hickory Lane was to come up, Titus said, "You seemed so content when Alma was with us."

Sylvia wondered what he meant.

"I mean, *really* happy . . . more so than now or when I picked you up tonight," Titus added. "Are ya sure somethin's not bothering you? You're awful quiet."

She groaned inwardly, wishing he hadn't brought this up. "Oh, I'll be fine," she replied.

"So there *is* somethin'." He looked at her, a concerned frown on his handsome face, and she felt trapped. No matter what she might say, she could get herself in a pickle. If she fibbed, she would be lying, and if she told the truth, she would be breaking her promise to Dat.

"Sylvie?" Titus touched her arm. "You can tell me anything."

She shrugged and wished that he would drop it.

"Is it somethin' I did . . . or said?"

"Oh, not at all," she replied quickly, not wanting to give him the wrong idea. "You've been so thoughtful tonight, Titus. But let's talk 'bout other things, all right?"

He nodded in agreement but fell silent the rest of the way. Truth be told, she didn't know what to say, and her thoughts flew back to her conversation on the porch with Dat, and how very different he and Mamma seemed.

And suddenly, Sylvia worried that she'd somehow let the cat out of the bag to Titus . . . even though she really hadn't revealed anything specific.

Even so, he knows something's wrong.

CHAPTER
Nineteen

*S*ylvia walked to Lois Peachey's for the canning bee the following Tuesday morning, still fretting about Mamma. Only a half mile away, the quick walk would do Sylvia good, and besides, she wanted to escape the house again. It alarmed her that she was thinking this way, though she had tried to get her mother to come along, too, as mournful and haggard as she looked. These days Mamma was hardly eating more than a few bites at dinner and even less at suppertime.

She's making herself sick.

The past few nights, Mamma had gone to bed very early while Dat had worked late—much later than Sylvia ever remembered. Ernie must have noticed, too, because he mentioned it when he helped her carry the trash out to the burn barrel yesterday afternoon. But Sylvia had shrugged it off and hoped her brother wouldn't bring it up again.

Truth be told, Mamma could look rather pleasant one minute, almost her usual cheerful self. Then when she thought no one was looking, her face would sag into a sad frown.

Sylvia breathed in the warm air, thinking ahead to school letting out for the summer tomorrow at noon. All the while, a great black cloud of birds was making a commotion in the large tree ahead. She wondered what it would be like to be a bird, flying high and free. No cares, except for finding food and shelter.

She dismissed that idle thought and realized that in two days, the May fourteenth Ascension Day picnic would take place at the schoolyard on Cattail Road. Volleyball nets would be set up, as well as all kinds of outdoor games, and plenty of food. *I can bake the chocolate cakes I promised Titus.*

As she contemplated doing her baking tomorrow evening, Sylvia saw a gray buggy not too far up the road, coming this way. Upon its approach, she could see Eva Kauffman with her youngest daughters, Lavina and Connie. The dark-haired girls waved, both smiling and wearing matching plum-colored dresses and aprons.

Slowing and then stopping the horse, Eva motioned for Sylvia to cross the road to them. "Where're ya headed, dear?" Eva asked, the driving lines held loosely against her black dress and apron.

"There's a canning bee at the deacon's house," Sylvia said as she crossed the road. "Aren't yous goin'?"

"Well, we were just heading to your Dat's shop," Eva answered. "Connie's havin' trouble with her bedroom wind-up clock. We thought maybe it could be repaired, instead of us buyin' a new one."

Connie nodded, her pretty brown hair parted perfectly straight down the middle. "Do ya think your Dat can make the alarm work again?"

"Oh, he can fix any kind of watch or clock, but he's been

backlogged since Preacher Zook's funeral. You might have to wait a week or so." Sylvia smiled.

"I'd wait a month," Connie said, her blue eyes bright.

Lavina gently poked her sister, as if to make her stop talking so much.

"Did ya bring your clock along?" Sylvia asked.

Connie leaned down to look in her burlap carryall, searching through it. Then, shaking her head, she looked disappointed. "I thought for sure I put it in," she said. "Sorry, Mamma."

"Another time, then," Eva said. "Guess we'll just head over to the General Store for a few sewing notions." She smiled at Sylvia. "Are ya sure you don't wanna come with us?"

It warmed Sylvia's heart to be included. "I would, but my cousins are expectin' me. Maybe another time?"

Eva glanced at her girls. "I think Lavina and Connie would really enjoy that."

"All right. I'll see to it." Sylvia waved as they headed down Hickory Lane, delighted by the prospect of having such thoughtful sisters-in-law not many months from now.

Sylvia glanced at Deacon Peachey's second-story balcony as she approached his lane, recalling that her father had once mentioned wanting to build something similar on their own home in the future. The deacon's farmhouse sat on seventy acres, including vast meadows and cropland. But what Sylvia liked best was the long screened-in porch that ran across the front and partway down one side of the house. She could just imagine sitting out there evenings, enjoying the breezes without the bugs.

Several carriages were already parked in the side yard close to the stable, and when Cousin Alma burst out the back door with the biggest smile, Sylvia knew something was up.

"Hullo!" Alma called. "You'll never guess what happened." Right there in the middle of the lane, Alma whispered in her ear.

"Well, that *is* somethin'," Sylvia answered quietly as Alma stepped back. "Danny's already asked ya out for next Sunday night?"

Alma's brown eyes squinted nearly shut. "*Jah*, just as I said." She walked with Sylvia toward the backyard. "You don't mind us doublin' up with ya again, after Singing?"

"How could I mind? You've been hopin' for this."

Alma grinned and lifted the hem of her skirt to head up the steps to the back door.

Following her inside, Sylvia smiled, thinking that this canning bee would be so enjoyable if she weren't carrying such worry in her heart for Mamma. Dat too. But at least Cousin Alma's happiness had lightened her spirits for the time being.

Later, during a short break when Lois Peachey served a large vegetable tray with multiple kinds of dips, Alma asked Sylvia, "Is your Mamma all right?"

Surprised, Sylvia replied, "Why should ya ask?"

"One of my brothers saw her out walkin' down the road with a teddy bear early one Sunday mornin'."

Sylvia shook her head. "Can't think why Mamma would do that. Must've been someone else—if your brother even saw right."

Cousin Alma shrugged and bobbed her head, seeming to accept that.

Sylvia forced a smile and went to get some fruit punch,

hoping that the subject of her mother wouldn't come up again.

That evening, during family prayers, Earnest sounded more expressive than he had lately. But except for the three meals they'd eaten together, he and Rhoda had not spoken two words to each other all day. He had been working over at Zooks' with Mahlon's sons to get ready for the farm auction, and Rhoda understood there was plenty to do. To be honest, she was glad Earnest was spending his time with Mahlon's family, even though it might be putting a crimp in his usually brisk clock business. Or maybe he *was* managing to stay on top of things—right now, she had no idea how late he worked, since he was sleeping over in his shop at night.

He could've moved to the spare bedroom downstairs, she thought, *but maybe he feared the children finding out.*

While finishing up some embroidery in her room, Rhoda saw Sylvia standing in the open door in her long white night-gown and matching summer duster. "May I come in?" her daughter asked, frowning and looking nervous.

"Sure, sit with me," Rhoda said, pointing to Earnest's easy chair.

Sylvia came and sat down, a solemn look on her face. "I just had to see ya . . . need to talk to ya, Mamma."

"Well, I'm here and so are you." Rhoda offered a smile. "What's on your mind?"

"I'm worried," she whispered with a glance at the door still standing ajar. "Do ya mind if I close the door?"

Surprised as she was by this, Rhoda nodded. "If it makes ya feel better."

Sylvia got right up. "Will Dat be comin' up soon?"

Rhoda wasn't going to say where Earnest had been sleeping. "He's workin' late to catch up some. He's been at Zooks' so much, preparin' for the big auction this Saturday."

"Oh, I wasn't sure just when it was."

"Just now I'm not sure I'll go," Rhoda admitted suddenly, surprising herself.

"Why . . . 'cause it's farm equipment and whatnot?"

"*Jah*, it's mostly that sort of thing."

"Then I guess there's no need for me to go, either." Sylvia gently touched her hand. "I'll stay home with you, all right?"

"That's awful kind," Rhoda said, her throat tightening.

"You're not gonna cry, are ya, Mamma?" Sylvia looked tenderly at her. "Sometimes when I see ya in the kitchen, I think you're on the verge of tears." Now Sylvia looked like *she* might be about to give in. "It hurts me to see ya like that."

"Don't worry, Sylvie. The Lord loves you and your brothers. And He loves your father, too. We'll get through this, one way or the other."

"Is this about what Dat told ya . . . 'bout what I found in the tinderbox?"

Rhoda nodded slowly, not wanting to divulge more. In order to protect their precious family, wasn't it as important to keep the dreadful truth from Sylvia as it was from everyone else?

They talked now about the various embroidery projects Rhoda wanted to do, and the plans she had for canning and whatnot this summer. "We'll keep real busy . . . and you and the boys can take turns runnin' the roadside stand again this year."

Sylvia nodded. "*Jah*, busy as bees." Then she rose and said, "*Gut Nacht*, Mamma . . . sweet dreams," and tiptoed out of the room.

Bless her heart, Rhoda thought, reaching for her embroidery again, aware of how very tired she felt.

CHAPTER

Twenty

*L*ate the next morning, Sylvia walked around Uncle Curtis's cornfield over to Mamie's, wanting to see Dat. Arbors of Preacher Mahlon's blooming pink rambling roses released a powerful fragrance worth drawing several deep breaths for, and Sylvia did just that as she passed by the deeply hued Old Garden roses. She had helped her father and Mahlon paint these very arbors the past few years, making sure they were nice and white.

As she'd hoped, she found her father, ready to head home for the noon meal.

"Surprised to see ya," Dat said.

"Want some company for the walk back?" Sylvia asked.

Dat was quick to agree, but she noticed his lips press together and wondered if he had an inkling what was coming.

Once they were heading out of Zooks' long lane, Sylvia said with as much confidence as she could gather, "Dat, what's wrong with Mamma? She's not eatin' much, and I've caught her crying."

Her father inhaled slowly, not meeting her gaze.

"What on earth did you tell her?" Sylvia pressed him. "This can't just be about one of your old girlfriends givin' you that pocket watch, can it?"

Dat looked down at his feet. "I loved another woman before your Mamma."

"I guessed as much, but why would Mamma grieve so over that?"

Shaking his head, her father groaned like he was ill. "I never wanted you to know." He grimaced and met her gaze. Several seconds played out before he sighed, as if releasing a terrible burden. "Sylvie . . . when I was a young college student, I married against my parents' wishes."

"*Married?*" The word stung her heart, and she had to look away.

Dat nodded. "The woman who gave me the pocket watch . . ."

"She's your *wife?*" Sylvia blurted out, terribly confused.

"She was, but Rosalind divorced me after a few months. And the worst thing is, I never told your mother about it . . . or the brethren. I was honestly afraid of losing the young woman and the community that I'd already come to care so much for. I realize that's not much of an excuse, but it's the truth." He coughed now and looked away again, as if ashamed.

"I wish I'd never asked," Sylvia said, unable to fully process this upsetting news and anxious to get home and be a comfort to her poor, dear Mamma. "Why didn't ya tell Mamma before you courted her? Why weren't ya fair to her?"

Dat was silent.

Sylvia sighed, pondering all this. Dat had seemed sincere just now, so open. And she told him so. "My whole life, I wished I could know you better, Dat. Really know you—about your family, who your friends were, what your modern life was like. And now I understand why you never told me."

He stared ahead, saying nothing.

"What'll the ministers do if they find out?" she asked suddenly, thinking Dat should come forward and make things right.

"That's just it: Your Mamma wants it to be kept quiet. And I agreed—you can surely understand why."

So, now Mamma and I are in the same boat, both keeping this secret, thought Sylvia, trying not to let her emotions overtake her. *No wonder she's lost her appetite and sits in her room alone at night. No wonder!*

When they arrived home, Sylvia hurried into the house, hoping for a private moment with her mother before Dat came inside. "I need to talk to ya, Mamma." She opened the utensil drawer to help set the table for all of them, since the younger boys would be home soon, out of school early for this last day. "Dat told me 'bout his first wife," Sylvia ventured.

Mamma's head jerked toward her. "He did?"

"*Jah,* so hard to believe. . . ." She wanted to embrace Mamma, let her know how much she cared.

"A shock, for sure, and I'm real sorry your father told ya," Mamma said quietly.

Sylvia opened the cupboard for the plates. "Am I s'posed to pretend like I don't know?"

Just then, Dat came in the back door and through the narrow hallway into the kitchen. He washed up at the sink and slowly went to sit at the head of the table. "Did I interrupt?" he asked, looking at Mamma.

"Sylvie was just sayin' that you told her about Rosalind," said Mamma, brushing her hands on her work apron.

Dat nodded, looking downright dejected. "I thought she should know."

"Well, this needs to be the end of it," Mamma announced.

Dat folded his hands on the table, glancing at Sylvia. "More harm could come to our family if we don't *schtill sei*," he said, an anxious look on his countenance.

Keep still, thought Sylvia, her shoulders knotting up. She placed the dishes on the table, her hands trembling.

Sylvia sat through dinner at noon with her family. With every speck of her, she was resolute about being strong for her mother, which just now meant sitting there and making herself eat the tender veal cutlet and mushrooms, creamy mashed potatoes and thick gravy, and perfectly seasoned string beans with ham bits, despite the fact that she had absolutely no appetite. But for her brothers' sake, she did not let on.

If Sylvia had allowed herself to give in to her pained aston-ishment and anger, she would have much preferred to run upstairs and cry. But this was Mamma's cross to bear, not hers. Even so, Sylvia would do whatever it took to bring solace to her mother. It was a promise she was making to herself even as she forked her string beans and ate them.

After the meal, Earnest stood out on the back porch, ques-tioning his decision to tell Sylvia anything, painful as it had obviously been for her. The delicious food Rhoda had gone to great lengths to make had held little appeal, and he had felt only sadness with every glance at Sylvia.

Presently, he leaned against the porch railing, watching Lily grazing in the meadow. Hearing a rumble of thunder, he saw the mare charge back toward the stable, galloping faster than he'd ever known her to do.

Earnest had work to do, but he'd lost interest. His first concern was for his family, as it must be. *I have to shake this off, keep myself going, for as long as Rhoda permits me to stay. . . .*

He heard the mail truck stop out front, so he made his way down the porch steps to the driveway. When he carried in the mail, Earnest went without thinking straight into the house, to the kitchen, and sat at the head of the table to read a letter postmarked Loveville, Maryland. He placed his old straw hat on his lap, curious who was writing him from the town where Papa Zimmerman had homesteaded so long ago.

Meanwhile, Rhoda was busy baking bread, as well as two pies. Considering her circumstances, she was still going forward with her household duties, not shirking from them despite her sorrow.

The kitchen was warm on this mid-May afternoon, and Earnest paused to wipe his brow with the back of his hand.

In the corner, he noticed Sylvia studying a recipe card. The two most important women in his life, working nearby, right there . . . it was almost too much for him. Yet to get up and leave the kitchen wouldn't be right, either. So, he sat there, aware of his own breathing, and opened the envelope.

He was surprised to see that the letter was from a master carpenter, an Old Order Mennonite man in need of help to repair a number of horse stables damaged by a recent storm.

When Earnest finished reading, he placed it on the table and leaned back in the chair, tentative, if not nervous, to bring this up to Rhoda. Considering her frame of mind, though, perhaps it was a good idea to give her some space. Besides, if he decided to accept the offer, they could use the extra money. On the other hand, he certainly did not want Rhoda to feel as if he was abandoning her.

"Sylvie, honey . . . I need to talk to your Mamma."

Rhoda glanced at Sylvia, who, without speaking, put down her recipe card, headed to the utility room, and closed the back door behind her.

Going to stand behind the wooden table bench, Rhoda asked, "What is it?"

He tapped the letter. "I've been contacted to help with structural repairs on some damaged horse stables in Loveville, Maryland . . . close to where my grandparents once lived."

"When would ya leave?" Rhoda asked immediately.

"This coming Tuesday morning. I'll hire a driver."

She brushed a hand across her forehead, then slowly nodded. "I think we could both benefit from some time apart." Studying him, she asked, "How long would ya be gone?"

"A little over two weeks," he replied, thinking he needed to find a way to call the Maryland carpenter, who must have gotten his name from the Hickory Hollow church membership roll.

Rhoda went to the oven to check on her pies. "What'll ya do 'bout the commissioned clocks you're workin' on?"

"Oh, I should be caught up on those orders if I work nights and early mornings before I leave," he said. "And the current inventory will suffice for market days and the showroom here during my time away."

Rhoda nodded. "Ya know how Sylvie likes to cover for you with clock sales."

"She's good at it," Earnest said, thinking that Rhoda seemed to be taking this news in stride. "You're not upset about my going, then?"

"I'll be all right." She opened the oven and removed the steaming pies, the aroma filling the kitchen as she set them on trivets on the countertop.

CHAPTER

Twenty-One

*V*ery early the next morning, Sylvia tiptoed down to the kitchen, thinking she should start on the cakes for the Ascension Day picnic. To her surprise, her father came through just then, hauling a large box and looking quite unkempt, and she wondered if he had stayed up all night working in his shop.

Dat set the box on the counter with a heave. "This is for your Mamma," he said quietly, then headed to the bathroom around the corner.

Curious, Sylvia went to read the writing on the box. *A new set of dishes!* She recalled that today was the anniversary of her parents' engagement—twenty years.

Her father had undoubtedly assumed no one would be up yet, not at this hour. But Sylvia had come down extra early, since her parents had talked last evening there in the kitchen, just when she'd planned to do her baking. Not wanting to disturb them, Sylvia had taken a long walk around the perimeter of their property, breaking into a run at points. When she returned, she'd felt too distraught to do any baking and almost wished she could skip going to the outing. And, seeing Dat looking so weary and disheveled now, she felt the same way—miserable.

"There won't be any cake for dessert if I don't keep my word," she murmured, still feeling sick over what Dat had told her yesterday. She hadn't slept well last night, either. And now here was this big gift from Dat to Mamma, a reminder of what had once been such a special day to both of them.

How will she react?

Leaving Eva Kauffman's cake recipe on the counter, Sylvia headed upstairs and slipped back into bed.

Rhoda awakened with the knowledge that this was not only Ascension Day, but the day that marked the twentieth anniversary of her engagement to Earnest, an occasion he had always insisted on celebrating. Last night, however, he'd said he would stay up late to catch up on orders before leaving for Maryland, so she did not anticipate any sort of celebration this year. *Just as well.*

Noticing Sylvia's bedroom door closed, she looked in on her daughter.

Sylvia raised her sleepy head. "I got up at dawn to dress, Mamma, but I felt so ill, I came back to bed." She explained that she wasn't going to bake the cakes she'd promised to take to the youth picnic.

"Oh, I'll bake them," Rhoda offered. "Glad to do that for ya."

"*Ach,* don't go to the trouble," Sylvia tried to insist before lying back down, all doubled up in her bed.

"You mustn't fret over the cakes."

"Will ya sit here with me?" Sylvia moved over to make space.

"You're takin' this awful hard, *jah?*" She touched Sylvia's forehead.

"I'm worried 'bout you." Sylvia pulled up the sheet.

Rhoda said, "You're fretting too much."

"Well, how can we ever trust Dat again?"

Rhoda had pondered this very thing but was surprised to hear her daughter voice it. "Honestly, 'tween you and me, I sometimes wonder now what else he might be hiding." It shook her that she'd admitted such a thing to her daughter. "But please don't repeat that."

"I never would." Sylvia closed her eyes. "All this makes me wonder . . . can anyone be fully trusted?" She paused. "Who *can* we count on?"

Rhoda sighed. "There's no doubting the Lord, Sylvie."

"Well, we can't see Him . . . can't touch Him."

"But we can *know* Him through the Good Book. *Ach*, my dear Sylvie . . . I doubt you'd be sayin' any of this if you weren't so upset." Rhoda leaned down to kiss her cheek. "Can ya rest awhile?"

Sylvia nodded. "I have one more question, Mamma."

Rhoda waited.

"Why do *you* think Dat didn't tell you 'bout his first wife?"

Rhoda had expected this. She rose to move to the window. Then, turning, she explained, "To your father's credit, he did offer to tell 'bout his old life before he asked to court me."

"He did?"

Rhoda nodded. "But I didn't care to know, and I told him that. I'd already begun to fall in love with him, too, and thought nothin' could change my mind."

"And now that you know, do ya wish you'd given a different answer?"

Rhoda went to her, sitting on the edge of the bed once more. "Oh, honey, I never would have had you or your brothers. . . . I can't go back and change the course of my life."

"*Nee*," Sylvia said, shaking her head. "I just wonder what would've happened if you'd known . . . if you'd have married Dat."

Rhoda realized that in order to do so, she would have had to leave Hickory Hollow and join Earnest in another church, away from the Amish life she so loved. With him being divorced, there would have been no other option. Her head spun at the thought.

"I've upset ya," Sylvia whispered.

"I love you, daughter. Never forget that," Rhoda said, patting her cheek, then leaving the room.

She walked downstairs, remembering just then how Earnest had said the same thing to her: "*I love you. Never forget. . . .*"

In the kitchen, she found him sitting on the wooden bench, already showered and dressed for work. He was eyeing a large box on the counter.

"What's this?" Rhoda asked, not knowing what to think.

"Open it." Earnest motioned toward the box. "I got it started with my pocketknife, to make it easy for you."

Surprised at the description on the side of the container, she wished he hadn't gone to any trouble. It just seemed so unnecessary.

Carefully, though, she removed the wrapping from the first plate and brought it over to the table and set it down, admiring the design. "A real perty pattern," she said, staring at it.

"The floral rim reminds me of you," he said simply. "And the bluebirds flitting here and there."

"Are ya sure we need—"

"It's long past time for a new set."

She couldn't argue with that. "I'll wash them, but what'll we do with the old ones?"

Earnest suggested discarding the cracked and chipped ones and saving the others to use for picnics or whatnot.

She ought to feel grateful, but it was just so strange to receive such an attractive gift—or any gift marking the years of their love—the way she felt. "*Denki*," she said. "You shouldn't've bothered."

After drinking a cup of black coffee, Earnest headed outdoors, and Rhoda got busy making scrambled eggs, toast, and sausage. Meanwhile, her gaze kept drifting to the box of dishes, which seemed to grow larger every time she looked at it.

After the family had eaten breakfast together, all but Sylvia, it took very little time for Rhoda to gather the ingredients for the chocolate cake, doubling the recipe to make two large sheet cakes, as Sylvia had planned.

Rhoda ignored the enormous box of new dishes, leaving it right where it was while she baked. Once the cakes had cooled enough for her to frost them, she called for Ernie to hitch Lily to the spring wagon.

It wasn't long before she and Ernie arrived at the schoolhouse grounds, where Titus Kauffman and his auburn-haired brother Jonah hurried over to help Rhoda with the cakes. "Sylvia wasn't feeling well," she announced. "She's real sorry to miss this outing."

Titus looked disappointed but thanked her for the cakes. "I hope she feels better soon."

"I'll tell her," Rhoda said.

Jonah went around to the driver's side to talk briefly with

Ernie, which Rhoda thought considerate. "You fellas have yourselves a nice picnic," she said, knowing it wouldn't be long before Ernie was one of this group, since he turned sixteen next February.

Titus thanked her and then, with a good-bye to Ernie, carefully carried one of the sheet cakes over to a long table where a few mothers were setting out a spread of food. Jonah carried the other cake, heading in the same direction as Titus.

It was ideal weather for a picnic, and Rhoda remembered the first time she had gone with Earnest to one such youth gathering, held years ago at Deacon Peachey's house. It was the day Earnest had decided it was all right to let the rest of the young folk know they were courting.

"Jonah just told me that some of the fellas are planning to help rebuild the horse barns in Maryland, too," Ernie mentioned, interrupting her thoughts.

"Is that right?" Rhoda replied, wondering if Earnest knew this. He had told the children last evening about the opportunity in Maryland, describing the vicious storm, which had been covered in many regional newspapers.

Thinking back on it now, Rhoda likened that storm to the invisible one that had ripped through her heart with Earnest's revelation. But unlike the Maryland storm, this one had done damage that might not ever be repaired.

CHAPTER
Twenty-Two

Sylvia heeded Preacher Kauffman's sermon three days later, thankful she felt well enough to be in attendance. And sitting there next to Mamma while Amos Kauffman preached from the fourteenth chapter of the Gospel of John, she recognized how much she was looking forward to marrying into this man's family.

Titus's father read now from the old German Bible, of which she understood little but listened intently anyway. His strawberry-blond hair and light brown beard were unlike any combination of hair Sylvia had ever seen. It was obvious where Titus had gotten his good looks, but she knew full well that being handsome had nothing to do with a person's heart.

"'Let not your heart be troubled, neither let it be afraid,'" Preacher Kauffman quoted. "Cling to the peace of God that passeth all understanding. And encourage one another in the faith," he said.

Like Ella Mae Zook does, Sylvia thought. *And like Titus does for me.*

Thinking of her beau, she was reminded of Mamma's thoughtfulness last Thursday in baking the cakes and taking them to the picnic. Sylvia could just imagine Titus's puzzled smile when he saw Mamma bringing them. And it felt as though it had been too long since they'd been together.

I'll see him tonight, Sylvia thought, hoping she wouldn't be troubled by the blues like on Ascension Day.

Sylvia smiled over at Ernie at the reins as he drove her to the Singing that evening. "Are ya lookin' forward to going, too, once ya turn sixteen?" she asked.

"Sometimes, *jah*. But pairing up . . . well, it seems kinda soon for me," he said.

"Maybe you'll change your mind in the next nine months."

He glanced at her. "You'll be hitched up for three months already by the time I have my birthday."

She nodded and smoothed her long apron. "Guess that means I won't be privy to whoever you're sweet on at youth gatherings."

"All the better!" Ernie laughed, slowing the horse a bit. "Say, why do ya think Dat's really goin' to Maryland when he's got so much work here?"

"You heard what he told all of us the other night."

Shrugging, Ernie nodded. "Just wondered what ya thought."

She had no idea what to say to that.

Ernie frowned. "All right, then, don't tell me."

"What's to tell?"

"Well, you work with Mamma all day . . . I don't. I've just noticed that she and Dat have been avoidin' each other lately."

She was relieved to see the farmhouse for the Singing come

into view. There was no way she would reveal anything about Dat's secret past to Ernie. "If ya believe in prayer, then maybe slip in one for them."

"Are you prayin' for them?" Ernie asked quite pointedly. She nodded.

"Okay, then, Miss Mysterious." He sighed and pulled up into the drive and came to a stop to let her out. "I s'pect you'll be ridin' home with your beau later."

"*Jah*," she said and watched Ernie back out of the driveway, feeling terrible, being so guarded about their parents. *Ernie's my closest brother, but what more could I say?*

Everyone cordially welcomed the small group of Amish youth from Smoketown to the Hickory Hollow Singing, including Titus and Danny, who went out of their way to invite the visiting fellows to sit with them on the young men's side of the long table. As far as Sylvia could tell, there were no apparent differences in their Plain attire, so she presumed the Smoketown *Ordnung* must be similar to Hickory Hollow's. *Just as well.* Surely one of the reasons to blend the two groups was for some of the young people to meet others from outside their district.

Sylvia sat with Alma and Jessie, singing gospel songs and hymns—livelier music than what was sung during Preaching services. Focusing on the lyrics, she let her fears slide away.

During the refreshment break midway through, quite a few people remarked about Sylvia's mother's chocolate cakes, adding that they'd missed Sylvia at the picnic. Embarrassed at being fussed over, Sylvia did her best to be polite.

As was his way, Titus sought her out at the tail end of

the refreshment time, mentioning he'd appreciated today's second gathering for baptismal instruction. He walked with her over near the open barn door. "It means we're that much closer . . ."

To our wedding day, she finished the thought. "The days will fly by once summer's here," she said. "Plenty to do to keep ourselves busy."

"I've been workin' hard for Dat, saving up for our rent and a deposit on a small house once we're married." Titus's face lit up at the telling. "We're talkin' about partnering at some point."

Maybe that's why his Mamm wants us to live there for the first weeks of our marriage, she thought. *Could that be?* She pondered this as the parent sponsors called for the last half of the Singing to begin.

After riding around Hickory Hollow for a while with Cousin Alma and Danny Lapp, Sylvia was delighted to be alone with Titus. He had been discreet about reaching for her hand earlier, but now that it was just the two of them, he slipped his arm around her, inching her closer as they rode along. "You seem happier tonight," he said, kissing her cheek.

She nodded, delighted by his affection.

Titus talked animatedly about their "*wunnerbaar-gut* future together," and when they came within a quarter mile or so of Sylvia's house, he slowed the horse to a walk and let the driving lines lie across his knee.

Turning to face her, he whispered in her ear, "*Ich liebe dich,* Sylvie. You know that, don't ya?" Then, looking deep into her eyes, he moved closer and kissed her.

The moment in his arms was so blissful, every care seemed to vanish.

Our first kiss! she thought, wishing he might kiss her again, but he nuzzled his nose against her cheek instead.

Then, picking up the driving lines, Titus signaled the horse to a trot.

"I've been thinkin' about us staying with your parents after we're married, before we move into our own place," she said.

"Are ya havin' second thoughts 'bout that?"

"Well, only that it's not what I'd expected."

He was quiet for a moment. "Still, this is what my Mamm expects. And what can it hurt? The main thing is that we'll be together."

She was puzzled by the dynamic between Titus and his Mamm. *Why doesn't he ask what I want?*

He changed the subject and talked about the kind of farmer he believed he would be, having been influenced heavily by his father's work ethic and wisdom all these years. But even as he rambled on about his future dream of running his Dat's big farm on his own someday, she stewed.

"I'm wonderin' what you'd say to this," she said, disrupting his topic of conversation.

"Sorry?"

"Will we always live according to what your family . . . well, your Mamm wants?" For some reason, just getting the question out winded her.

"I just think it will make her happy to have us there," Titus said slowly. "And I want to do the right thing by my parents."

But what if that means ignoring Amish tradition?

Much as she disliked the idea of departing from the norm,

she did not say more about it, but when it came time to step out of his courting buggy, the memory of his fervent kiss earlier had started to fade.

All during the next day, Sylvia recalled the strain between her and Titus last night. She felt it while she was cooking with Mamma and cleaning upstairs, and while picking strawberries with her brothers. Titus's desire to stick up for his Mamm's wants and expectations made her uneasy.

Late that evening, after Sylvia had gone to her room and was in her duster, she heard the tapping of pebbles on her window and looked out. Below, she saw Titus with a flashlight, motioning for her to come down and talk to him.

Raising the window, she poked her head out and said she would be down shortly, then closed it and pulled down the shade to dress. Fortunately, she had not taken her hair down, which made it possible for her to be presentable much more quickly.

What's he doing here? she wondered, rushing to pin her long apron over her dress.

When she met him out in the side yard, he asked if she'd take a walk with him. And, curious to know what was on his mind, she agreed, and they headed toward the meadow, out behind the barn.

"Since your Dat's goin' to Maryland, you know about the need for workers to help down there," Titus began.

"*Jah*, they're leavin' tomorrow morning," she said, curious why Titus was bringing this up.

"So, I got to thinking and decided to go, too. We could put the money to *gut* use, toward getting our own place."

He must be thinking that I'm not keen on staying at his parents'
home as newlyweds.

"That's fine," she told him. "And it'll give you the chance
to spend some time with your future father-in-law."

Titus laughed. "I'll enjoy that, for certain."

They walked a bit farther, Titus reaching for her hand. "I'll
miss ya, Sylvia," he said. Then, stopping, Titus kissed her, but
she only let him once.

"I'll miss ya, too," she said.

Twenty-Three

ollowing breakfast the next morning, while Earnest
was still sitting with his family at the table, he read
a short psalm, then bowed for silent prayer before leaving for
Maryland.

Young Tommy seemed to take his leaving the hardest, staring over at Earnest, then coming to sit on his knee. Rhoda
seemed unfazed, however, and who could blame her?

Oh, but it pained him to leave her when she was still sorting
through all this. Even so, he couldn't have known this chance
for extra work and money was coming—the timing of the
construction job seemed providential in more than one way.

When Earnest signaled the end of their silent prayer, he
said good-bye to each of the children, then to Rhoda, reaching
gently to hug her as they all stood. He was thankful she did
not stiffen in front of the family.

Sylvia inched back, as if worried he might approach her
with a personal good-bye or a verbal reminder to keep quiet.

Though this filled him with regret, he was mindful to spare her that.

Then, clearing his throat, he picked up his suitcase and headed out the back door as soon as the passenger van pulled up. "I'll be home before you know it!" Earnest called to them where they lined up on the porch.

Sylvia was standing next to her Mamma, her mouth turned down, as low in spirits as Earnest had ever seen her.

Just then, Tommy broke away and dashed down the steps, running to him and squeezing him around the waist. "I wish *I* could go, too," he said, looking up at Earnest.

"When you're older, son."

A smile spread across Tommy's face as he nodded, eyes brightening.

"I'll be in touch very soon, dear," Earnest said now, looking at Rhoda, who offered a restrained smile as she raised her hand in a delicate wave.

The next day, and the next, Sylvia juggled her chores with customers dropping by to look at her father's beautiful clocks. And fourteen-year-old Connie Kauffman came in a pony-drawn cart with her little wind-up clock, too. Sylvia assured her that she would have her father look at it as soon as he returned from Maryland.

"Titus went, too," she said with a little grin. "Did ya know?"

Sylvia merely smiled, not letting on that her big brother had been over here fairly late the night before he left.

"I know yous are engaged," she whispered, "so you can tell me."

"*Jah*, your brother told me" was all she said before showing Connie around the shop.

Connie seemed drawn to the large grandfather clock in the corner. "Oh, would that ever look nice in our front room!" she exclaimed. "I'll tell Mamm 'bout it."

"It'd be a *wunnerbaar-gut* present for Christmas, maybe," Sylvia said, thinking how surprised and pleased her father would be if she managed to sell it while he was away.

"Wish I had enough money saved up to buy it for her," Connie said, her smile showing her dimples.

"Well, even if ya don't now, someday you might—it's an expensive piece, ya know—and my father's always building new and different clocks. You could even custom order one years from now, or decide on something more affordable."

Connie looked at her. "You're so nice, Sylvie." She grinned. "Okay if I call ya that, too? Titus says it's your nickname."

"Of course." She had to smile at Connie's adorable manner. "Titus took stamps along with him, by the way."

"Did he, now?"

Connie nodded. "I wonder who he plans to write to." She let out a little giggle.

Thinking of Dat just then, Sylvia wondered if he'd taken along some stamps, as well. It made her feel sad again, thinking about her parents so far apart for the next two weeks.

Earnest, Titus, and four other men from Hickory Hollow attended the gathering that Sunday morning in the front room of the rented house where they were staying. Loveville, Maryland, was Old Order Mennonite territory, so there were no Amish districts to join in worship on this fine Lord's Day. However, Earnest had heard numerous horse-drawn carriages on the back roads that morning, a few even before sunrise.

The familiar sound reminded him of spending time with Papa and Grammy Zimmerman not far from there.

Three different men took turns standing before them to read passages from the Good Book. They also sang from memory the familiar *Ausbund* hymns—the songs of the seventeenth-century Anabaptist martyrs—and later knelt to pray.

The impromptu service was altogether unlike the ones that took place back home in Hickory Hollow, but it was an assembly to honor God, and Earnest didn't mind at all the shortened version. He had yet to do a thorough job of making things right with the Lord, but he had tried in his fumbling way.

The memory of seeing his wife's small hand waving so slightly to him as he left last Tuesday played repeatedly in his mind. But he struggled with any real sense of repentance. It seemed downright dishonest, considering that nothing had been resolved.

Later, following a hearty meal, Earnest took out his lined tablet and began to write to Rhoda in the privacy of his room. He hadn't written to her since they were courting, and close as they had always been, it felt strange to do so now. Even so, he wanted to keep in contact with her, in large part because he was concerned about her. So he wrote about the trip there and described the jovial farmer who was renting the large *Dawdi Haus* to all the Hickory Hollow men. The farmer, he'd come to realize, was his great-uncle Martin Zimmerman, a retired Mennonite preacher and the younger brother of Earnest's beloved grandfather. *What a small world, indeed!* And he wrote that the men's meals were being provided, too, at no extra charge.

Meanwhile, Titus Kauffman was off exploring the area with a few other young men, eager to get back to work tomorrow on the rebuilding. Earnest had been a bit leery about Titus coming, but what Titus didn't know about Earnest's past would never hurt him.

A few days passed, and Rhoda made a point of making a special dessert for Sylvia and the boys—a lusciously moist and sweet bread pudding—and she was already planning to bake a two-layer carrot cake with a thick buttercream frosting for next Saturday.

The early strawberries were ripening fast now, which meant Rhoda had no trouble keeping busy. There was more fruit than what was needed for making oodles of jam to store down cellar, so there was plenty to sell. Sylvia and Ernie took turns tending the roadside stand, and the sight of Sylvia out there reminded Rhoda of the first time she'd ever laid eyes on charming Earnest. *Such happy, happy days,* she thought.

A letter from Earnest arrived, and with him working such long hours in Maryland, she was surprised he was able to make time to write. The letter primarily seemed like a chronicle of his days, but what she found most interesting was the fact that the men were staying next door to Earnest's own kin. "What a surprise," she murmured, wondering if Earnest had ever kept in touch with *that* relative.

It surprised Earnest how quickly he and Great-uncle Martin Zimmerman had reconnected. Every other night or so, Earnest found himself drawn to go over and talk with the former minister who'd served the horse-and-buggy Mennonites in the area.

So far, Earnest had managed not to divulge to Martin the specifics of his past life before he became Amish, and it didn't seem that the man knew about his short-lived marriage, either. He'd explained his attraction to the Hickory Hollow community only in terms of wanting a simpler life—one like his Zimmerman grandparents had—so much so that he'd been willing to leave behind his so-called "fancy ways."

To this, Martin smiled and tugged on his tan suspenders. "After all this time, I just assumed you vanished into thin air," he said, sitting and rocking there in the front room, the windows all raised to let in the sultry evening breeze.

"It felt like that to me, too, for a while," Earnest admitted. "I have a daughter and four sons," he said, changing the subject. "Sylvia is the firstborn."

Martin asked how he liked being Amish.

"It hasn't been the easiest thing I ever set out to do."

"Well now, I wasn't askin' that," Martin said, glassy eyes scrutinizing him.

Earnest sighed. "Actually, I've had some very good years."

"And now?"

Not wanting to talk about his and Rhoda's current circumstances, he simply said, "I made some terrible mistakes, and they've caught up with me."

Martin nodded, rocking slower now. "We've all done that, to be sure, but thankfully there is a Savior . . . waiting to forgive." He ran his stubby fingers through his silky white beard.

Forgive? How do I forgive myself, Earnest thought, *when my family continues to suffer? And there's no end in sight?*

Martin stopped rocking. "I s'pect you're cautious about opening up to someone like me . . . Mennonite that I am."

Smiling, Earnest recalled how frank Papa Zimmerman's younger brother could be sometimes. "I've never been one to talk much about how I feel," he acknowledged.

"That must run in the family," Martin replied with a quick smile. "Though it must've skipped your Papa, 'cause he was one talkative fella."

Earnest remembered. "I miss him and Grammy all the time."

"Say, would ya like to go and see where they're buried while you're here? I'd be glad to hitch up and take ya over there. Just say when."

"Would you?" Earnest was truly touched. "*Denki*, Martin . . . Uncle Martin, I should say."

"*Ach*, I'm too old for such formalities. Just call me Martin, or Preacher. Whatever suits ya."

When Earnest said good-night and walked back to the *Dawdi Haus*, he realized how much better he felt. Spending time with Martin seemed like a godsend after losing touch with his family so long ago.

Sylvia was pleased to see not just a letter from Titus in the mailbox, but one from Dat for Mamma, and she ran up the driveway, waving both envelopes as she rushed into the house.

Mamma didn't look as excited as Sylvia felt when she went into the spare room down from the kitchen and sat on the bed to open her letter. She began to read:

Dear Sylvie,

How are you? I imagine you're busy picking early straw-berries and selling at a good price—the first pickings are always best!

Here, we're making good headway on the horse stable I've been working on with your Dat. Like you said, he's pretty quiet, but I like partnering with him in this project. I know

*I've said this before, but I can't tell you how honored I feel
that someday he'll be my father-in-law. Most people can't
make the leap from being fancy to Plain, at least not with
much success. He's a very good man, indeed.*

Sylvia stopped reading and groaned. *Titus can never know
the truth,* she thought, almost wishing she hadn't received this
letter. It stirred up all the turmoil she'd experienced before
Dat left.

She read on, more reluctantly now, and discovered that
Titus had welcomed the change of scenery but felt bad about
leaving his father with so much of the farm work. *While here,
I've thought about what you said—about our first weeks as newlyweds, Sylvia. I'm trying to work through that in my mind . . .
how to please my parents and you, my fiancée. I hope you can
understand, and maybe this time apart will give us both a chance
to contemplate all of this.*

Sylvia was glad he couldn't see her grimace as she finished
reading, then folded the letter and put it back in the envelope.
Wondering, then, if Mamma's response to Dat's letter was more
positive, Sylvia leaned back on the bed and prayed for God's
will to be done between her parents. *And for Titus and me,*
she added, more unsure than before. Could she trust Titus to
take her side, once they were wed?

Rhoda had taken her letter from Earnest outdoors, and
there she sat on one of the several rockers, reading the account
of her husband's frequent visits with his elderly relative, a
former Mennonite preacher, of all things.

Is Earnest seeking counsel from him? Connected as she was
to her husband, she felt as if her life was spinning out into

unfamiliar realms . . . out of control even further. She had no idea how to reel things back in. *Oh, to look through innocent eyes at the Earnest I once knew!* she thought. *I loved him so dearly then. Can I love him that way again?*

As the days passed and more letters came, Rhoda began to piece together that Earnest was, undeniably, receiving spiritual guidance from his great-uncle, though without exposing his past, or the pact he'd made with Rhoda to keep silent.

She was relieved that Earnest had someone to talk to, as much as he surely missed Mahlon Zook. But even though she thought it was good of him to write, Rhoda did not take time to pick up pen and paper and reply. *What would I say?*

CHAPTER
Twenty-Four

Wednesday morning, after the house was cleaned, Rhoda took herself off to visit Ella Mae. Since Earnest had been writing about talking with Preacher Martin Zimmerman, Rhoda, too, wished she could take some time to do the same here with the Wise Woman, before Earnest was to return this coming Friday.

Or is it too risky? she wondered. *Even with Ella Mae?* But no, if there was anyone she could trust, it was her dear friend.

While Rhoda took a seat across the small table adorned with its pretty yellow rose place mats, she sipped iced peppermint tea and let her guard down a bit. "To tell you the truth, I've been cryin' my eyes out lately."

"Sorry to hear it, Rhoda . . ." Ella Mae started, as if waiting to hear why, but when Rhoda didn't offer specifics, the Wise Woman didn't press. "Maybe ya just need to cry," Ella Mae said thoughtfully. "'Tis better than bottlin' up emotions . . . that can make a body sick."

Rhoda nodded. "I just don't know how we—I mean, I—can get through this."

"Well, whatever *this* is, the Lord sees ahead, dearie." Ella Mae took a breath. "Your situation is no surprise to Him— He'll walk right with ya and never let ya fall."

"I've *already* fallen." Rhoda said this convinced she was guilty of going against the *Ordnung* in urging Earnest to keep quiet about his past.

Ella Mae sipped her tea slowly, looking at it, then over at Rhoda. "Have ya fallen so far that the Lord can't reach down and pick you up?" She paused, then went on. "Will ya trust Him to carry you?"

Rhoda sighed. "I'm sorry, but you can't possibly know what I'm talking 'bout."

"*Nee*, but *He* knows."

Lifting her tumbler, Rhoda took a drink, the minty taste soothing her.

"I tell ya what . . . why not take a long walk and just talk to your Savior like He's walkin' alongside ya. I used to do this all the time, before I got up in years—walk and talk with Jesus, our elder *Bruder*."

Rhoda smiled. Even without knowing much at all about Rhoda's difficulties, Ella Mae sure knew how to get to the bottom of things. "I want my happy life back," she ventured, inching closer to telling Ella Mae something more significant.

"Remember, you are God's hands and feet to your husband," Ella Mae said quietly. "Forgiveness is one of the greatest forms of love."

This startled Rhoda. How far into her heart could Ella Mae see? "I don't understand," she sputtered. *How does she know this?*

Ella Mae set her tumbler down and wiped her thin lips with the paper napkin. "Usually a woman doesn't cry her eyes out, like ya said, if her marriage is on solid ground."

While Mamma went to visit Ella Mae, Sylvia took out a pen and stationery and sat at the kitchen table to write to Titus, thinking that, while it was too late to send it to Maryland, it could be waiting for him on his return. She tried several times to simply tell him how she'd passed her time but soon realized there was a certain tone in her words and phrases that she could not conceal.

I must be upset with him, she thought, crumpling up her third attempt and going to the wastebasket under the sink. "What's wrong with me . . . with *us*? Do I expect too much from Titus?"

She wandered upstairs to her bedroom and stood there, surveying the space. It would be plenty big for her and her husband-to-be, even had a nice-sized closet, which not all the bedrooms in this house had. Why did Eva think they shouldn't stay here, in her parents' home, like other Amish brides? Was she having trouble letting go of her eldest son?

Going to the window, Sylvia looked out at the family vegetable garden, thinking she should go and weed it again.

And as she did, she found herself praying for Mamma, believing the Wise Woman was the ideal person for her to visit.

Once Rhoda was home, she took Sylvia up on her offer to make dinner and hurried out for a walk, exactly as Ella Mae had suggested. She started to pray but felt embarrassed about speaking words into the air when always before she'd prayed silent rote prayers.

After a few excruciating moments of this, Rhoda sensed she was finally growing more comfortable telling the Lord everything troubling her. And somehow, He was there in the gentle breeze, listening to every word she whispered. He was also there in the fragrance and the cascading beauty of the blooming wisteria growing along the horse fence in the pasture where Earnest and little Sylvie had planted them years ago.

But most of all, His presence was firmly rooted in her heart. This spoke volumes to her pain, encouraging Rhoda to pour out her sadness, her anger, and her deep frustration. "Help me love Earnest the way You do, Lord," she prayed, thankful the dear Savior was a friend to the brokenhearted.

The walk was a long one, but when she finally reached home, Rhoda hoped she would not need to cry again tonight.

Thinking about his arrival home at the end of the week, Earnest headed over next door to talk with Martin. He'd gone with Martin last Sunday afternoon to visit his grandparents' graves, and the experience had affected him differently than he had anticipated. Standing by the small white matching headstones, he'd felt a sense of peace rather than sadness. Were they rejoicing in heaven, as Grandpa Zimmerman had often said he looked forward to doing one day?

Now seeing Martin at the back door, waving him inside, Earnest greeted him and thanked him again for going to the trouble to take him by horse and buggy to the old cemetery.

"Mighty glad to do it," Martin said as he poured some coffee for both of them. "Most younger men stay as far away from a graveyard as possible."

Earnest nodded slowly.

Martin cocked his head sideways. "Ya look like you're carryin' the weight of the world on your back." He put the two coffee mugs on the table.

Earnest picked up one of the mugs and went to sit down. "There's no way out, that I can see." He sighed. "After running away from my former English life, I'm afraid it's finally caught up with me."

"Well now, when ya run away, you never really escape, do ya? You only fail to deal with whatever made ya run in the first place. Ain't that right?"

Earnest knew that was true.

"Have ya considered confessin' your shortcomings to God?"

Earnest acknowledged that he'd tried.

"Listen, son." Martin headed for his rocking chair there in the kitchen, where he sat down with a great sigh. "God doesn't love you 'cause you live a good life. He doesn't even love you because you're generous with your time and money." Martin drew a deep breath, eyes softening. "God loves you, Earnest Miller, because He's your heavenly Father . . . and it's His nature to love."

Earnest had heard words like this before from Papa Zimmerman—so long ago, he'd forgotten.

They talked further, and Martin said he wondered if Earnest hadn't been hungry for God when he joined the Amish church. "More so than just for a new way of living." Martin studied him. "Have ya ever considered that?"

"I was raised to believe that a person needs faith, but it never really took."

Martin nodded. "But why do people need faith, do ya think? Do you understand what it means to have a heart made new by the Lord himself?"

Earnest listened, but there were other things on his mind. "I'm concerned that if I were to confess my wrongdoing to the deacon, it would turn my family's lives upside down."

"It seems as if things are *already* topsy-turvy," Martin suggested. "Besides, what's the worst that could happen if ya told the truth?"

Earnest thought on this. "I really don't know. But it could affect my daughter's chances to marry her fiancé," he confided. "He's an Amish preacher's son, a highly respected young man. I wonder if he and his family could look past it." He took a sip of coffee.

Martin Zimmerman was slow to respond, his brow deeply furrowed. "Well, is her young fella a man or a mouse?"

Earnest was captivated once again by Martin's frank approach.

"You wouldn't want your daughter with a man whose love is shallow or dependent upon things goin' smoothly, *jah?*"

"I doubt Sylvia would see it that way. . . . She's quite taken with him."

"That may be so, but you're not doing her any favors, Earnest, by postponing your confession only to protect her. You don't want this fella to someday *regret* marrying your daughter."

Earnest could see the wisdom in Preacher Martin's perspective, yet part of him still warred against that.

"Besides, is it Sylvia you're concerned about harming . . . or is it yourself?"

Earnest's conscience was pricked, to be sure. The old minister's words were worth pondering seriously.

Martin continued, now rocking in his chair. "Are ya familiar with this verse in the Psalms? 'I am come into deep waters, where the floods overflow me.'"

"I may have read it," Earnest said, wishing he had read the Good Book more often for himself . . . not just to his family.

"During difficulties, it can be hard to imagine that a deep flood will retreat, given time. Or that in a dark night, the way forward can be found by simply puttin' one foot in front of the other."

Preacher Martin offered to pray for Earnest, and bowing his head, Martin asked God to make him willing to be corrected with grace and to accept healing for his wounded spirit, as well as for the Holy Spirit to give him courage to do the right thing—come clean before the Lord and the Hickory Hollow brethren. "No matter how it impacts Sylvia and her fellow."

At Martin's amen, Earnest knew that it *had* been Providence that brought him to this out-of-state job, where he had become reacquainted with this old sage and brother of his grandfather Zimmerman.

"One last thing," Martin said, leaning forward. "I encourage ya to pray for Rhoda. The upheaval over whatever it is you've done has certainly spilled onto her. She is, after all, heart of your heart."

Earnest nodded, eager to include an apology to dear Rhoda in the letter he had already begun writing that evening. He would also do his best to pray for her. Talking man-to-man with Martin had given Earnest some solid direction, and he shook his hand firmly, thankful beyond words.

On the way out the door, Earnest noticed Titus Kauffman eyeing him from the walkway over near the woodshed. *He must wonder why I spend so much time conferring with a Mennonite minister,* thought Earnest, hurrying his steps.

It crossed his mind that consulting with someone outside Amish circles was frowned upon, but he dismissed the possibility of being reported to Deacon Peachey. There were more important things on Earnest's mind this night.

That evening, after the children were in bed, Rhoda sat upstairs in her room and offered thanks to God for breathing life into Ella Mae's words. She prayed for Earnest, too, having reread through each of his letters. It was curious, really, how much time her husband seemed to be spending with this Mennonite relative of his, and how comfortable he seemed in taking advice from him. True, the man was his great-uncle, but he was nonetheless an outsider, and that, along with everything else, made her feel nervous.

She wished she had written at least one letter to Earnest while he was away. Still, she hadn't known what to say . . . till now.

Last of all, she prayed that the Lord might plant the seed of a forgiving love in her spirit, the kind of love He extended daily to His children, wayward or obedient.

Dear Lord, soften my heart toward Earnest.

Twenty-Five

By Earnest's best estimate, he and the other men would arrive back in Hickory Hollow by eleven that Friday night. He had no reason to expect Rhoda to wait up for him, given the way things had stood when he left, and since she hadn't replied to his letters.

Riding in the passenger van with the other men, Earnest noticed how quiet Titus seemed to be, even withdrawn. Having Titus as his roommate for their time in Maryland had been a good experience, and Earnest had come away with the impression that Titus would be a good husband for Sylvia. Now, though, when he tried to engage Titus in conversation, the young man acted strangely distant, unlike the Titus he had come to know over the years.

He might just be worn out, Earnest thought, staring at the dark landscape, the twinkling lights of the small town vanishing as they rode toward Pennsylvania. His thoughts drifted to some of Uncle Martin's remarks during the numerous visits.

"*God knows everything about ya, Earnest . . . even how many hairs are in your beard. You don't have to figure out how to reveal yourself to the Maker of heaven and earth. He already knows what makes ya tick. . . .*"

During his final meeting with his great-uncle, Earnest had come to an important conclusion—his twenty-year-old secret was going to tear him and Rhoda apart. Maybe not tomorrow, maybe not next week, but eventually.

Even worse, the possibility of being nominated for Mahlon's vacancy hung over his head. *It's too dangerous to allow my name to be included in the lot for preacher!*

If ever in the future the People became aware of his deception—and if they knew that both Rhoda *and* Sylvia had harbored his dishonesty—the consequences would be much greater than if he came forward now.

But will Rhoda agree? he wondered.

Heavyhearted, he considered what might lie ahead for him. What sort of church discipline might he face? He'd heard of Katie Lapp's severe shunning. And what about dear Rhoda, and the probable loss of her good standing amongst the People? Would her family and friends stand by her? And poor Sylvia, as well, how would she suffer?

Shifting in his seat, he squinted at the cars racing past on the opposite side of the road, their bright headlights shining into the passenger van. Sighing wearily, he knew that no matter the kind of misery he and his family might have to undergo, he had to do the right thing.

If Rhoda agrees, all the better, he thought. *At least we'll be unified in that.*

205

Sitting in her room, Sylvia nervously realized that her father was returning sometime that night. She had grown so close to Mamma these weeks, feeling sorry for her as she was. Never before had she shared her heart like she had on the morning of Ascension Day—asking such direct questions. Yet Mamma had been the best listener, almost reminding Sylvia of the Wise Woman.

She reached for her Bible and read two psalms, hoping the words and the inspiration might calm her before going to bed. She'd wanted to stay up, just to hear the van pull into the driveway and Dat arriving home, knowing it meant Titus was home safely, too, but she had to be out at the roadside stand early tomorrow morning. It was her turn, and Ernie was going to market with Aunt Ruthann and one of her boys to help set up for the day. Sylvia had been invited to go, as well, but declined, wanting to be close to Mamma since Dat would be back. The peace of the house was at stake, and even though she was only one of the children, she needed to know that Mamma was all right.

It was much later than Earnest had predicted when he arrived at the farmhouse. A small lantern was lit on the kitchen table, and seeing it gave him a ray of hope. Was it there to welcome him home?

A note caught his eye, and he saw that Rhoda had suggested that he *not* sleep on the floor in his shop tonight. Surprised but pleased, he carried his suitcase of laundry down to the wringer washer, then returned to the kitchen and put out the lantern. His heart pounded as he headed up to his and

Rhoda's room. If she was still awake, he wanted to talk about his decision to confess.

The sky was beginning to grow light just as Earnest rolled over and looked at the clock on Rhoda's dresser at five-twenty the next morning. He dozed another minute or so and was suddenly aware of Rhoda's hand gently resting on his arm. Turning to face her, he smiled sleepily into her beautiful face. "I missed you," he whispered.

"When did ya get in?" she asked.

"Close to midnight."

"*Willkumm* home, Earnest," she said sleepily.

"My home is where *you* are, love." Oh, he wanted to kiss her, but he didn't dare. Not yet. Not till he knew she would accept his affection again. "I have a lot to share with you."

"I do, too," she said, pulling the lightweight blanket up over her arm.

He was curious but forged ahead. "As you know from my letters, I spent a lot of time talking to my Mennonite uncle."

Her eyes widened suddenly.

"And I have no right to ask this of you. . . ."

She smiled, which gave him the courage to simply lay it out. "I'm worried our secret keeping is going to tear us apart," he said.

Her face softened with tenderness. "And I believe the Lord wants us to confess, too," she said, explaining that she had been walking and praying every afternoon. She paused and looked at him. "I believe we're s'posed to make things right before the Lord and the brethren."

He sighed, deeply relieved.

"You don't know how much better that makes me feel," he said, struck that they'd both come to the same conclusion while apart.

"But what'll happen to Sylvie . . . to her and Titus?"

He remembered Martin's encouragement regarding this and shared some of their conversation. "If Titus Kauffman is anything like his father, he's a strong young man and will be true to his engagement."

"I've wondered if Titus could stand up to Amos, if he's told to back away from her." Tears came to Rhoda's eyes. "It hurts me to think how sad Sylvie would be if . . ."

"Let's not borrow trouble," he said, wiping her tear away with his thumb.

She blinked and looked at him for the longest time, as she often had before his secret was laid bare—back when she'd trusted him without reservation.

"I understand how hard this is," he whispered. "I've wronged you in many ways."

"You've apologized repeatedly," Rhoda reminded him. "Now it's time for us to find a way to move past all this pain . . . with God's help."

"*Jah*," he said, still holding back from taking her into his arms.

"Whatever happens, we must trust God to help us, Earnest."

Sunlight flooded the room, and a robin began singing at the top of its little lungs. In that moment, he couldn't imagine loving her more.

Rhoda smiled and breathed a sigh of relief, he felt sure. "Ernie's headed off to market to help Ruthann, so I'd best be gettin' up and cookin' some breakfast for him . . . and for you."

Earnest was reluctant to leave his close proximity to her but rolled out of bed nevertheless. "After breakfast, I'll hitch up, and we'll head over to the deacon's."

"No sense waiting," Rhoda said, not hesitating.

The secret's been eating away at her, too, Earnest thought as he pushed his feet into his old brown slippers.

Earnest wiped the beads of perspiration from his upper lip, aware of the trepidation yet also a sense of resolve as he lifted the driving lines in the carriage and signaled Lily to move ahead. Rhoda, sitting next to him, was the picture of calm and serenity. She believed God *wanted* them to confess, he recalled.

Stopping at the end of the driveway to see if the road was clear, Earnest was startled to see Deacon Luke's horse and carriage appear and make the sharp turn into the lane. The deacon halted his horse and waved to Earnest to back up.

What's going on? he wondered, doing as the deacon indicated and halting Lily in the side yard. Then, climbing out of the carriage, he got out to talk to Luke.

"Can ya spare the time to sit down with me, Earnest?" Luke said from the driver's side of his buggy. He sounded quite firm, and Earnest knew something was up.

"We can talk privately in my shop," he replied, returning to his waiting horse and carriage to let Rhoda know. Rhoda didn't ask why the deacon had come, though Earnest could tell by her expression that she was curious.

The men tied their horses to the hitching post, and the three of them walked across the yard to Earnest's shop, where he closed the door and invited Luke to hang his straw hat on a wooden peg. Earnest pulled up a chair for Rhoda, as well. Then, going to sit in his work chair, he looked fondly at his wife, knowing she was nervous.

"Why's he here?" she whispered.

"I don't know," Earnest said quietly.

Deacon Luke sat down, a frown on his ruddy face as he looked straight at Earnest. His thick gray hair matched his stick-straight beard. "I'm here on a church matter—a complaint from someone who worked alongside you in Maryland."

Surprised, Earnest recalled the good fellowship he'd had with the other men there, Titus Kauffman included.

Luke continued. "I understand you had a number of private sessions with a Mennonite minister?" he asked. "Quite frequent, too?"

Earnest knew there was no denying it. "*Jah*, my great-uncle Martin Zimmerman."

"So it's true, then."

"We were discussing—" Earnest stopped, and taking a deep breath, he caught Rhoda's eye. She looked terrified. "My talks with Uncle Martin helped me see the flaws in my thinking . . . brought me to the realization that I must confess my sin of deceit," he said. "He instructed me to seek forgiveness from the brethren," Earnest added, emphasizing this.

It was Luke's turn to look confused. "Forgiveness? For what? I'm talkin' about taking counsel from an outsider," he clarified. "And to be frank on this, Preacher Kauffman met me early this mornin' over at my farm to relay what his son Titus observed."

So it was Titus, Earnest thought sadly. "Well, you don't know the half of it," he said, ready to get the confession out in the open.

"Maybe you should inform me," Deacon Luke demanded.

"Rhoda and I were on our way over to your place . . . to talk to you," Earnest said, wringing his hands, thinking that his plan had been turned on its head. Even so, he began to tell of his first marriage as a young college student, and the subsequent divorce against his will. He told of having withheld this truth from even Rhoda and his closest friend, Preacher Mahlon, as well as from the People. "I've asked God to forgive me." Earnest looked at his dear wife. "And Rhoda, too." He turned to the deacon. "And now I humbly ask for *your* forgiveness."

Deacon Peachey's brown eyes seemed to grow darker by the second. "You were divorced when ya came to Hickory Hollow seekin' to be Amish?"

"*Jah.*"

Luke ran his thick fingers through his beard, frowning hard. "Then you had no business joining church." As he said it, Luke looked befuddled, having always been so fond of Earnest. "You surely knew that."

Rhoda's face was pale. And it killed Earnest to drag her through this again.

"I'm here to confess . . . to say that I'm sorry," Earnest said, his voice faltering. "And willing to do whatever is required to demonstrate my sincerity."

Still frowning, Luke nodded. "What reason do ya have for living this deception these many years?"

Earnest's eyes met Rhoda's momentarily. Then, focusing solely on the deacon, he said, "I wanted a new life after my first wife left me and married another man." He paused for a breath. "And although I had planned to tell the truth about my past, I became afraid of losing my new life with the People. . . .

It brought me such hope and healing in the aftermath of my disastrous marriage." Earnest sighed and shuffled his feet where he sat.

Deacon looked at Rhoda. "And, Rhoda, you knew of this?"

Rhoda's lower lip quivered as she stated how she'd recently learned the truth—and how wicked she'd felt keeping Earnest's secret these past weeks. "It was my idea to keep quiet about it and not come forward to the brethren," she admitted, her voice breaking. "Both Earnest and I have realized how wrong that was. I've offered my confession before the Lord."

The deacon took his time, folding his hands, his eyes blinking as he stared at the floor. Finally, he pursed his lips and gave Earnest a serious look. "I will meet with the bishop and fill him in on what you both have confessed."

Earnest nodded.

"But I can't say what will be done. You came to us an outsider, Earnest, and you certainly convinced us that you were genuinely interested in becoming one of us. We trusted you. . . ." Luke paused, wearing a serious frown. "You shared the confidence of the ministerial brethren, particularly Mahlon Zook, and now you're telling me that you lied from the beginning. Not only to the ministers, but to your wife and children."

"And I'm deeply sorry," Earnest whispered.

Turning to Rhoda, the deacon continued, "I am, however, closing the issue with you today, Rhoda, for your failure . . . but a lesser offense than your husband's." He offered her a reassuring smile. "I appreciate your penitent heart." Then, looking again at Earnest, his stern expression returned as he stated, "I can only say that Bishop John will be greatly disappointed that you deceived the People as you did . . . as well as for seeking frequent counsel outside the church while you were in Maryland." He went on to instruct Earnest not to attend the next week's Preaching service, when Bishop John would surely name him to the church membership as a transgressor.

CHAPTER
Twenty-Six

S ylvia had gone out to water Promise, the deacon's mare, as well as Lily, both horses still hitched to their carriages, a half hour after her parents and Deacon Peachey headed into her father's shop. Initially, she'd shivered at the sight of the three of them looking so somber as they walked together. *What caused the deacon to show up out of the blue?*

A large hawk flew over the backyard, and its hoarse screech alerted Sylvia as it landed on the roof, staring down at something in the thicket, probably a squirrel.

"Shoo!" she called. "*Nix nutz.*" *Good-for-nothing pest,* she thought.

Sylvia turned back to the horses, giving each a sugar cube and some gentle stroking, like she'd learned to do from Dat. She thought of unhitching Lily to lead her back to the stable but wasn't sure if her parents might still be planning to go somewhere once the deacon left. Anymore, there were too many questions spinning around in her head, questions that seemingly had no answers, nor any hope of one. Although it would be easy to fret, Sylvia refused to give in to worry.

Suddenly, there was a swoosh of wings, and Sylvia saw the hawk glide straight toward the ground, intent on a helpless squirrel. Turning her head, Sylvia did not want to see the outcome, even though she was a farm girl and around animals all the time. She had always wondered why there were such vicious critters just waiting to pounce on their prey.

Some moments later, Sylvia watched through the kitchen window as Dat and Deacon Peachey ambled across the backyard to the deacon's horse and carriage. Sylvia had been gathering up the trash but was now reluctant to open the door and walk over to the burn barrel behind the side of the barn. Should she wait till the deacon was gone? And where was Mamma now? Had she stayed in the shop?

Sylvia wanted to go over there in the worst way but realized she had better keep her nose out of this.

That evening, Sylvia was still wondering what on earth had transpired earlier between the deacon and her parents when she hurried outdoors for a walk, hoping to follow Mamma's example and use that time to pray.

She admired the lovely lavender bushes off to the right-hand side of the driveway. Dozens of bees buzzed around the blossoms, gathering nectar. She didn't want to risk being stung but was tempted to go over and sniff the fragrance. Moving a little closer, she breathed in the scent, grateful to God for such beauty as she headed toward the road.

She had walked about a half mile when she saw Titus riding

this way in his black open buggy, waving his straw hat and grinning.

"Want to ride with me, Sylvie?" he called, halting the horse.

His jovial expression and eagerness drew her across the road, and he met her with a welcoming embrace. "I missed seein' ya."

"How'd ya know I'd be out walkin'?"

"Oh, just took a chance," he said. "Otherwise, I was goin' to wait till dark and toss some pebbles up against your window, like before."

She smiled as she stepped into his courting carriage, surprised at how upbeat he was after the things she'd said before he left for Maryland. *Almost too cheerful . . .* Tonight, she wouldn't bring up any of that business about where they would stay as newlyweds. She simply wanted to enjoy being with him.

Titus held her hand until twilight fell, and then he slipped his arm around her and asked why she hadn't written back. "I hoped you would."

"I started a couple letters to you but wasn't sure what I wanted to write. And later, I didn't think a letter would get to you, not before you were home again." She still had wanted to send one to him . . . sometime.

Titus leaned over and kissed her cheek. "My time away seemed longer than I expected," he said. "I kept thinkin' about you, wanting to see you again." He glanced at her. "And, something else, Sylvie. I don't see why we can't compromise and spend the first three weeks after we're wed at your parents' house and the last three at mine. Or whatever you'd like. How would that be?"

She liked the sound of this. Yet Titus had seemed so adamant before—what changed his mind? *"Jah,* that might work," she said happily.

And all during the rest of the evening, he was so remarkably cheerful and attentive, it made her wonder if just missing her had been enough to change his perspective.

Late that Saturday night, Sylvia slipped over to see her father in the clock shop. There, she found him polishing the glass covering the large face of the grandfather clock that Connie Kauffman had been so enamored with.

"Dat?" she called softly. "Just hopin' you might tell me that everything's gonna be all right." She mentioned seeing the deacon come by unexpectedly that morning. "I hoped maybe you or Mamma might've said something before now."

Moving toward her, Dat offered a small smile. "Things will be in time, I hope." He set down the cloth on the worktable. "I meant to talk to you, and I'm glad you asked, Sylvie, since it's only right that you hear it from me."

"Hear what?" She held her breath as Dat explained the decision that he and her mother had made.

"I'll soon be under church discipline. It means I won't be permitted to attend Preaching next Sunday." His voice was low. "I don't know if I'll be put off church permanently or temporarily . . . but your Mamma and I know it was right for us to confess to the deacon."

"Mamma confessed, too?"

He nodded. "For joining in my deceit, keeping my former marriage confidential since I told her about it."

Sylvia frowned. "But what about me?"

"*Nee*, no confession is necessary from you, since you're not baptized yet."

She looked at him, her dear Dat. With all that was on him,

he was not downhearted, as she might have expected. "You said you might be excommunicated? Mamma too?"

"My discipline is in Bishop John's hands now, but *nee*, your Mamma is not in danger of that."

Sylvia was relieved for her mother but had to ask, "What's the worst that can happen to ya, Dat?"

"I could be shunned for life," he said.

Sylvia trembled at his words. "Oh, Dat." She dreaded what this might mean for him—for all of them, really. "When will ya know?"

"The bishop might visit me before next Sunday, or I might be told after church." Dat reached to touch her shoulder. "But I don't want you to worry, Sylvie. This is in the brethren's hands. I sinned and must pay the penalty."

"Do my brothers have any idea?" she managed to say.

"I'll talk to them soon, so they understand why I won't be at church."

She felt an urge to hug him, but that was frowned on at her age. "I love ya, Dat, and always will. I want you to know. . . ." She swallowed hard. She didn't want to think of their family being split apart, but surely that would happen if he was permanently excommunicated.

On the Sunday Earnest was not allowed to attend Preaching, Rhoda got into the family carriage and picked up the driving lines. Except for the occasional illness and Earnest's time in Maryland, she could not remember having gone without him since their wedding. It felt ever so strange.

Sylvia sat next to her in the front seat, dressed in her pretty blue dress and white organdy apron, with Tommy, wearing one of his new white Sunday shirts and his black trousers and black coat, perched next to Sylvia. The rest of the boys were in the second bench seat, all of them mighty still.

Earnest had talked with them yesterday at breakfast, explaining that he would be staying home from church at the deacon's request because of something wrong that he did a long time ago.

"*You're bein' punished?*" Tommy had asked, eyes big, eyebrows raised.

Earnest had been visibly shaken but told Tommy that he planned to tell them everything they needed to know, once they were home from Preaching. Rhoda had agreed that it was better that way.

Tommy hadn't asked another question, though he had scrunched up his face as if more was on his mind. Ernie and Calvin had grimaced, but neither spoke. Adam, on the other hand, sat stiff and straight-faced as he picked at his scrambled eggs.

It was Rhoda whose heart was breaking . . . for her dear children, who would soon know the startling truth about their father's past. She and Earnest had privately discussed how to best handle this, not wanting the children to hear it from the grapevine, which had a way of spilling the beans, even about something as hush-hush as a bishop's pronouncement at a members-only meeting. That being the case, they planned for her to bring the children right home after the fellowship meal so Earnest could sit down with them and summarize his past, explaining the need for church discipline.

Almost as soon as his family departed for Preaching, Earnest heard another carriage coming up the driveway. "A visitor on a Preaching Sunday?" he murmured, glad he'd dressed appropriately—nice enough to attend church, though of course he had been told to stay home.

Rising from his chair in the front room, Earnest wandered to the back of the house and looked through the screen door. When he saw Bishop John stepping out of his enclosed gray carriage, Earnest's breath caught deep in his throat. Adrenaline raced through his veins. "Hullo, John," he called, stepping barefoot out on the porch.

John's demeanor was staid as he walked toward the house and up the back steps. "Wanted to talk to you before ya hear it from Rhoda."

Earnest clenched his teeth. "Have a seat," he offered, motioning toward the rocking chair nearest John.

"*Nee* . . . won't stay long." John was the picture of a well-dressed Amish minister in his white shirt, black trousers, vest, and frock coat—longer than an ordinary coat and with a split up the back. "Your family's off to church, *jah?*" John asked.

Nodding, Earnest suspected why he'd come. "I'll be talking with my children when they return home," he volunteered.

"I see." John seemed to gather himself, glancing at the porch floor, then at Earnest. "After prayer and discussion with Preacher Kauffman and Deacon Peachey, I've decided on a six-week *Bann.* During that time, you will not eat at the same table as any church member, nor can you take money or any other object directly from another church member's hand. When you attend worship in two weeks, you'll need to sit with your head bowed and cover your face during the entire first sermon, and you won't be able to share a hymnal with any church member. You'll also meet with the ministers at the beginning of church, and every day or so one of us will drop by to encourage you during this time of chastisement, supportin' you in the hope that you see it through to the final Sunday of the sixth week . . . and the day of your public kneelin' confession."

In all the years Earnest had known him, Bishop John had never sounded so solemn.

Earnest inhaled slowly, sending air deep into his lungs. He felt terribly embarrassed, his pride wounded. This short-term exile was a serious matter with strict guidelines, but all the same, he wanted to thank John for not casting him aside for life. He would have to do exactly as he was told if he wanted to return to being a member in good standing.

"It's my desire to extend peace and fellowship to you in the name of the Lord at the end of this *Bann*," Bishop John said. "But it is a grave offense to deceive God . . . and the church. A grave offense, indeed."

Earnest understood and watched him walk back out to his horse and carriage, relieved that his preacher friend Mahlon didn't have to share in the difficult ordeal just ahead. *How I would have disappointed him, too. . . .*

CHAPTER
Twenty-Seven

*S*ylvia could sense the tension coming from her mother during the second sermon. Mamma's hands were clasped so tightly in her lap. She couldn't help wondering how strict the discipline would be, the memory of Dat's words ringing in her memory—he could be shunned for life.

As soon as the benediction was read and the closing hymn sung, the unbaptized would be ushered out so the membership meeting could begin. Sylvia was not qualified to attend the meeting, of course, but she also did not want to stand outside with any of her other cousins, worried what she might be asked.

Just now, thinking about that, Sylvia wished Ernie had been the one at the reins when they'd pulled into the lane this morning before worship. *Maybe then Dat's absence wouldn't have been so noticeable,* she thought woefully, wishing she could simply go and sit under one of the big willow trees behind the barn. *To pray . . .*

The day's mugginess was getting to Rhoda. She could not bear to look at the bishop when he rose to speak after the youth and children exited the house. She heard John Beiler's wisely chosen thoughts as he began, the words penetrating her heart when Earnest's full name was stated for the congregation to hear, and his sin of deception called out.

"Our brother, Earnest Miller, was married to an outsider before he came lookin' for peace here in Hickory Hollow, more than twenty years ago."

A muffled gasp rippled through the congregation. Torturous as this was, Rhoda bowed her head, wishing she had stayed home with her husband.

"Earnest's first wife divorced him and married another man. Yet Earnest remained silent, never once revealing this as a seeker who desired to follow the Lord in holy baptism to join this church." The bishop paused to mop his brow with a white handkerchief. "Earnest's deceit over the years hardened his heart, and the father of lies had a strong foothold."

Rhoda glanced up just then to see the bishop's gaze fixed on the back wall, not making eye contact with anyone. Grateful for her sister Ruthann's hand on hers, she prayed silently for her own sake, lest she start to weep.

The bishop lowered his voice as he continued. "We will encourage our brother Earnest to put on a humble attitude before the Lord God and the church when he returns to Preaching service two weeks from today. In the meantime, I urge you to stop by his house to encourage him to remain strong in the faith and continue to abide by the Old Ways during the next six weeks of this temporary *Bann*. And please, all of you, remember Earnest in your daily prayers."

Rhoda wondered what the womenfolk around her were

thinking. *Earnest pulled the wool over poor Rhoda's eyes. . . .* She tried her best to shut out the terrible thoughts. *I mustn't let my imagination take over.*

When the bishop brought the meeting to a close and the older women filed out on the side where the womenfolk and young children usually sat, Rhoda's eyes caught Ella Mae Zook's. The kindly woman gave her the dearest look. *Now she understands why I've been struggling so,* thought Rhoda, remembering how helpful to her the last visit had been.

Rhoda did not trust herself to look Eva Kauffman's way as the preacher's wife walked out, and in that moment, Earnest's secret crashed against her heart. *What will Titus be told?* While as an unbaptized youth he was not present, people sometimes talked, and Rhoda was concerned about that for her children's sake. *Sylvia's especially.*

She rose and waited for the women in front of her to form a line and head out of the front room, then through the large sitting area and the kitchen. Rhoda squinted into the sunlight as she exited the farmhouse, wishing she could skip the common meal and go home straightaway with her children.

Sylvia walked past the school-aged youngsters, their round faces and long-lashed eyes observing her more closely than she'd like. Or was she just imagining things? *Nee,* she thought, *they don't know what's being discussed inside . . . or who's being named a sinner.*

Her own brothers were over near the stable, and when it looked possible to avoid her teenage girl cousins, Sylvia made a beeline toward the barn and around to the back, where she leaned against the rough wooden siding, crying silently. It was best to get it all out before the shared meal, and she did, the tears coursing down her cheeks. Alas, she did not have a hankie along, since she'd left her purse with Mamma in the house.

She could not erase the image of her father's face that morning, white as the Sunday shirt he wore. She had watched him closely, the man who had always treated her with kindness, love, and respect, even though some Amishmen were disappointed in having a female firstborn. Sylvia had never known Dat to treat her that way, though, always going out of his way to include her. *Sometimes even more so than Ernie when we were younger,* she realized just then, which made her fight back even more tears. Oh, she loved her father so!

She remembered all the hours learning how to properly groom the horses, Dat guiding her little hands to hold the curry brush, as well as the times she'd watched him build the exquisite clocks his customers had bought through the years. Her father allowed her to open the door and welcome them in when he was bowed over his work desk, putting on the final touches. *He's always trusted me,* she thought, *and hasn't minded having me underfoot.*

There had been plenty of days, too, when he'd asked her along to town, or to hop in the spring wagon to pick up flour at the nearby mill, or to visit an ailing relative, if Mamma was busy.

Will I ever recover the good relationship Dat and I had before I looked in the tinderbox?

When she was certain the meeting was over, Sylvia rounded the other side of the barn, heading toward the backyard, where

Connie Kauffman bumped into her. "*Ach*, sorry," Sylvia said, reaching out for Connie's arm. "Are ya all right?"

"*Jah*," Connie said, staring at her face. "But . . . are *you?*"

"I'm fine, really." Sylvia nodded as if to convince herself. "Say, your clock is all fixed . . . I could walk over and bring it to you this evening."

Connie's eyes lit up. "That's *wunnerbaar-gut*, but ya don't have to." She frowned, her head slanted now as she studied Sylvia. "Ain't ya goin' to Singing?"

"Prob'ly not." Though she'd been the one to bring up her plans, Sylvia disliked being cornered by Titus's little sister. Walking now, she had to change the subject. "I'll see ya after supper," she said, keeping her eye out for Mamma, wanting to go over and stand with *her*, even though it was not customary. Typically, the married women either helped in the kitchen to serve the food or clustered on the porch or in the yard. The teenage girls usually stood together in circles of conversation here and there, though today Sylvia made sure she didn't look their way too long, not wanting one of her many cousins to view that as an invitation to come over and talk. Of course, the cousins who were already baptized had no business revealing what the bishop had pronounced at the meeting. It was understood that anyone who talked about what was said in the members-only meetings was also at risk for church discipline. Once the People dispersed to head home, though, gossip sometimes began, and the thought made Sylvia nearly ill.

Rhoda was touched when Hannah, at church for the first time since her recent miscarriage, came to talk with her on the side porch. "If there's anything I can do," she started by saying, but Rhoda waved it off. "Come now. You've always been there for me, *Schweschder.*" Hannah reached for Rhoda's hand. "I mean it."

Rhoda motioned for them to walk toward the front of the house. "How are *you,* Hannah? I'm glad to see ya out of the house again."

"Well, you know how a person feels after talkin' with Ella Mae, *jah?*"

Nodding, Rhoda truly did.

"I was reluctant to believe it, but I'm starting to feel somewhat better." Hannah gave her a small smile. "I've been finding ways to keep myself busy, making food for a few new mothers."

"What a *gut* idea," Rhoda said, glad that Hannah seemed to be finding a more constructive path for living with her grief.

"By the way, our sisters all know 'bout my loss now, but I didn't feel the need to tell any of the other womenfolk." Hannah smiled tentatively.

Rhoda reached to give her a brief embrace. "I'm ever so thankful you're feeling more yourself again."

"I'll be keepin' *you* in my prayers now," Hannah said, appearing as if she was ready to head back inside.

"Well, please pray mostly for Earnest," Rhoda urged.

Shaking her head, Hannah looked at her with compassion. "I don't know how you're managing."

"*Ach,* there'll be plenty of counsel ahead for us." Rhoda certainly hoped that was the case. She'd known of other couples who, when one of the spouses was under a temporary *Bann,* received frequent visits from the ministers. "But we do need a lot of prayer. . . ."

Hannah squeezed Rhoda's elbow. "You drop by anytime, ya hear? Our door's always open."

"Same for you, *Schweschder.*"

At the shared meal, Mamie Zook sat next to Rhoda, not saying much, but her presence was a comfort. Just knowing that Mamie was still grieving the loss of her husband brought a sweetness to their fellowship as they ate together. Ruthann and Hannah also sat nearby, as well as Rhoda's mother. Their talk was of gardening, filling birdfeeders, and attending canning bees. No one mentioned a single word about Earnest.

Later, while waiting for their road horse to be hitched up, Rhoda noticed Mamie coming in her direction, like she wanted to talk further. Rhoda stepped away from her children to greet her again.

Mamie leaned near. "I'll keep you in my prayers."

"I should be the one encouraging *you*," Rhoda replied, clasping the dear woman's hand.

"Oh, but you have . . . and you *are* by bein' such a thoughtful neighbor," Mamie said. "You've always been. You and Earnest both . . ."

Hearing Earnest spoken of so kindly put a lump in Rhoda's throat, and when she could see that their carriage was ready, she smiled at Mamie. "*Da Herr sei mit du,*" she said, making her way back to her waiting children.

"The Lord bless you, too," Mamie called. "All of yous."

Once they were settled in the buggy, Sylvia whispered, "Mamie's the dearest woman, ain't so?"

Rhoda nodded as she picked up the driving lines. "Are we ready to go?"

"I am," Tommy said, squeezed in beside Sylvia. "And I can't wait to see Dat!"

"He'll surely be looking for you, too . . . might even be sitting on the front porch watchin' for us," Rhoda said, trying to sound cheerful. But she had to wonder how Earnest would manage to tell their children about his first marriage.

CHAPTER
Twenty-Eight

*D*uring the ride home, Sylvia hoped she hadn't seemed short with Cousin Alma during their brief encounter before the light noon meal. She really hadn't been disinterested in Alma's chatter about doubling up again with their boyfriends after Singing tonight. But Sylvia hadn't had the nerve to tell Alma she felt like staying home that evening . . . not wanting to open the door to questions about Dat.

I should've said I wasn't going. Sylvia shifted in her seat.

"You all right?" Mamma glanced at her, concern written on her face.

"Just wishin' this day was over," she whispered.

"Well, let's not wish our life away, *jah?*"

Nodding, Sylvia realized how selfish she must seem to Mamma, who had to be the one suffering most. "Sorry, Mamma . . . really, I am."

She could not imagine sitting in Titus's father's carriage tonight, listening to the jokes between Danny and Titus and making small talk with Cousin Alma, too. All of that was perfectly enjoyable on a normal night, but the thought of it now felt overwhelming.

Sighing, Sylvia's thoughts retreated to a bitterly cold February evening when Titus had taken her out for a ride in his father's sleigh. Over the back roads, then through the fields, they had flown . . . almost literally. Both of them had bundled up in multiple layers of clothing and black earmuffs, Titus in his father's heaviest wool coat and black leather gloves. She had marveled at the white-blue ring of haze around the full moon . . . the way her breath hung in the air like frost before her eyes. Even though they were having such a wondrous adventure, she'd tried not to laugh too hard, because every time she took a breath, a sharpness pricked her lungs. *"We should've wrapped our faces with woolen scarves,"* Titus had said, and Sylvia agreed while enjoying the speed of the ride.

On that night, she'd felt so nervous and naïve and unsure of herself, Titus being the eldest son of well-known Preacher Kauffman. Later, however, when she thought back on their first handful of dates, Sylvia was thankful Titus had been so pleasant around her, without any pride. They could talk for hours and then discover that it wasn't just fifteen minutes, as it seemed. *"There's a name for that,"* Titus had once pointed out. *"Prob'ly somethin' the English made up."* He'd chuckled.

"Ah . . . *soul mates?"* she said hesitantly.

"Jah, that's it."

At the time, she had merely smiled, thinking it was too early in their dating relationship to decide such a wonderful thing.

Back at the house, Sylvia was glad when Dat came out to help Ernie and Adam unhitch Lily, greeting all of them as he rushed across the yard. Just seeing him come so swiftly did her heart good.

Sylvia followed Mamma into the house, glancing over her shoulder at her father. Calvin and Tommy were close behind, not talking one bit, unusual to be sure.

How can Mamma be so calm? Sylvia thought as they headed to the front room for the family meeting. She wondered how long before Titus spoke to her about Dat's discipline. *If he hears about it, he surely will.*

Prior to the family meeting, Earnest stared at the streaming light in the front room, wondering if he ought to begin with prayer. Considering his children's reactions were pending, it seemed like a necessity. Rhoda had already spent time praying for each of them and their responses to what they were about to hear. Inspired by that, Earnest began by asking them to bow their heads.

When his prayer was done, he cleared his throat and raised his head, and his children unfolded their hands, their eyes on him. "What I'm going to tell you will surprise you," he said in *Deitsch,* bracing himself. "You might not want to believe it." Pausing, he added, "What I did a long time ago was wrong, and I'm sorry that knowing it will hurt you. If I could spare you, I would. But my silence all these years is one of the reasons I'm being disciplined by the ministerial brethren."

The children sat in close attention, the younger two boys looking completely puzzled. Earnest despised to think how this revelation could affect all of them.

But still he continued. "When I was a teen, I dated a girl named Rosalind."

Sylvia's eyes met his from where she sat in a chair close to

Rhoda, arms folded as though to shield herself. To the right of Earnest, Ernie and Adam fidgeted with their suspenders, clearly anxious, while Calvin and Tommy sat cross-legged on the floor not far from Earnest's feet, eyes wide.

Generalizing the rest of it, Earnest spoke slowly, looking at each one as he explained. "After a short while, I married Rosalind, a marriage that neither of us was prepared for. *Glotzkopp*, that's what I was, ignoring my father's wise advice."

Frowning, Tommy covered his gaping mouth. Ernie and Adam, meanwhile, stared down at their bare feet, as if mortified. As for Calvin, his face turned a deep shade of red.

"This is an awful shock, and I'm sorry. With every ounce of my being, I am." Earnest coughed, trying to regain his composure.

When he was able to speak again, he said, "The marriage didn't last long." He did not put the blame on Rosalind, nor say that she'd left him for another man. "And then I came here."

Earnest went on to reveal that he had kept all of this from the Hickory Hollow ministers, and from their mother, too, from the time they began dating. "I was wicked not to be honest about my past," he said. "Instead, I tried to hide it from everyone, and it's eaten away at me all these years."

Tears welled up in Tommy's eyes, and the older boys looked baffled. Adam's knuckles were white as he tightened his fists against his knees.

"The ministers will counsel me during the next six weeks while I'm under the *Bann*," Earnest told them. He paused and then asked the children to remember him in their prayers. He looked at Rhoda. "With the ministers' help . . . and God's, your Mamma and I are workin' through this together." Earnest returned his focus to the children. "I'm asking each of you to forgive me for deceiving your Mamma . . . all of you, really."

Sobbing, Tommy jumped up and ran into Earnest's arms. "You're still my Dat, ain't ya?" he asked, and Earnest reassured his son.

As Sylvia sniffled where she sat, Ernie and Calvin looked at each other, apparently still trying to grasp this news. But Adam rose and left the room without saying a word.

"If you have questions, just ask me," Earnest said, setting Tommy, who was rubbing his eyes, on his lap.

Ernie ran his hands through his hair. "When did Mamma learn all this?"

"Not long before I left for Maryland," Earnest replied, concerned that Ernie and the others might think he'd left on purpose those weeks. He sighed. Indeed, there was so much that could have been said to help them through this, but also so little that *should* be said.

Sylvia did not linger, instead hurrying upstairs to her room, where the floodgates opened. She could have wept the rest of the day, but she had to get ahold of herself. Her brothers were in shock, and her own hope of a happy future could be in jeopardy of splintering apart, too.

An hour or so later, Mamma knocked on the bedroom door, bringing up a plate of food—a ham and cheese sandwich, some grapes, and potato chips. "In case you want to eat somethin' before goin' to Singing."

"I won't go with swollen eyes." Sylvia covered her wet face with her hands.

"Well, if ya change your mind, your father is willing to give you a ride."

Sylvia shook her head. "Not tonight . . . I just can't."

"I told him it'll take some time." Mamma sighed and went to stand in the doorway. "For *all* of us."

Sylvia worried what the *Bann* would do to her father's good name, temporary though the excommunication was to be.

Something had been bothering her about the deacon's visit last week. She hadn't said anything to her parents, but now that she and Mamma were alone, she asked, "How did the deacon know to come over here last Saturday?"

"Well, your father was seen visiting his Mennonite uncle quite often while in Maryland."

Frowning, Sylvia shook her head. "But he's Dat's kin."

"True, but your father was getting spiritual advice from a retired minister outside the confines of the People," Mamma said, looking more worried than Sylvia would have predicted. "Word of those visits got back to the Hickory Hollow brethren."

"So one of the other men must've reported it," Sylvia said, thinking aloud. *But who?*

Mamma nodded, then quietly excused herself to return to the kitchen. And Sylvia could hardly wait to get outside for an especially long walk.

Twenty-Nine

*T*he neighbors' cows were grazing in the far meadow as Sylvia left the house. Mamma had encouraged her to splash cold water on her face before stepping out. *She doesn't expect me to go to Singing,* Sylvia thought gratefully while walking toward Hickory Lane carrying Connie Kauffman's wind-up clock in her canvas shoulder bag.

Sylvia took her time, knowing the road would be rather empty, at least of buggy traffic, since most folks who'd gone to church were settled in for the evening. And *die Youngie* were already sitting at the tables, getting ready to sing.

Dat's putting on a good front, but he's really wrestling with all of this, she thought, remembering how frightfully serious he'd looked this afternoon during the family meeting.

Sylvia tried, but it was hard to put herself in her mother's shoes. In fact, it was impossible. *She's got to be concerned Dat won't get through the* Bann, Sylvia thought. Surely during the days of his Proving, her father had never imagined that the refuge he thought he'd found here could possibly shut him out.

Turning onto West Cattail Road, Sylvia walked along the dirt shoulder, listening to the throaty bullfrogs near a small pond up yonder. Within a couple of hours or so, the meadowlands would be filled with hundreds of twinkling lightning bugs. She passed a cluster of honeysuckle bushes and was tempted to do what Dat had taught her as a little girl—what his grandpa Zimmerman taught him—to pull out the stamen and lick the tiny drop of syrupy nectar at its end. This melancholy evening, however, it was enough to simply take in the familiar scent.

"Not sure where Sylvie went off to," Rhoda told Earnest when he asked.

They found themselves alone in the kitchen, the boys having gone to the stable after supper.

"Sylvie must be taking Connie Kauffman's alarm clock back to her," Earnest said, leaning on the counter. "But she seemed upset."

Rhoda nodded, not wanting to add more to her husband's burdens. Now that they weren't supposed to sit at the same table for six weeks, Earnest had eaten out on the back porch during supper while Rhoda sat with the boys indoors . . . Sylvia brooding upstairs in her room.

Toward the end of the supper hour, Deacon Luke had dropped by to talk with Earnest, joining him on the porch to offer some spiritual encouragement at the outset of his temporary excommunication, or so Earnest had shared with Rhoda.

"What do you think will happen between our daughter and Titus?" Earnest asked. "Will she find out that Titus reported me to the brethren?"

Rhoda shrugged. "Hard to say. It's all too much to carry." She glanced toward the window. "I've had to give it up to God."

"Well, evidently Preacher Kauffman hasn't decided if he'll tell Titus that I was married before coming to Hickory Hollow. But certainly not his younger children."

Rhoda turned her head to look at her husband. "He hasn't decided?" She felt sick at the realization. "That means he might?"

Earnest nodded. "*Jah*, Deacon mentioned it today when he dropped by." He opened the clear glass cookie jar, reached in for a snickerdoodle, and took a bite. "It remains to be seen if Amos Kauffman breaks the rules of the *Ordnung* and reveals the reasons for my excommunication."

Rhoda pondered that while wringing out the washrag and going over to wipe down the front of the gas-run fridge. She knew plenty of folk who gossiped and were never found out by the ministers. But Amos *was* a minister, of all things! "We'll have to hope and pray that nothin' deters Titus and Sylvia."

"*Jah*, more pray than hope, I'm thinking," Earnest said, looking concerned, then glancing at his cookie. "Did Sylvie bake these?"

Rhoda smiled wryly. "She'll certainly be a bride who knows her way round a kitchen."

Earnest's smile waned as he went to sit alone at the table.

Rhoda opened the cookie jar and took out a second snicker-doodle for him. "I know ya want another one." She went over and set it down in front of him, then sat on a chair some distance from the table, noticing how drained Earnest looked. "You've been getting up even earlier than usual. Can't ya sleep durin' the wee hours?"

"My inner alarm clock has been waking me up," he said.

"And I've been working to replenish my clock inventory, looking ahead to the autumn tourist season in a few months." He finished off his cookie.

"But how can ya have enough energy for the day with just a few hours' sleep?" Rhoda asked. "Not that I'm tryin' to discourage ya from your work."

He chuckled, eyes softening. "I'm surprised you brought this up." He drew in a deep breath. "Honestly, I wasn't sure we would ever talk this freely again."

I wasn't sure, either, she thought, uncertain how to respond. So she mentioned the children. "Well, our family does need our constant love and care right now."

Earnest leaned his elbows on the table. "Speaking of family, I wouldn't have thought I'd have to be concerned about Adam," Earnest said. "But after today, I'm not so sure."

Rhoda nodded. "He did take it very hard." *They all did, but Adam seemed to be the most affected,* she thought.

They talked further about how needed the ministers' visits and prayers were going to be during the weeks ahead. "Really, though, it falls to me to bring the children along," Earnest said quietly with a glance toward the screen door. "If they can ever trust me again."

Rhoda studied him, believing that what she was hearing and seeing was an indication that he hadn't hardened his heart but was willing to work to heal the wounds he'd caused. But she and Earnest still had a lot to overcome.

Lost in thought, Sylvia turned toward Preacher Kauffman's lane. She picked up her stride, then going around to the back door, she knocked and saw Connie coming to greet her.

"As promised, here's your clock," Sylvia said, removing it from her shoulder bag.

"*Denki*, Sylvie . . . ever so much!" With a giggle, Connie pressed the clock against her cheek. "Come in and have some goodies."

Thanking her, Sylvia said she needed to get home. "Enjoy your clock. My father says there's no charge."

"Really?"

Sylvia nodded. "It didn't take him long at all."

"Well, tell him I appreciate it, okay?" Connie was all aflutter.

"I will." Sylvia said good-bye and made her way out to the lane and down to the road.

She breathed in the air this early evening, grateful for this chance to walk and delighted to see Connie's happy response to the clock. *My little sister-in-law-to-be*, Sylvia thought, walking more briskly now.

Watching the road and wishing she could talk to her best friend, her fiancé she'd become so close to, she also realized at the same time that it was wise not to have attended Singing tonight.

I'm torn betwixt and between, she thought, especially when it came to her father's *Bann*, which Dat had told the family about that afternoon. And while she hadn't been permitted to attend the membership meeting, her heart had been quite present all the same. Of that she was ever so sure.

She had walked a short distance when she saw an enclosed carriage coming this way. The horse was moving faster than a trot, and its speed brought the carriage close to her in no time at all. She wondered if someone was sick or late getting home, but she couldn't make out who was inside as the horse and buggy sped by.

She thought of her brother's angry response earlier, leaving the front room in a huff. *We all have knee-jerk reactions.* She wouldn't soon forget how upsetting it had been to discover the pocket watch and its inscription. *I've had more time than my brothers to mull all of this,* she thought, still wishing Dat would have gotten rid of the watch years ago.

CHAPTER
Thirty

*E*arnest made a point of going out to the stable and talking with Adam, but his son was obviously in a bad way.

"We work together with the livestock every day," Adam said, his voice cracking. "We talk 'bout different types of feed, shoeing horses, and goin' to farm auctions. Sometimes, you've talked a little 'bout what it was like to be fancy, but never once have ya said you were married before Mamma." His eyes glittered accusingly.

Adam had never spoken up to Earnest like this, but he couldn't fault him. His son was visibly smarting after learning the truth. "Listen, Adam, I don't expect you or anyone to excuse me for concealing my past. I was wrong; that's all there is to it."

"Well, it ain't settin' right with me," Adam said, his shoulders rising sharply, then falling. He flicked a piece of straw out of his thick hair. "And I don't wanna hold a grudge, Dat, but is there anything else ya haven't told us?"

Earnest shook his head. "I've tried to walk in your shoes,

wondering how I'd feel if I were your age." He glanced toward the meadow. "Just know I love you . . . and I'm workin' closely with the ministers to reconcile myself."

Adam's eyes searched his, then looking down, he murmured, "You can't know how I feel, Dat."

Earnest watched him exit the stable, and there in the stillness of the evening, Earnest looked back at the house. The golden glow of gaslight lit the kitchen and Sylvia's room— Rhoda must have lit a lamp for her, awaiting her return.

Such hardship my family's going through, and all because of me, he thought, dismayed at the heat of Adam's anger . . . worse than Earnest had ever feared.

Rhoda showered downstairs and got ready for bed, Earnest having already gone up to their room. She removed all the pins from her *Kapp* and took down her hair bun, brushing her hair briskly on all sides. That done, she washed her face in front of the mirror in the small bathroom.

Going out to sit on the back porch in her bathrobe, she stared at the sky, watching the stars appear one by one as the sky grew darker. She offered a prayer for her daughter, wishing she would arrive home soon, hoping to talk to her before bedtime.

Rhoda had become accustomed to their close mother-daughter relationship, something she had often wished for. And now, in the midst of her sadness over Earnest's past, she was finding unexpected comfort in Sylvia's loving care.

She made her way back to the kitchen and sat at the table drinking the rest of the milk in her glass. She ate one more cookie, deciding not to wait for Sylvia to return. *Maybe she's out in the stable grooming Lily,* she thought.

At last, Rhoda climbed the stairs and quietly opened the bedroom door, where she saw Earnest asleep in bed, having left the small lantern on. At the sight, she felt both torn and relieved. This lack of intimacy was what she required now, yet she would do what she could to ease his pain. *Earnest is at his lowest, but I can't help feeling distant,* she thought. And she could not see into a future when she could open her heart again as a wife to him.

Sylvia stayed up late reading, and when she was ready for bed, she put out the gas lamp in her room and flung back the bed quilt. Recalling her conversation with Mamma, she was in no mood to read the Good Book, nor did she kneel to pray, not even saying her silent rote prayers when she was lying on the flat of her back, staring at the shadows on the far wall. So much had happened today, starting with having to exit the temporary House of Worship, knowing what Dat was about to face. She pressed her lips together, wondering who had told on Dat's doings down in Maryland.

Over the next few days, Sylvia noticed multiple visits from the bishop and deacon, but none yet from Titus's father, Preacher Kauffman. None of the farmers who were close friends with her father had dropped by yet, either, and neither had any of the Riehl uncles. For the most part, it seemed that the menfolk had not taken to heart the bishop's request to encourage Dat in the faith during his shunning.

But she was committed to doing her part by praying for him, just as the ministers and others surely were. The hardest part, at least for her, was eating with Mamma and the boys at the table inside while Dat sat alone on the back porch or took his food out to his shop. After the first meals, it began to take its toll, not only on Dat, but on all of them. Most times, they sat and ate silently from the pretty new anniversary plates, Ernie and Adam wolfing down their food to finish quickly and get on their way to chores. It was not only strange to see Dat's empty chair at the head of the table, but downright sad.

Friday, June nineteenth, after purchasing fresh eggs from Aendi Ruthann, Sylvia returned home to find her mother sweeping the front porch. She couldn't help noticing how drawn Mamma's face looked, yet somehow she managed to keep up with her chores, the daily routine she always followed.

A fresh breeze blew across the yard and dipped down toward the driveway as Sylvia carried the wicker basket filled with the newly gathered eggs. Inside, she placed them in the fridge and poured some meadow tea, feeling very thirsty.

She noticed the crispy squares Mamma had made while she was gone to get eggs and visit with Cousins Alma and Jessie. Her mouth watered—she knew the ingredients by heart, a delicious mix of peanut butter, rice cereal, chocolate and butterscotch chips. *Mamma's determined to keep the family well fed.*

Going upstairs to her room, Sylvia sat at her small writing desk, staring at her pretty box of stationery, wondering if she ought to write to Titus. After all, it had been nearly two weeks since the Saturday Deacon Peachey had come so unexpectedly. Surely by now Titus had heard something of Dat's temporary *Bann,* she thought, glancing out the open window and wondering if she ought to be worried at Titus's lack of communication. "Did he miss seein' me at the last Singing?" she murmured, guessing they wouldn't be going out tomorrow evening for their Saturday date, after all. "Did Connie tell him I dropped by with her little clock?" she whispered.

She heard the mail truck before she actually saw it, and wanting to help Mamma out, she hurried downstairs and down the driveway to the mailbox near the road. To be expected, a batch of letters had arrived for Mamma—she was so faithful with her circle letters and whatnot. But Sylvia also saw a letter with Titus's handwriting and smiled, eager to read it.

"I'll put your mail on the kitchen counter," she called to Mamma, who'd moved to sweeping the walkway between the front porch and the driveway.

"*Denki!*" Mamma bobbed her head and kept sweeping.

The minute Sylvia put the mail inside, she took her letter and hurried outside and over to the field lanes, barefoot and heading for a little stream in the back of the meadow. There, she waded up to her knees, enjoying the coolness, with Titus's letter safely tucked in her dress pocket. It was as though she needed to calm herself before reading it, and she honestly didn't know why. But something was downright odd about its arrival today. *Unless Titus does plan to take me out tomorrow evening.*

She sighed, not wanting to be a worrywart, but with everything going on related to Dat's *Bann*, she hardly knew what to think. Surely Titus had something to say about all of this.

She stepped gingerly over the stones and up the grassy bank to the shade tree nearby. There, she sat down, pulled out the letter, and began to read.

Dear Sylvie,

How are you? It's been a while since we talked, and I missed seeing you at the last Singing. But I guessed you needed some time to yourself.

I really wish I could see you this Saturday, but I can't get away for our usual date. There's so much to do here at the farm, but I'll see you at the next Singing for certain. Okay?

Also, thanks for returning Connie's little clock. She is a happy girl to be sure.

With love,
Titus

He seems cheerful and upbeat, just like he was the last time I saw him, she thought, scanning the letter again. But to think that he was canceling their date this late in the week, something he'd never done before.

Her thoughts flew back to when he'd said they must always be honest with each other, and she couldn't help wondering if he was being entirely honest with her now. Was he *really* too busy to spend time with her tomorrow?

It had been such a long time since she'd seen him, but since then, her suspicions had only grown stronger.

"*Ach,* I'll see him at Singing, like he said," she whispered, refolding the letter and lying back in the deep grass, listening to the gurgling stream, tempted to wade in it again and simply skip suppertime. It was still so upsetting to eat inside the house while Dat ate alone on the porch. And, she thought, if it bothered her this much, what was it doing to her father?

Rhoda was alone in the kitchen the following Thursday morning. Sylvia had scurried off to Mamie Zook's to help make blueberry pies for an upcoming fundraiser to offset the cost of repairs to the one-room schoolhouse.

She had been working to peel two quarts of ripe tomatoes, preparing them for a tomato corn relish recipe Mammi Riehl had given her as a newlywed. As she worked, she recalled the Scripture verse that Bishop John must have written down for her husband, one that she'd seen lying on Earnest's bedside table that morning. First John, chapter one, verse nine: *If we confess our sins, he is faithful and just to forgive us our sins, and to cleanse us from all unrighteousness.*

It was hard to know the condition of one's heart—certainly for the purpose of judging. She felt called to pray for her husband, hoping that he was still open to accepting valuable spiritual input from the brethren.

He hadn't made any negative remarks to her, but it was still early in the *Bann*, and already she sensed his restlessness and his low spirits. He had, after all, worked more than two decades to establish his excellence as a clockmaker, trusted friend and confidant, and all-round good man. She couldn't know for certain, but she was starting to think her husband's business was at risk. For one thing, only two Amish customers had dropped by since the bishop had declared him shunned, and there'd been no sales. And Adam had mentioned to Rhoda privately last evening that he'd seen an Amish neighbor up the road hauling a grandfather clock—one Adam was certain had not come from his father's shop—in the back of his spring wagon. Rhoda wouldn't think of bringing this up to Earnest, of course, but she assumed it indicated at least one lost sale.

This troubled her. Typically during a temporary *Bann*, church members were encouraged *not* to "starve out" the shunned person. But Rhoda wondered if because Earnest had been looked up to, perhaps even erroneously put on a pedestal, some folk were uncomfortable doing business with him now. She just didn't know what to think.

CHAPTER
Thirty-One

The last Sunday in June arrived, hot and sultry, and with it Dat's required attendance at Preaching, the first time since the bishop declared him excommunicated.

When Sylvia and the other baptismal candidates were dismissed to join the congregation downstairs after class, she spotted her father in the second row, behind where the ministers went to sit, bowed low. She felt overwhelmed with sadness and embarrassment to see him up front, sitting that way to show humility.

She hoped her brothers weren't feeling as gloomy as she did just now.

Before this, Sylvia had had no firsthand experience of a shunning, although she'd heard about Katie Lapp, a young woman who had been shunned decades ago. She knew, though, that just like at home, Dat was not allowed to sit with anyone for the common meal today after Preaching. Rather, he was expected to stand on the porch or out on the lawn, available for the other men to talk with him and hopefully encourage him. *To think he has a whole month more of this!* thought Sylvia, her heart going out to him, even though, according to the way of the People, the discipline was considered essential.

The Ordnung *teaches us how to live,* she thought where she sat next to Mamma. Sylvia had learned in baptism class that it was not a list of *rules* to follow but rather a set of *expectations* for conduct. And while the *Ordnung* was unwritten, it honored the memory of older folk in the community . . . the source of the wisdom in the long-held tradition.

Sylvia's brother Ernie dropped her off at the Sunday Singing that evening. And as she entered the barn for the gathering, she suddenly felt self-conscious. Oddly, if it was not her own imagination, she could feel the glances of the other youth.

Is everyone staring at me?

She tried very hard not to let it bother her, spotting Andy Zook smiling across the haymow at that moment. He waved, seemingly unfazed by her presence, and she waved back. Then she happened to see Mel Kauffman looking her way—Titus's close cousin who'd double-dated with her and Titus a while back. At first, he seemed to study her, but then, when he noticed her looking at him, he turned away. Trying not to take this to heart, Sylvia walked toward Linda Mast, one of Uncle Curtis's teenage cousins, who blinked her eyes awkwardly at Sylvia and turned her fair head.

This ain't going so well.

Taking her seat with Cousins Alma and Jessie, she assumed that most of *die Youngie* had either seen or heard that her father was seated up front during Preaching that morning, bowed over in contrition. *The grapevine has spread this, if not the fact that Dat deceived about his past,* she thought, heartsick that some were likely gossiping about her father . . . and their family. *Me included,* she thought, not looking for Titus, who she assumed was sitting with the other young men, not far from her.

Oh, Sylvia thought, *I should've stayed home!*

It was clear to Sylvia that Titus was taking the long way to her house, slowly trotting the horse past the General Store, where a low-spreading mimosa tree would soon produce bright, rosy pink blossoms. As a girl, Sylvia had marveled that the tree could rain down powdery blossoms at the slightest breeze. Now in the darkness, she saw only the outline of its delicate branches.

Oddly, she felt relaxed, even though Titus had yet to mention anything about her father's temporary shunning. Titus did glance at her every few minutes, the driving lines taut in his hand, and she felt sure he had other things on his mind. *Or does he expect me to bring it up?*

Drawing a deep breath, she said at last, "I'm glad this week's nearly over."

Titus looked at her and nodded. "But tomorrow's a new beginning, my Mamm always says."

I wish that were true at our house, she thought. What with the *Bann* underway, every time one of the ministers arrived to admonish Dat, it was a reminder to the whole family of what he had done.

"I'm glad we're together tonight," Titus said, disturbing her musing.

Not in the mood for romance, Sylvia could not dismiss the

thing that had nagged at her since the morning Deacon Peachey came rushing into the driveway to see her father. "Titus, did ya spend most of your time in Maryland with my Dat?"

He turned to look at her. "Like I wrote in my early letter, we partnered on the rebuilds. We even shared a room."

She was conscious of a shift in his tone as he seemed to stiffen, his arm still around her. "Just curious."

He nodded, mum.

She held back a moment and wondered if she dared stick her neck out. But then curiosity overruled, and she asked, "Did ya happen to know that my Dat was spending evening hours with his great-uncle?"

Titus was quiet for a moment. "The retired Mennonite preacher?"

"*Jah.*"

He removed his arm from around her and held the driving lines with both hands now. "I enjoyed spending time with your father, Sylvie," he said, changing the subject. "I've always liked bein' around him—you know that."

That's not what I asked, she thought, fixing her gaze on the back of the horse and the occasional carriages coming toward them.

"Speaking of your father, I noticed he was absent from Preachin' two weeks ago," Titus said unexpectedly.

"*Jah.*"

"And there was a members meeting afterward." Titus glanced at her. "Do you know why the meeting was called?"

What's he doing? she thought. *Surely he saw Dat bowed during Preaching this morning!*

"We're not members, are we, you and I?" she replied, her answer as vague as he'd been earlier.

"Not yet."

She refused to say that a *Bann* had been put on her father. While the excommunication was temporary, it was a shunning all the same. Thankfully, Titus didn't ask anything more about that, and she had decided not to talk about it with him anyway, wanting to act like she was already a baptized church member. *If the members aren't permitted to discuss it,* she thought, irritated, *then the daughter of the shunned man shouldn't, either.*

Just then, Titus mentioned a hike the youth were planning at Landis Woods next weekend. Sylvia merely listened, finding it strange that he had changed the subject so drastically.

And when he kissed her good-night while they sat on the shoulder of the road in front of Sylvia's house, she could think only about getting back to her wounded family.

"What's the hurry?" Titus asked, reaching for her hand.

"Oh, just tired, I guess."

"Well, would ya like to go on that hike with me, and with Alma and Danny, too?"

Sylvia looked at him sitting there in the dim light of dusk, the driving lines lapped over his knees, and she really just wanted to ask him straight out if he had been the one to tell the brethren about her father's meetings with his great-uncle. It wasn't *his* fault that her father was being shunned, of course, but she felt Titus should have been honest with her.

But she wouldn't let on how angry she was. Furious, really. "I know for sure I'm gonna be busy this week," she said, wanting to stay close to Mamma, helping around the house and at the roadside stand.

Titus seemed to take this in stride, which was a relief. Then he mentioned a few other activities coming up, including a volleyball game and that some of the youth were getting together to go fishing in the Susquehanna River. He seemed to want to keep her from leaving, talking on about all the fun they would have together the rest of the summer.

But Sylvia's mind wasn't on any of that.

Did you report my father? she wondered when they said goodnight at last. *And even worse, not tell me the truth about it?*

Ten days passed, and once the house was clean that Wednesday, Sylvia sat down at the kitchen table to study for her classes, wanting to be as conscientious a candidate now as she had been each day since the first Sunday.

Mamma was just across the kitchen, rolling chicken pieces in a mixture of flour, seasonings, and butter before baking.

"Mamma, do ya remember this from your baptism instruction?" she asked, then read aloud Ephesians, chapter four, verses twenty-three and twenty-four: "'And be renewed in the spirit of your mind. And that ye put on the new man, which after God is created in righteousness and true holiness.'"

"I do remember." Mamma turned to look at her, shaking the pieces of chicken in a bag filled with the coating mixture.

"I'm curious 'bout the meaning of 'be renewed in the spirit of your mind.' Do ya know?"

Mamma set down the bag of chicken and walked toward the table. "You're a thinker, Sylvie. *Des gut.*" She smiled. "I think the Apostle Paul meant that we aren't able to separate ourselves from sin and live a holy life on our own strength. The only way is to surrender our hearts and minds to our Savior. If we do that, God renews our hearts and makes us more like Him."

Sylvia listened and wondered if the brethren were encouraging Dat to do what the verse instructed. "I s'pose we can encourage each other best when we remind each other of this, *jah?*"

Mamma nodded. "And we can be thankful for those who come alongside us when we've fallen." She returned to the counter and picked up her brown bag and began shaking it again. "We're a community of believers who lift each other up, remember."

Sylvia was glad she could talk with Mamma about the things she was learning, but she also wondered why a wayward person like her father had to be put through such a tough time before being accepted back into the membership.

CHAPTER

Thirty-Two

A week later, after Thursday breakfast, Earnest hitched up and headed over to the hardware store. His wife and daughter had gone to a spaghetti sauce–making bee around the same time he'd left the house. *They've become very close,* he thought, glad Sylvie was such an attentive daughter.

He thought of how often she had come over to spend time with him in his shop, prior to his secret being exposed. Those days were distant now in his mind as he poured his energy into following through with the *Bann.* Six weeks felt like an eternity, but he was determined not to resent the brethren. *I had it coming. . . .*

A black-topped carriage was heading this way, and Earnest recognized it as an Old Order Mennonite buggy, like his Zimmerman grandparents'. As he liked to do, Earnest waved at the elderly couple, his former customers.

To his surprise, neither returned his wave and, all the more astonishing, the man and woman quite noticeably turned their faces away. This knocked the air out of Earnest, and he wondered if word hadn't gotten out that his was not meant to be a permanent *Bann*—ousted for life. *What if folks are talking behind the bishop's back?*

He observed the familiar expanse of cornfields, trying to pull himself together, his horse moving at a steady trot.

At the store, Earnest took out his list of hardware items, and one by one quickly located what he'd come to purchase. While folding his list and stuffing it back into his pocket, he was suddenly aware of two men talking on the other side of the aisle. He couldn't see them from his location, but their voices were clear enough, especially when his own name was spoken just then.

"Such a fine, upstanding man we all thought Earnest Miller was. The best clockmaker in all of Lancaster County, and honest as the day's long," a man was saying. "'Least, we thought so."

"*Jah*, to think he kept it from his wife for that long," the other man said.

"And those Millers were such a *wunnerbaar-gut* family, too," came the reply. "All those fine young sons . . . and Earnest's daughter, always so kind."

"Ain't that the truth . . . so well thought of all these years. 'Tis a horrible shame that everything he's worked for has been ruined."

Mortified, Earnest leaned closer to the shelves, unable to lay eyes on these men. Neither voice rang a bell for him, and he stood there, dismayed. Given the bishop's warning, it was horrible to realize that news of his excommunication had spread to another Plain community. It was all he could do to hold himself back from hurrying up the aisle and around to confront the men. And, had he not been an Amishman for two decades, he might have done just that.

Eventually, Earnest managed to recover his composure sufficiently to push the cart over to the cashier, hoping the gossiping men had left the store.

Rhoda was delighted Sylvia had come with her to Hannah's, where Ella Mae Zook and some of the other older women, including Rebecca Lapp and Mamie Zook, were present for the sauce-making bee.

It was heartening to see Hannah looking so refreshed while at her kitchen table mincing garlic cloves. On the stove simmered several large kettles of tomatoes and homemade tomato soup, filling the air with a delicious, homey smell.

During their midmorning break—an excuse for some treats—Hannah served fresh cherries, pretzel sticks, cookies, and sweet breads. Thankfully, Hannah's past sorrows seemed far from her mind. Like the other older women there, she was lavishing attention on Sylvia, who was the only young woman present. And thinking of all the stress her dear family was currently enduring, Rhoda was glad. *This time is really good for her, dear girl.*

Once everyone was seated at the tables set up in the large sunny kitchen, where every window was pushed wide open, Hannah shared her hope to crochet baby afghans to give to expectant mothers in the area. "Wouldn't that be a nice fall project for us, after the harvest?" Hannah asked, her eyes shining.

Rhoda was a bit surprised her sister was up for something like that. "That's a great idea," she said, the first to speak up.

Ella Mae raised her hand, then put it down and looked around, her eyelashes fluttering. "Ach, I forgot we ain't in school."

The women laughed, including Sylvia.

"So I take it you're interested in makin' a cradle afghan, Ella Mae?" Hannah asked from where she sat across from the Wise Woman.

"You saw my hand go up, *jah*?"

Another wave of laughter skittered around the room.

"'Tis a *gut* idea, Hannah," Ella Mae said at last. "One we can all help with."

Rhoda nodded and agreed to make one, as well, hoping that one day not too far off, she would be crocheting afghans for Sylvia's babies.

When they stopped that afternoon for some lemonade and cookies, Ella Mae walked outdoors with Sylvia, who wandered over to the shady side of the wraparound porch. "How are ya doin'?" she asked.

Sylvia suspected she was referring to her father's shunning, so she was glad they could talk privately.

"I'm tryin' to be strong, mostly for Mamma," Sylvia confided, realizing she must have attracted Ella Mae's notice due to her sad countenance today. "And for my brothers, as well." She didn't mention how seemingly miserable Adam had become, hardly speaking two words when Dat was present in the room.

Ella Mae nodded. "'Tis awful hard on a family when one member suffers." Her eyes welled up. "I went through the temporary *Bann*, too . . . years ago."

"Oh?" Sylvia had never heard this.

"Scarcely anyone remembers now . . . most of my immediate family has since passed on." Ella Mae shared that she had fallen for a young man who hadn't yet joined church and didn't

seem interested in doing so. "This fella was later known as Ol'
Isaac Smucker . . . the elderly man who sold his clock business
to your Dat. But back when he was a teenager, Isaac got to
runnin' with a wild bunch, and I liked goin' with him in his
fast car—even though I was already baptized. Imagine that!"

Curious to hear more, Sylvia motioned to two rocking
chairs, not wanting Ella Mae to have to stand for too long.
"How'd he get straightened out?"

"Well, if ya really wanna know, after a time, I insisted he
settle down and heed the Lord's call on his life. And since I
had gone through a six-week *Bann* because of my association
with him, he perked up his ears and did just that." Ella Mae
chuckled. "Guess I played a small part in getting him right
with God and the church."

"Dare I ask if you two courted after that?"

"*Ach*, we nearly got ourselves hitched, but we parted ways
after my father took me aside and suggested I step back and
give the relationship some breathing room." Ella Mae smiled.
"Thank goodness I listened, 'cause later I met the man I was
s'posed to wed."

Sylvia was spellbound. "I never would've guessed you ran
around after you were baptized. Or that you were ever shunned."

"'Twas *der Hutsch* of my youth, but that and the *Bann* kept
me from making an even worse mistake. I'm grateful to this
day to God and to my wise father."

Sylvia shook her head, surprised. "Strange as it might seem,
it's a relief to hear it all turned out fine for you . . . like my
Dat's not alone in this."

"*Ach nee* . . . a number of folk in this district have been
shunned, truth be told. The youth can be especially *schpankich*
at times. Why, even some of the ministers got off the straight

and narrow before they were ordained." Ella Mae glanced heavenward. "Only our Lord lived a spotless life. And 'tis a blessing to have the love of the People at such a needful time, ain't so?"

Agreeing, Sylvia nodded. "You're such a help to me."

"Well, don't be shy about comin' over to see me, if ya ever wanna talk more."

Then, hearing Mamma calling to them, Sylvia said, "I guess we should get back inside." She offered a hand to help Ella Mae out of the rocker, but the woman refused, clucking as she managed to pull herself to a standing position. Together, they walked around the corner and to the back door, where Sylvia's mother waited, smiling.

Earnest wanted to talk with Rhoda before bedtime, so after supper, when she and Sylvia were done redding up the kitchen, he approached his wife in the sitting room, where she was reaching for the newspaper on the big hassock near her comfortable chair. "Would you like to take a walk?" he asked, his voice raspy with uncertainty.

"Well, if ya don't mind, I was lookin' forward to just sitting here awhile and reading," she said, glancing up at him. Her hair was a bit untidy on the sides where it had been twisted that morning into her hair bun.

"Just a short walk?"

"I'm all in," she replied.

"All right, then." *She does look tired,* he thought as he turned to leave the room. But he'd felt sure this would be a good evening for a walk, since she had been over at Curtis's place with Hannah and the womenfolk. Even so, he was disappointed.

He trudged back to his shop and sat in his work chair, staring at the note that had arrived in the mail from a long-time acquaintance, not far from here, who'd written to Earnest to say he was no longer interested in a custom-built grandfather clock. Earnest hoped this wasn't the first of many such notices. He could not stay afloat if his business fell off any more than it already had.

I'll be relieved when the Bann is over, he thought, looking down at the cupboard where the tinderbox was hidden. *Rhoda sure didn't know what she was getting into when she agreed to marry me,* he thought, standing up and going to the screen door to look out. *But I'm not that foolish young man anymore.*

He could see Ernie and Adam going from the barn to the stable, Ernie with a piece of straw hanging out of his mouth. And Adam looking down at his bare feet as he came along behind his brother.

He recalled Adam's remark to him. *"Is there anything else ya haven't told us?"*

The question had struck him hard, circling in his mind till it gave him a headache. *Adam's sorely put out with me,* he mused. But then, looking out at the woodshed, the meadow, the beautiful landscape so familiar to him now, he hoped he could get through till the final Sunday when Bishop John asked him the expected questions in front of the church membership.

It had been humiliating to overhear the men at the hardware store, and to see the couple in their buggy looking away . . . and to be shunned from eating at Rhoda's table. It wasn't just painful—the foreignness of it seemed almost wrong to him, given the way he was raised, though he hadn't let on to anyone that he felt that way.

He eyed the woodshed again and recalled the time he'd

caught Ol' Isaac Smucker out there puffing on a cigarette after Earnest gave his gentleman's handshake on this property. Isaac hadn't minded getting caught; in fact, he'd boldly offered Earnest a smoke. Even though he'd always liked the smell of tobacco, Earnest had refused. As he recalled, Isaac had relayed then how he often pushed the limits of the Old Ways, yet it was clear that the elderly clockmaker had become well respected, even loved, amongst the People. *His honesty saved him*, Earnest thought, pushing the screen door open and moving toward the area where the sun shone on the porch. *And eventually he gave up his smoking habit. Was it on his own . . . or did the ministers convince him?*

Earnest leaned against the porch rail. Just now, he didn't care to go out and help with the evening chores, and there was really no need to, not with the boys working. It was Rhoda's affection he wanted. It had been weeks since they had been even close enough to kiss, let alone to hold each other as they fell asleep. He yearned for her, and the thought of living without her love made him feel dejected. At the same time, he did not fault her for keeping her distance.

Thirty-Three

*R*hoda could see Earnest heading this way across the side yard from her easy chair near the sitting room window. Dusk was another hour or more away, and it had been relaxing to read by the light of the waning sun. Occasionally she glanced out to see the boys cutting up and calling back and forth to one another, having fun doing chores. For the longest time, Sylvia had been sitting out front on the porch writing a letter, presumably to her beloved Titus. *Maybe she, too, needs a reprieve from the day,* Rhoda mused, recalling how very quiet Sylvia had been at Hannah's earlier. *It was good of Ella Mae to seek her out,* Rhoda thought, grateful for the woman's tender heart.

Earlier, while doing the dishes, Rhoda had considered staying up later again so that Earnest was asleep when she came to bed. The ongoing lack of the intimacy they'd once enjoyed really wasn't something she could talk about yet. But in the weeks since his startling revelation, she sometimes felt it was an achievement for her to simply keep house and keep up with meals, doing her very best to make this place the home it had always been—or something like it.

We're all just holding our breath till the Bann's behind us.

Friday was particularly demanding for Sylvia. Even before the sun rose, she'd gotten up with the early birds to churn butter with Mamma. They had also baked bread and extra desserts for Sunday, an off-day from church, since they were planning to visit several relatives. As was her way, Mamma wanted to have some goodies to bring along.

Presently Sylvia tended the roadside stand, rearranging the remaining produce after a visit from an enthusiastic group of tourists. Sylvia thought ahead to seeing Titus tomorrow evening, wondering how that would be.

As for her father, he'd seemed less talkative than ever before and often looked disheartened while going outdoors for their awkward mealtime arrangements. She supposed that she or one of the boys could go out there and eat with him, since none of them were baptized church members. But when she came close to talking to Mamma about it, she simply could not do it, not wanting Mamma to misunderstand her reasons.

Lately, she found herself thinking more and more about how she'd opened the tinderbox and stirred all of this up.

If only I'd left well enough alone.

Earnest opened every window in his shop and left the door standing open to the screen that evening, hoping for some cross-ventilation. Then he removed the tinderbox from the low cupboard and took out his family photos—his parents'

engagement picture and their wedding photo, followed by several school pictures of his sister, Charlie, and himself. He admired the Yankees ball cap and the prized ticket his father had spent hard-earned money to purchase, surprising him with a trip to Yankee Stadium on his eleventh birthday.

Earnest twiddled the key chain, a birthday gift from his best pal in seventh grade. Last of all, he studied the red crocheted tree ornament from his little sister, recalling how many hours Mom said it had taken for Charlie to have it ready by Christmas Eve.

He studied his high school diploma, and the letters from his Papa and Grammy Zimmerman. He had felt compelled to examine these items again. And to remember . . .

But Earnest had left Rosalind's pocket watch, wrapped in its protective cloths, inside the tinderbox. There was no need to bring that out to gnaw at his memory. *Why did I keep all this?* he wondered.

Thinking back on his boyhood with his loving family, he was hit with a wave of longing to see sweet Charlie again. How he missed his little sister!

Leaning forward, Earnest located her first-grade school picture and peered at her little pixie face. "She had Mom's heart-shaped face," he murmured, "and Dad's thick head of hair." He wondered if she would still be involved in his life, had she lived. Would she have kept in touch after he left for Hickory Hollow?

I'd like to think so, he mused.

Sighing, he reached for what Mahlon Zook had always called the Good Book and turned to the verses Bishop John had urged him to meditate on first thing in the morning and before retiring at night. As he had every day these past weeks,

Earnest read each one aloud, then recited the last one a second time. "'For we ourselves also were sometimes foolish, disobedient, deceived, serving divers lusts and pleasures. . . .'"

Nodding his head, Earnest whispered, "Pretty much describes me."

In the wee hours, Earnest dreamed of Papa Zimmerman and the large fishing hole where Earnest had learned to cast off and reel in. And, like the ever-changing clouds, the dream evolved into young Earnest holding the end of a skipping rope, the other side tied to the yard fence as little Charlie jumped and chanted a silly song while he turned the rope over and over again.

Earnest reveled in the lovely dream, then rose to dress for the day. As had become the norm, he headed to the shop before dawn to work on a cherrywood mantel clock special ordered by an Amish fellow he'd met at market. *More than likely, he hasn't gotten word of my shunning.* Earnest hoped that was true as he stained the wood to the desired hue. *I have to earn a living somehow.*

Later, when Rhoda and Sylvia were up and ready to serve breakfast, he went to sit on the back porch to eat apart from his family—his required routine these weeks. *My discipline,* he thought solemnly.

Young Tommy came outside carrying a heaping plate of hot biscuits and gravy, one of Earnest's favorites. "*Denki.* Tell your Mamma that, too," he said, accepting the plate, and Tommy bobbed his head.

"How much longer must ya eat alone, Dat?" Tommy asked with a frown, his hair still uncombed.

"Just eight more days."

"That's a whole week and one whole day," Tommy muttered, then turned toward the back door. "Adam's real sad 'bout it . . . doesn't understand why ya can't eat with us."

"Adam said that?" Earnest was surprised. *Better than being miffed like he has been for the past weeks,* he thought. "Have him come out here a minute."

Very soon, Adam wandered out, standing there without suspenders, his trousers baggy around his skinny waist. "Tommy says ya wanna see me, Dat."

"Bring your breakfast out here, son. *Kumme esse.*"

"With you?" Adam blinked and glanced back at the door. "I'm allowed?"

Earnest motioned for Adam to go and get his meal. "Tell your Mamma I want your company." *I need it. . . .*

A hesitant smile appeared, and Adam turned to hurry inside.

While he waited for his second-oldest son to join him, Earnest wondered if and when Amos Kauffman might stop over again to talk. So far the man had only come twice to pray and admonish Earnest. Considering that Titus was the one who'd reported Earnest to the bishop, it was hard not to rule out the notion that Amos might be feeling ill at ease around Earnest. Perhaps that was the reason Amos had been rather scarce.

It was midmorning when Earnest walked over to the house and asked Rhoda to come with him to the clock shop. "I'd like to show you the things I saved from my days as an *Englischer,*" he said.

Rhoda stopped washing windows and went with him, her little white work apron over a long black one, and her navy blue bandanna sliding back on her head.

Hoping this was a good idea, he showed her the contents of the tinderbox, beginning with the family pictures.

"Why'd ya keep these?" she asked, looking a bit surprised and confused.

"I couldn't part with them." He explained that they were the last vestiges of the best parts of his old life. "All but the pocket watch, of course, and I've already told you why I kept that."

"Oh . . . thought ya might've sold it by now," Rhoda said, looking with interest at the Miller family pictures.

"I'm ready to sell it, *jah*."

"Maybe use the money as a dowry for Sylvia?" Rhoda smiled momentarily as she glanced up at him. "What would ya think of that?"

Earnest nodded, noticing she seemed quite taken with one of the photos of his sister. "That's Charlie . . . well, Charlene. She was such a vivacious, happy girl . . . liked it when I bought her bubble gum." He chuckled a little. "We used to have bubble-blowing contests, you see. Usually I was the one who ended up with gum plastered on my face."

Rhoda continued to study the photo. "She died so awful young."

"It nearly killed my parents." He wanted so badly to slip his arm around Rhoda, but he hung back, not wanting to spoil this moment. "I wish they could have known *you*, Rhoda."

"I would've liked that, too," she said, examining each photo at length. "I can see why you'd want to keep these, but I'm not sure what Bishop John would say. Though he *has* become more accepting in the past few years."

"That's partly why I wanted *you* to see all of this. Tell me what you think, Rhoda."

She fingered his high school diploma, then thumbed through the letters but didn't open the envelopes. "These things won't cause any concerns, but the pocket watch from your first wife prob'ly will."

"Then I'll go into town soon and talk to a jeweler," he said, glad for Rhoda's kind demeanor.

"All right, then."

"I appreciate your help."

She nodded. "I enjoyed seein' what your family looked like." A brief smile crossed her face. "It was also nice to see into your heart a little, too, Earnest." With that, she moved to the screen door and headed back to the house.

Quietly, he returned everything except the pocket watch to the tinderbox, thinking that he and Rhoda had made some small steps forward. *At last* . . .

CHAPTER
Thirty-Four

Sylvia's outing with Titus on Saturday evening involved another double date with Cousin Alma and Danny Lapp, and the four of them played volleyball with other young people at the farm of James Zook, one of Mahlon's married grandsons. On the same team as Titus, Sylvia was relieved to be surrounded by others and tried to let herself join in the fun, setting up the ball for his hits. Alma and Danny were on the opposite team, whereas Cousin Jessie and her beau, Yonnie Zook, played against each other, and Sylvia noticed him glancing Jessie's way quite a lot.

During a break in the play, James and his young sons brought out slices of watermelon for everyone, and right away a number of the young men began a seed-spitting contest, Titus, Danny, and Yonnie cheering them on.

They're trying to impress us with their good manners, Sylvia thought, sweet watermelon juice dripping on her bare feet.

⌒

Much later that evening, when Sylvia was alone with Titus, she breathed a prayer, waiting for the right moment to bring up what was on her mind. Titus had been uncharacteristically reserved tonight, but Sylvia knew it was vital that they talk.

The horse's *clip-clop-clip* matched the timing of Sylvia's heartbeat as she tried to think how to start the discussion with Titus.

"Did ya have a nice time tonight?" he asked then, breaking the stillness.

"*Jah.*"

"How are things goin' at your house?"

My parents are trying to survive, she thought, somewhat peeved that he should ask. How did he think they were going? "My father's workin' through the *Bann* . . . carefully following the ministers' instructions."

Titus glanced at her, then looked away. "My Dat told me that your father was married before comin' here as a seeker."

She jerked her head around to face him. "He told ya?"

"He thought I should know." Titus was slow to continue. "It was all very confidential, just between him and me." His voice sounded strained. "Dat told me only because of our plans to marry. And I vowed not to tell anyone else."

Sylvia felt ill. "Even so, I'm real surprised."

"Well, we'll be married in four months, Sylvia," he said. "You can't keep something like that quiet from family."

He's right, she realized.

"Mamm urged me to tell you that I know," Titus said.

"Your Mamm? So telling me wasn't your idea?" This set Sylvia off! And while Sylvia was expected to be compliant in her relationship with her fiancé, she couldn't help wondering why he always chose to do what his mother suggested. "Seems to me your Mamm's still leadin' the way."

Titus turned to look at her. "What're you sayin'?"

As important as it was, she couldn't simply blurt out that she wished *he* would be the one to decide things for them.

"I was just relaying what Mamm said, Sylvia."

She reached down for the hem of her long apron and fanned herself with it, the night so hot and sticky. "I know ya want to please your parents, *jah?*"

"I'm just doin' what I believe they want me to—they're not insisting I do things a certain way, Sylvie. Please don't mistake that."

She looked at him, the air tight in her chest. At this rate, she feared his mother was likely to run their marriage, and with her parents' rocky relationship right now, it was all too much. And it didn't help that Titus hadn't told her whether or not he had been the one to tell on her father. "Honestly, Titus, I don't think I know you as well as I should."

"That's ridiculous." He sounded perturbed.

"I'm not sure it is. Please . . . I need time to think things over," she replied, the words spilling out now. She remembered what the Wise Woman had said about giving her long-ago relationship space to breathe. "Wouldn't it make sense for us to step back from seein' each other . . . 'specially with so much focus on my father right now?"

Titus nodded. "I believe you're right," he said, not putting up any kind of argument.

Her mind was in a whirl as she recalled what Titus had said weeks ago about nothing but death keeping them apart. Yet *she* had been the one to bring this up tonight. Even so, the fact that Titus was so quick to agree meant he must have been thinking similarly. "All right, then," she said at last.

He signaled the horse to turn into Dat's driveway, where their good-byes for the night felt more like good-bye forever.

Even before Titus came around to offer to help her down from the buggy, Sylvia got out, lifted her skirt, and ran up the long driveway and into the house.

Rhoda wasn't necessarily alarmed the next day when Sylvia slept in and didn't join her brothers and Rhoda at breakfast. But when Sylvia finally did come dragging downstairs in her bathrobe and slippers, looking like she hadn't slept all night, Rhoda was terribly concerned.

As the day progressed and Sylvia was too tired to go visiting with the family, Rhoda felt certain that something had happened between Sylvia and Titus. *Have our worst fears come true?* she worried. She even mentioned it to Earnest after they arrived home from Rhoda's parents'. "This isn't like our girl to burrow away."

Earnest nodded. "She was fine yesterday . . . as fine as any of us are these days."

"I thought so, too," Rhoda agreed.

They didn't say much more, and after a time, Rhoda excused herself to go for a walk. Once more taking Ella Mae's good advice to heart, she headed out to the meadow, her favorite place to pray these days. *Our poor Sylvie . . .*

Earnest watched Rhoda hurry across the side lawn, past the stable, and up toward the grazing land. He wanted to walk with her, but the wall between them discouraged him. He feared it might become all the more fortified if he imposed himself in hope of breaking it down.

Opening the Good Book on his lap, he believed that it was his duty—if he could—to do whatever it took to help ease Rhoda back into the way things used to be. It was one of the main reasons he had been rereading certain passages from Bishop John's list of recommended verses, also taking the time to read the chapters around them.

But the verses he kept going back to were found in Psalm thirty-one: *In thee, O Lord, do I put my trust; let me never be ashamed: deliver me in thy righteousness. Bow down thine ear to me; deliver me speedily: be thou my strong rock, for an house of defense to save me. . . .*

"How wrong I was to think the Amish life, or any lifestyle, could be my strong footing," Earnest whispered as he sat there on the porch in July's oppressive heat. It was as if a new understanding had emerged in his heart. His yearning to turn over a new leaf more than two decades ago had not led him to the peace his soul longed for—that was too much to expect of Hickory Hollow and its Amish tradition.

He recalled all the years Papa Zimmerman had taught him Scripture, and bowing his head, Earnest began to pray. "O Lord, lead me through to my public confession next Sunday. Help me stay on the path so that I hear the bishop's words of restoration."

Sitting there, Earnest watched the sunlight play on the trees nearest the meadow, his eyes trained on the return of his wife. *My darling bride . . .*

CHAPTER

Thirty-Five

The following morning, after Sylvia helped pin the washing to the clothesline, she assured Mamma that she was well enough to take Lily and the carriage over to the General Store to stock up on sugar and spices for the canning coming up.

Mamma agreed but tilted her head, seemingly scrutinizing her. Sylvia hadn't talked about the painful conversation with Titus just yet, but she would very soon. *Some secrets aren't best kept,* she thought, heading to the stable to get Lily out of her stall.

Dat must have noticed, because he came out of the shop to help her hitch up. She could tell he was as worried about her as Mamma seemed to be. But he didn't say much other than "I'm glad to see you must be feeling better."

"I believe I am."

Her father led the mare into position, then backed her into the parallel shafts. Sylvia helped hook the tugs and traces, still reeling from the events of Saturday evening.

When Lily was hitched up and ready to go, Dat said, "Be careful out on the road."

"I will," she promised and thanked him for helping her. Then, turning back to him, she said, "Dat?"

He gave her a quizzical look. "Are you sure you're up to going on your own?"

"*Jah,*" she assured him, "but I just wanted to say that . . . uh . . ." She'd lost her courage. Why was it so hard to talk to him anymore?

"What is it, daughter?" He pulled on his beard, concern in his eyes.

"I still feel bad . . . for opening the tinderbox," she said, wanting to be honest.

Dat went over to double-check the horse's harness, like he was contemplating what she'd said. *Is he upset?* she wondered as she watched him run his hand over Lily's mane, then pull a sugar cube out of his pocket to give her. *Maybe I shouldn't have dredged this up.*

"Just wanted ya to know," she added softly.

"You might find this hard to understand," he said, walking back to Sylvia, "but I'm glad you opened it." He paused and held the buggy door for her. "It gave me the very push I needed . . . the kick in the pants, really." Dat's brow creased as though there was more on his mind, but then he simply nodded. Before she discovered the pocket watch, he would likely have engaged her in a short conversation, but Sylvia reckoned those days were over. *He was never one for many words, anyway. . . .*

She climbed into the carriage and picked up the driving lines. "I won't be gone long," she said.

Dat took a step back. "Don't forget, Sylvie, you'll always be my little girl," he said before closing the door securely.

278

Encouraged, Sylvia signaled Lily to move forward, down the long driveway. At the corner, where Mamma had planted lavender years before, Sylvia noticed a big black barn cat rolling around in the middle of the bushy shrub. The animal's frolicking brought a smile to her face.

"At least Dat doesn't hold a grudge toward me," she murmured, her heart lighter.

On the way, Sylvia tried to focus on the summertime landscape. The Amish neighbors' yards were all mown and edged meticulously, the flower beds well cared for. Coming up on David and Mattie Beiler's, she enjoyed seeing Mattie's many petunias—white, pink, and burgundy—spreading cheer along the opposite side of their house from Ella Mae's small abode. And, passing by the Wise Woman's place, Sylvia was tempted to stop in and see her on the way home.

I wish I had the time. . . .

During the noon meal, not only did Adam go out on the porch to eat with Dat, but Ernie also joined them, which made it strange for the four of them left inside. *If we all went out there with Dat, poor Mamma would be left alone,* thought Sylvia. *Like we're choosing sides.*

"Your brain's workin' on something," Mamma said with a glance at her.

"Oh . . . I'm all right."

"If you'd like to walk with me after the kitchen's redded up—"

"*Nee,* I'm fine," she replied. Calvin and Tommy were sitting across from her at the now sparsely occupied table, obviously all ears.

"If ya change your mind," Mamma said, "you're welcome to join me."

Her brothers glanced at each other, and Sylvia guessed they were wishing to go walking with Mamma, instead of stacking wood with the older boys.

During the rest of the meal of baked ham, chow chow, scalloped potatoes, and corn on the cob, Sylvia realized how thankful she was for her parents' kind consideration of her and her well-being. Truth be told, she was counting the hours till Dat's public confession before the church membership. The *Bann* had been difficult for the whole family, but soon they would be back together at mealtime. And hopefully, life would be peaceful again.

Saturday afternoon, Sylvia hurried out to get the mail, fleetingly wondering if she might hear from Titus. She recalled again how silently they had ridden to her house a week ago this very night. Of course, it really wasn't his place to contact her first, she knew, given how she'd left things. But they'd never even talked about how long this time apart should last, and the way Titus had so quickly agreed to it still troubled her. *I suppose I should reach out to him. If so, what would I say?*

There was a collection of letters for Mamma. But as anticipated, there was no letter from Titus. The world around Sylvia had spun apart last Saturday night, and as each day passed, it seemed like even the landscape looked less bright, less green . . . less appealing.

She plodded back to the house and placed the mail on the kitchen counter, then returned to weeding and hoeing the vegetable garden while Mamma took her daily walk. Sylvia also weeded the flowers surrounding the house and along the walkway to the back-porch steps.

When her mother returned to help take down the washing and fold it, Sylvia noticed her wiping her eyes with a hankie. *I should've gone walking with her.*

The next morning, Sylvia felt uncertain enough about seeing Titus at baptism class that she sat at the far end of the row of other young women, so as not to be in his line of vision. It was far more important to concentrate on the ministers and not be distracted.

When the morning's session was over, she made her way downstairs with the other youth and joined the congregation, suddenly feeling nervous. Following the service today, her father would kneel before the bishop and openly confess his sins to the membership. She had felt this same knotted, tight feeling before Bishop John Beiler's pronouncement six weeks ago—at least she hadn't had to suffer through hearing *that*. Necessary though the *Bann* was as part of Dat's restoration, it was enough to have endured its restrictions and seen its effect on her family.

Dear Mamma, she thought. *Will today open the wound all over again?*

After the children and youth left to go outdoors, the membership meeting began. Rhoda wasn't the only one silently weeping as Earnest knelt and confessed his sins before the People. Sniffling came from many on the women's side. And if Rhoda wasn't mistaken, there was a catch in Bishop John's voice as he asked the first question. "Earnest Miller, do you believe that your discipline was rightly deserved?"

"I do," Earnest replied.

"And do you honestly ask for patience from the Lord God and this church?"

Just as after the first question, Rhoda held her breath.

Earnest nodded. "I do."

Bishop John looked pale as he asked the third question more slowly. "Finally, is it your sincere desire to promise to live an exemplary life, with God's help, as you vowed to do at your baptism?"

Earnest said with apparent confidence, "I do."

The bishop wiped his eyes with his white handkerchief, then stated that he believed the Lord above had pardoned and removed Earnest's sins. He asked that the congregation "be kindly encouraging and caring toward Earnest and his family in the coming days and weeks."

Then, extending his hand to raise Earnest from his knees, the bishop offered a kiss as a sign of peace and reinstated relationship. Various ones in the congregation shed tears, but Rhoda did not let her gaze linger long. It was a precious time of purification—and healing—for the entire membership.

Everyone seemed to go out of their way to welcome Earnest back to the table at the shared meal; sitting amongst so many friends and relatives, including brother-in-law Curtis Mast, was something he had greatly missed. He nodded politely at Judah and Edwin Zook as they leaned over their end of the table to make eye contact with him and smile. Judah was known to have a perpetual twinkle in his eye, and it was there for Earnest now.

These are my Amish brothers. . . . With a grateful heart, he pondered the process that had led to his restoration to full membership and to such good fellowship with those around him. But his dearest thoughts were of Rhoda.

While checking on the livestock that afternoon, Earnest was pleased to see Adam coming to join him—the first of his sons to change clothes and venture out to help water and feed.

"Looks like I'm your right-hand man again," Adam declared as he removed one of his work boots and emptied the dirt out of it before putting it back on.

Sensing what he meant, Earnest smiled and patted his son's shoulder. "You always were," he insisted. "Nothing could ever change that." He noticed the stable door opening and the other boys walking in.

"Many hands make light work," young Tommy called out, all smiles.

And Earnest could feel that a change had taken place—the church discipline had not only restored him in the eyes of the community . . . but in his own sons' eyes, too.

Instead of spending time upstairs in her hot room, Sylvia went out walking in hope of visiting Ella Mae Zook, who had invited her to drop by anytime.

"'Tis so nice to see ya again," the Wise Woman greeted her. "My peach pie's coolin' on the counter, so if you'd like some with your iced peppermint tea, that'd make my heart ever so glad."

"Sounds delicious, but I really didn't come for a dessert." Sylvia smiled and pulled out a chair at the table, where Ella Mae motioned for her to sit.

"Well, I'm not much one for eatin' pie alone . . . are you?"

Sylvia had to grin. "*Nee*, not really."

They talked about the fact that her father had been restored to a right relationship with God and the church. "I've already noticed a spring in Dat's step," she confided. "But he's not the same."

"No matter how short or long it is, excommunication is stressful, even frightening. But in the end, confession's mighty *gut* for any soul. . . . I certainly know this to be so." Ella Mae stood at the counter cutting her pie into six large slices. "You remember what I told ya 'bout my own *Bann* as a teenager."

"*Jah*, I do. But I'm looking forward to, well . . . for things to return to normal."

"Well, things'll never be exactly like they were, I'm sure ya realize. How can they be?" She paused, blinking and pulling out her hankie from beneath her sleeve. "When hurtful things are revealed, it leaves a wound that only the Lord, and time and tenderness, can heal."

"So are you sayin' I should be patient?"

Ella Mae turned to glance at her. "That's exactly what I mean." She brought over two pretty dessert plates with very generous pieces of pie on each. "Here we are, Sylvie . . . I've always liked your nickname."

"My father gave it to me when I was little."

"Well, it suits ya." With a little bob of her head, Ella Mae sat across the small table from Sylvia, looking over the top of her spectacles. "Your father's always been real fond of ya. I remember when you were born, he carried you around every chance he could, whenever your Mamma needed extra rest."

Sylvia loved hearing this, even though Mamma had told her the same thing years ago.

"Oh, and when you were toddlin' about," Ella Mae continued, "he would lift ya high on his shoulders, holding on to your little dimpled hands while you just giggled up there . . . his little girl."

"I can almost picture that," Sylvia said with a sigh. "I've always felt close to Dat. But not since I got all of this started . . . with his excommunication an' all."

"*You*, dearie?"

Without telling everything, she explained to Ella Mae about finding the heirloom tinderbox full of her father's memorabilia. "One of those items was something Dat never expected anyone to discover."

Ella Mae seemed to take this in, tilting her head as if in deep thought. "Well, since the dear Lord has forgiven your father's sins, isn't it time you forgave yourself?"

Sylvia swallowed hard. "I can forgive others, but it's harder to forgive myself."

Ella Mae nodded. "I want to share somethin' with you. In the book of Micah, the prophet writes, 'And what doth the Lord require of thee, but to do justly, and to love mercy, and to walk humbly with thy God?'"

Sylvia felt as if Ella Mae were searching her heart with her eyes.

"Tonight, before ya slip into your bed, will ya talk this over with the Lord?"

Sylvia wanted to—in fact, she'd tried to repeatedly. The

pressure was ever so burdensome, but she hardly knew how to answer.

"Remember, we can shine the brightest in our suffering an' pain," Ella Mae said quietly.

She's right, Sylvia thought as she watched her pour more cold peppermint tea.

"You did want more, ain't so?" Ella Mae asked, smiling broadly.

Later, during her walk home, Sylvia looked forward to helping Mamma make supper and to sitting down at the table, all of them together once again.

Things will be better now, she thought. *Surely they will.*

CHAPTER
Thirty-Six

*F*our days passed and, from what Sylvia could tell, her family was slowly but steadily returning to their previous routine, even though Dat's inventory of beautiful clocks was not selling quite as quickly as was typical. The consequences of her father's past deceit, and his tarnished reputation, had caused deep scars amongst the People.

Just as Ella Mae predicted, Sylvia thought.

As before, Preacher Kauffman and Deacon Luke resumed their social visits with Dat, both men taking turns coming over and chewing the fat, especially during these hot and humid evenings. Sylvia brought out homemade ice cream and ice-cold root beer—the best ways to keep cool—then left the men alone to talk, having noticed Preacher Kauffman somewhat less engaged, seemingly standoffish, maybe feeling awkward. She couldn't be sure, but she guessed there were some fences to be mended where Preacher Kauffman was concerned.

Meanwhile, Sylvia had kept busy picking tomatoes to sell at

the vegetable stand. There were tomatoes of all shapes, sizes, and colors in Mamma's enormous garden, enough to keep tourists coming back for more. She even had a silly dream about tomatoes overrunning the house—tomatoes rolling about everywhere.

The sweet corn harvest was also in full swing in Hickory Hollow, and Mamma served corn on the cob or cut corn swimming in butter nearly every suppertime.

This evening, though, Sylvia was on her way over to help Cousin Alma start cleaning house for the Preaching service her family would soon be hosting.

When they were alone upstairs washing floors, Sylvia confided in Alma about Titus. "Wanted ya to hear it from me, since you and Danny doubled up with us a lot."

Thankfully, Alma didn't react dramatically. She just quietly said, "Well, sometimes steppin' away for a little while can help a relationship." Alma's face was flushed from the heat. "If it's meant to be, things'll work out in the long run."

Titus has to become independent of his family, Sylvia thought, feeling strongly about that. "At some point, he and I need to discuss all of this and come to an understanding, so we can decide 'bout our future."

"With the Lord's help," Cousin Alma added, her brown eyes shining.

Sylvia nodded. "Most definitely." She was glad Alma understood and hadn't asked, even jokingly, who she and Danny Lapp would double-date with now. No, her cousin had handled the whole thing with grace. *She's ready to court on her own*, thought Sylvia.

In an attempt to beat the day's muggy heat on this last day of July, Sylvia and her family had gotten up at four-thirty to do their outdoor chores. By the time she took her turn at their vegetable stand that midafternoon, she was ever so thankful for the dark green awning Dat had erected over the roadside stand years earlier.

The air was thick when a red sports car pulled into the driveway a few yards and stopped. Out stepped a tall woman in white jeans and a blue-and-white-striped blouse. She smiled at Sylvia as she came over to look at the produce. "Everything looks delicious," she said, removing her sunglasses.

"The cherry tomatoes are real hearty this year," Sylvia said, engaging in the sort of small talk she was used to with customers. "Are ya from round here?"

The fancy woman shook her head. "Actually, I'm in the area looking for a clockmaker by the name of Earnest Miller," she said, pushing back her light brown hair on one side. "Might you know where he lives?"

"*Jah*," Sylvia said. "He lives here."

"Are you acquainted with him?"

Sylvia wasn't sure what to make of this. "Well, I'm his daughter, Sylvia."

The woman's lips parted, as though she was surprised, if not shocked. The scrutinizing gaze she gave Sylvia felt strange even though Sylvia had long since adapted to *Englischers* staring at her and her Plain family.

"So . . . you're *Amish*?"

Sylvia nodded.

"Oh no . . ." the woman murmured. Then, glancing toward the house, the woman's color seemed to pale.

Something's wrong, Sylvia thought as she studied her, noting her long dark eyelashes.

"Would it be possible to speak with your father?" the woman asked.

"I'll have to check," Sylvia said, and it crossed her mind that the woman looked familiar somehow. But how could that be when she didn't seem to recognize *her*? "Does my father know you?"

"I don't believe so, but I can't be sure until I speak with him."

How odd! Sylvia thought.

Abruptly, the young woman turned away, looking back at her car. "Now that I'm here, I think this might be a mistake."

She seemed so troubled that Sylvia reached out and touched her arm. "Are you all right, miss?"

She straightened as though gathering a measure of courage. "I should at least tell you my name. It's . . ." She smiled with obvious uncertainty. "I'm Adeline Pelham."

"Adeline," Sylvia whispered. "That's a perty name. I can't say I've ever met an *Englischer* with that name before."

The woman smiled, but the expression seemed less happy than pained, and another awkward moment dragged by.

"Wait here just a minute," Sylvia said, seeing a couple more cars pull onto the shoulder near the roadside stand. She needed to get one of her brothers to spell her off, and she dashed up the driveway to the backyard. Spotting Calvin, she called to him. "Can ya go down to the vegetable stand right quick?"

"Somethin' wrong?"

"Just go!"

"Ain't my turn," Calvin muttered, but he headed toward the driveway anyway.

Sylvia hurried to Dat's shop, where Mamma was setting

a tumbler of lemonade on the worktable. *Ach,* she thought, wishing her father were alone.

Sylvia pushed open the screen door, perspiration on her neck and face. "There's a young woman parked in the driveway—an *Englischer*—who wants to see ya, Dat."

Turning in his chair, he nodded. "Bring her here to the shop."

"Well . . . but I told her to wait down there." Sylvia lifted her long black apron and wiped her face and neck with the hem. "Hope I did the right thing."

Her parents exchanged confused looks. Then Dat got out of his chair. "I'll see about it. I need some exercise, anyway."

After he left, Mamma gathered up yesterday's newspaper, redding up a bit. "Maybe she wants to purchase a clock," she said absentmindedly.

"I don't think so."

Mamma looked at her just then. "Are ya feelin' all right?"

Sylvia shook her head. "Somethin's strange 'bout this." She tried to pinpoint just where she had seen the fancy woman, but hard as she tried, she could not place her.

The sun was beating hard on the blacktop, and Earnest was glad he'd worn his work boots instead of going barefoot. The woman near her car was fanning herself with a black folder, and he happened to see her red toenails peeking out from white sandals. "Hullo," he called to her. "What can I do for you?"

"Are you Earnest Miller?" She looked him up and down.

"I am, and who might you be?"

"Adeline Pelham." She paused, still staring at him. "Uh . . . my fiancé helped me locate this area. Hickory Hollow, right?"

Earnest gave a nod and waited expectantly. Something struck him—a familiarity, a feeling so strange he immediately dismissed it.

She pursed her lips. "You know, I had this all planned ahead of time—what I wanted to say—but I'm afraid it falls flat, now that I'm standing here, talking to you face-to-face."

"I don't understand. How can I help you?"

She seemed to steel herself. "I believe you knew my mother, Rosalind Ellison . . . from Hilton Head, South Carolina."

Rosalind? Instantly he recalled the image of the young, beautiful blue-eyed woman he'd fallen for much too quickly. But wait . . . had this woman just said that Rosalind was her *mother?*

"Before she died, my mother told me that she was once married to you," Adeline explained.

"*Rosalind* is your mother?"

Adeline nodded. "Yes . . . she passed away four months ago."

Shocked to hear it, Earnest was unsure how to respond. "I'm sorry for your loss."

More awkward silence followed as he tried to make sense of why Rosalind's daughter would be seeking him out. "You look very much like her," he said softly, observing the set of her blue eyes, the similar engaging smile.

"People have said that." Adeline nodded, clearly embarrassed. "But my mother, now, *she* was beautiful."

He shifted his weight. "You know, it's been so long since I saw her, more than twenty years. . . ." Earnest pondered the passage of time. "Again, I'm very sorry to hear of her passing."

"There are no words. . . ." Adeline said, glancing away, then back at him. "I loved her so much—we shared everything, really."

Sylvia was standing near one of the front room windows, watching Dat and the tall *Englischer*, noticing the shape of the woman's pretty face and thinking again how very familiar she looked. *Where have I seen her?*

Her father folded his arms abruptly, and she could see his expression suddenly change. Something was definitely troubling him.

Sylvia shook her head and muttered under her breath.

"What're ya fretting about?" Mamma asked.

"I think that woman might be a relative of Dat's—a cousin, maybe. I can't be sure." She stared at Adeline. "Actually, she kind of resembles a girl in some photos Dat has."

"Charlie, ya mean? But that's peculiar," Mamma said, joining her at the window. "I didn't think any of his family knew where he lived—so how'd she find us?" Mamma watched for another minute or so. "Ya know, I think I'll go out there." She sounded quite determined.

"Oh, I'm sure Dat can handle this," Sylvia suggested gently.

But Mamma merely shook her head and headed out of the room.

Ach . . . nee, Sylvia thought, feeling prickly with stress, though she did not know why.

Earnest listened carefully there in the scorching sun as Adeline explained why she'd come. "My mom was ill for more than a year before she died from a serious lung condition, but up until then, she lived a very comfortable and happy life." She sighed. "My stepdad was very good to her . . . and to me, until he passed away when I was twelve."

Earnest hugged himself all the harder.

"After his death, my mother showed me my birth certificate. . . ." Adeline paused.

Where's this leading? Earnest thought, feeling lightheaded.

She inhaled deeply, as if steeling herself. "Your name is listed as my father." Her face crumpled like she might tear up. "And so I find myself here in an Amish village too small to be on any map, talking to you." Her eyes met his.

Earnest was floored by this news. *There must be some mistake!*

Then he stopped himself, thinking now of Rhoda's likely reaction to this news—if Adeline's declaration were true. *Rhoda will be devastated all over again.*

At that moment, he heard someone behind him and turned to see his wife coming down the driveway.

CHAPTER
Thirty-Seven

"Everything all right?" Rhoda asked, taking note of the pretty young woman as she walked toward Earnest.

Her husband unfolded his arms quickly, touching Rhoda's elbow as he introduced her to Adeline Pelham. Then, looking at Rhoda, he said, "And this is my wife, Rhoda Miller."

Adeline extended her smooth hand to Rhoda. "I apologize for just showing up like this."

Curious, Rhoda offered a smile and faced Earnest, who was frowning, his bangs damp with perspiration. "I'm afraid there's no easy way to say this, Rhoda," he began quite deliberately.

Rhoda caught the woman's anxious look and wondered what was going on.

Earnest continued with a nod toward the young woman. "Adeline here believes she might be my daughter."

Rhoda stepped back slightly, unsure if she was hearing him right, eyes on Earnest as she tried to comprehend his strained expression. She blinked, then exclaimed, "Ach, what a surprise that would be!"

"Certainly, though, Rosalind would have *told* me about a

295

pregnancy before she left," Earnest insisted, folding his arms across his chest again.

Adeline flinched, anxiety registering on her pretty face. "Perhaps it was wrong of me to come—"

"Wrong?" Rhoda said, regarding Adeline and trying to remember the family photos Earnest had shown her in his shop, particularly the ones of Charlie. "I wonder if I see a resemblance between Adeline and your sister, though. Do you, Earnest?" She looked at him intently, hoping she wasn't speaking out of turn.

Adeline clutched a photo album. "I brought my birth certificate," she said breathlessly.

Earnest looked at Rhoda, clearly seeking her input.

"Why don't ya come to the house and have some cold lemonade," she said to Adeline.

Adeline suddenly looked relieved. "Are you sure?"

"*Jah*, no sense standin' out in this sweltering heat," Earnest agreed, leading the way, his shoulders slumped.

Adeline walked alongside Rhoda, her dainty sandals making clicking sounds on the pavement, and Rhoda scarcely knew what more to say.

How is this even possible?

"It's nice to meet you," Adeline said to Sylvia as the four of them stood in Mamma's kitchen. "*Each* of you." Adeline smiled again at Dat and Mamma.

Dat was clearly shocked at Mamma's generosity—inviting the strange young woman into the house. Just now, he looked at Sylvia and shook his head as he took his seat at the table.

Over lemonade and a dish of salted almonds, Adeline began to explain that, after months of deliberating, she had driven all the way from South Carolina to Lancaster County. Then, just as quickly, she handed the photo album to Dat, her birth certificate on top.

Sylvia clasped her hands firmly beneath the table as she sat there, completely stunned by the news that the young woman before her might be her own half sister.

Taking several sips of lemonade, Adeline said, "I knew that I eventually had to find you. Before she died, Mom encouraged me to do exactly that, warning me that it could be difficult." She stopped to take a breath. "You see, Mom had tried to find you when I was born, but you had vanished."

A silence fell over the room, and Sylvia heard the bray of a mule in the near distance. But she could still scarcely grasp what she was hearing. And how was Dat taking all of this? There was so much astonishing information to absorb! And how could such a jaw-dropping revelation help her parents' relationship when it was just starting to get back on track? Holding her breath, she kept her gaze on her father as he paged through the album.

Dat's face grew more ashen as he turned each page. When he was finished, he looked at Mamma with sadness in his eyes before handing it to her. "I had no idea Rosalind was expecting a baby," he said. "It's hard to understand why she didn't want me to know . . . when she was pregnant."

"I don't blame you," Adeline said, looking miserable. "I'm still trying to process all of this, too."

Dat and Mamma exchanged glances.

"Well, you must stay with us, dear," Mamma said, breaking the silence, "at least for supper, if not the night."

At that, Sylvia nearly fell off her chair, and Dat's mouth literally dropped open.

Adeline looked at Mamma, seemingly shocked. "I really don't—"

"You've traveled such a long way," Mamma said.

Sylvia could hardly believe her eyes and ears. Mamma had invited this English stranger to eat with them . . . and to spend the night!

Meanwhile, Dat wasn't actually staring at Adeline, but close to it.

"*Kumme mit* . . . I'll show ya where you'll be sleepin'," Mamma told Adeline. "Earnest will help ya bring in your things later."

Sylvia got up from the table, too, and left the kitchen, stepping back outside. Calvin undoubtedly was wondering where she'd gone. After all, it was her turn to help customers, not his.

Hurrying down the driveway, she tried to understand what had just taken place. *I have a half sister who's an Englischer,* she thought, her head still spinning.

Nevertheless, she managed to put on a smile as she took Calvin's spot at the vegetable stand, thanking him before he scurried away.

"A dollar and a half for a pint of cherry tomatoes," she told the middle-aged female tourist he had been helping. After so many years of working the stand, Sylvia could automatically recite the price of everything there without having to stop and think.

But now the rest of her brain was in a dense fog. *My father has another daughter. . . .*

While Adeline was getting settled in the spare room, Earnest asked Rhoda to come with him to the utility room. There, he closed the door leading in from the narrow hallway.

"You amaze me, Rhoda," he said, longing to take her hand. "This girl's an outsider—apparently even my *daughter*—yet you've opened our home to her." He looked at his wife, thinking how deeply upsetting this must be for her. *And just when things were starting to calm down.*

"Adeline's the spittin' image of your sister, ain't so?" Rhoda replied, looking at him with tender eyes.

Earnest nodded and glanced out the row of screened-in windows, toward the barn and beyond. Then, looking at her, he said, "You were so kind to her."

"It's the right thing to do, Earnest." Rhoda smiled up at him, reaching to touch his arm. "Ain't easy, believe me . . . but there's no doubt she's your flesh and blood."

In that moment, his love for Rhoda knew no bounds. He reached for her hand, and she accepted. And for the first time in months, he had hope that at long last they were on the path to peace and eventual reconciliation.

Epilogue

*S*unshine glistened on the west side of the large trees near the meadow gate that evening as I headed that way, barefoot. While Dat, Mamma, and Adeline were talking in the house, I'd decided to go for a walk . . . missing Titus.

I tried to picture what I would tell him on such an earth-shattering night, if things weren't so unsettled between us. Would I have the nerve to talk with him about my father's other daughter, appearing out of nowhere? Was our relationship strong enough to openly share such personal things? Honestly, I wasn't sure anymore.

Skipping back in my memory to our early days, before I uncovered the secrets in the tinderbox—back before I realized that Titus must have believed it was his obligation, as a preacher's son, to report Dat's counseling sessions with his Mennonite great-uncle—I remembered imagining what it would be like to go out in Titus's rowboat on a clear and moonlit night.

Titus had been the one to bring up the idea, although

we never got around to going. But now, thinking of him, I recalled how he'd described pushing the oars slowly and steadily through the water as we moved along. Just Titus, me, and the Good Lord's love shining down on us.

I'd imagined Titus picking some white wildflowers for me, so I could hold them as he rowed across the glossy lake, the moonlight making the blossoms all the whiter. And I wondered now what it would be like for Titus to kiss me in the rowboat, the moon high above us, the water all aglimmer. Would we feel as close as we did before Dat's sin was exposed?

I glanced at the house, far in the distance now, and had no desire to hurry back. It was disquieting to have weathered the tempest of Dat's excommunication, and then miraculously find we had all survived, only to get hit by this whirlwind called Adeline, as fancy as her name.

As the evening sun slipped toward the horizon, I had only one recourse . . . to turn to God in prayer, remembering all the times Mamma had come out here to walk this same dirt path around Dat's big green meadow.

Dear Lord, please help my parents make it through this new and unforeseen storm, I pleaded with my heavenly Father. *Please help us all, I pray.*

The Millers' Story Continues...

*A*s the only daughter, Sylvia Miller has always held a special place in her Old Order family, one Adeline Pelham jeopardizes when she shows up at the Millers' Hickory Hollow farm. It isn't that Adeline means to be a threat, but her very existence is a reminder of the painful secret that has so recently upended the Miller household. And with Sylvia and her mother still struggling to come to terms with that news, this is a challenging time to welcome an outsider—especially *this* outsider—into their midst.

Can God allow something good to come out of the mistakes of the past? Or does Adeline's arrival mark one too many surprises for the Millers and their Amish community? Find out in *The Timepiece*, the compelling conclusion to *The Tinderbox*, available September 2019!

Author's Note

If I had more space here to write about the many Amish folk who assisted with research for this book, it still would not be sufficient. Of course I wouldn't publish their names, but they certainly know who they are, and my heart is overflowing with appreciation for their exceptional kindness, generosity, and time.

I'm grateful, as well, for the opportunity to visit with the delightful clockmaker's wife at Kauffman's Handcrafted Clocks in Ronks, Pennsylvania—a must-see for all my reader-friends!

It was really terrific having Dave, my husband, accompany me to Lancaster County for an incredible week of research and fellowship with Amish and Mennonite friends, including my own dear Buchwalter relatives. I had loads of fun brainstorming the conclusion to *The Tinderbox*, which is entitled *The Timepiece* and releasing September 2019.

I offer abundant thanks to my steadfast editors, David Horton, Rochelle Glöege, and Elisa Tally, as well as to my amazing reviewers, Ann Parrish, Dave Lewis, Barbara Birch, and my Plain consultants. The Bethany House marketing team also deserves a standing ovation!

Enormous gratitude goes to my beloved friend and former teacher colleague Martha (Marty) Nelson, who faithfully prayed for me while she was so very ill during the writing and research of this book. A true gem!

Special thanks—and love—extends to my daughter Julie, one of my greatest encouragers and helpful beyond belief! Hugs and kisses across the miles to my sweet twinnies, Janie and Jonathan, who cheer me on with their thoughtful phone calls and handwritten notes.

To my dear prayer partners, including the group at Bethany House Publishers, my wonderful church, and my own extended family—Buchwalters and Joneses alike—thank you! I'm also indebted to my sister-writers whose constant support from afar and faithful prayers make this busy writing life possible.

As you may know, I cherish my loyal readership. It is a true honor to write for you, my dear reader, hoping this story will touch your heart as it did my own. If you ever have the opportunity to visit my beloved Lancaster County, I hope you'll take time to drive (or walk) the back roads and visit some of my very favorite shops, all of which influenced my latest novel: Smucker's Quilts, Lapp Valley Farm, Zook's Homemade Chicken Pies, Shady Lane Fabrics, and the Old Candle Barn, just to name a few.

Now, to the Lord above, I offer up my greatest tribute. *Soli Deo Gloria*—to the glory of God alone.

Beverly Lewis, born in the heart of Pennsylvania Dutch country, is the *New York Times* bestselling author of more than one hundred books. Her stories have been published in twelve languages worldwide. A keen interest in her mother's Plain heritage has inspired Beverly to write many Amish-related novels, beginning with *The Shunning*, which has sold more than one million copies and is an Original Hallmark Channel movie. In 2007 *The Brethren* was honored with a Christy Award.

Beverly has been interviewed by both national and international media, including *Time* magazine, the Associated Press, and the BBC. She lives with her husband, David, in Colorado.

Visit her website at www.beverlylewis.com or www.facebook .com/officialbeverlylewis for more information.